Away from the millionaire mansions and expensive beaches of Sardinia's north coast are the Sardinian mountains, lair of an unsubmissive, clannish, and hard people with no love of the law. In these flinty mountains a murder has been committed. The victim, Oscar Burolo, had built an impregnable villa with the latest in high-tech surveillance. But an assassin had somehow slipped through, and now Burolo's dead. Aurelio Zen of the Ministry of the Interior has been assigned to the case, but the list of suspects soon develops into a dangerous rogues' gallery of neoterrorists, Machiavellian politicians, an artistic son, a venal co-worker, and a perverted lion tamer—all with ample reason to kill the victim . . . and the police investigator. For as Zen gets closer to the solution, a killer gets closer to *him*.

VENDETTA

Two-time Gold Dagger Award–winning suspense author Michael Dibdin pulls the veil off an intricate, disturbing portrait of Italy, the human heart, and the dark nexus of anger, resentment, and corruption—the personal vendetta.

VENDETTA

Michael Dibdin

BANTAM BOOKS

New York · Toronto · London · Sydney · Auckland

*This edition contains the complete text
of the original hardcover edition.
NOT ONE WORD HAS BEEN OMITTED.*

VENDETTA

*A Bantam Crime Line Book/published in association with
Doubleday*

PUBLISHING HISTORY
Doubleday edition published December 1991

Bantam edition / February 1993

*CRIME LINE and the portrayal of a boxed "cl" are trademarks of
Bantam Books,
a division of Bantam Doubleday Dell
Publishing Group, Inc.*

*All rights reserved.
Copyright © 1991 by Michael Dibdin.
Cover art copyright © 1993 by Tom Sciacca.*
Library of Congress Catalog Card Number: 91-14472.

ISBN 0-553-29639-6
Published simultaneously in the United States and Canada

*Bantam Books are published by Bantam Books, a division of Ban-
tam Doubleday Dell Publishing Group, Inc. Its trademark, consisting of the words "Bantam Books" and the portrayal of a rooster, is
Registered in U.S. Patent and Trademark Office and in other coun-
tries. Marca Registrada. Bantam Books, 666 Fifth Avenue, New
York, New York 10103.*

PRINTED IN THE UNITED STATES OF AMERICA

RAD   0 9 8 7 6 5 4 3 2 1

TO MOSELLE

VENDETTA

Rome

WEDNESDAY: 0150 — 0245

AURELIO ZEN LOUNGED ON the sofa like a listless god, bringing the dead back to life. With a flick of his finger he made them rise again. One by one the shapeless, blood-drenched bundles stirred, shook themselves, crawled about a bit, then floated upward until they were on their feet again. This extremely literal resurrection had taken them by surprise, to judge by their expressions, or perhaps it was the sight of one another's bodies that was so shocking, the hideous injuries and disfigurements, the pools and spatters of blood everywhere. But as Zen continued to apply his miraculous intervention, all this was set to rights, too: the gaping rents in flesh and fabric healed themselves, the blood mopped itself up, and in no time at all the scene looked almost like the ordinary dinner party it had been until the impossible occurred. None of the four seemed to notice the one remarkable feature of this spurious afterlife, namely that everything happened backwards.

"He did it."

Zen's mother was standing in the doorway, her nightdress clutched around her skimpy form.

"What's wrong, Mamma?"

She pointed at the television, which now showed a beach of brilliant white sand framed by smoothly curved rocks. A man was swimming backward through the wavelets. He casually dived up out of the water, landed neatly on one of the rocks, and strolled backward to the shaded lounging chairs where the others sat sucking smoke out of the air and blowing it into cigarettes.

"The one in the swimming costume. He did it. He was in love with his wife so he killed him. He was in another one, too, last week on channel five. They thought he was a spy but it was his twin brother. He was both of them. They do it with mirrors."

Mother and son gazed at each other across the room lit by the electronically preserved sunlight of a summer now more than three months in the past. It was almost two o'clock in the morning, and even the streets of Rome were hushed.

Zen pressed the pause button of the remote control unit, stilling the video.

"Why are you up, Mamma?" he asked, trying to keep his irritation out of his voice. This was breaking the rules. Once she had retired to her room, his mother never reappeared. It was respect for these unwritten laws that made their life together just about tolerable from his point of view.

"I thought I heard something."

Their eyes still held. The woman who had given Zen life might have been the child he had never had, awakened by a nightmare and seeking comfort. He got up and walked over to her.

"I'm sorry, Mamma. I turned the sound right down . . ."

"I don't mean the TV."

He interrogated those bleary, evasive eyes more closely. "What, then?"

She shrugged pettishly. "A sort of scraping."

"Scraping? What do you mean?"

"Like old Umberto's boat."

Zen was often brought up short by his mother's

ability to knock him off balance by some reference to a past which for her was infinitely more real than the present would ever be. He had quite forgotten Umberto, the portly, dignified proprietor of a general grocery near the San Geremia bridge. He used the boat to transport fruit and vegetables from the Rialto market, as well as boxes, cases, bottles, and jars to and from the cellars of his house, which the ten-year-old Zen had visualised as an Aladdin's cave crammed with exotic delights. When not in use, the boat was moored to a post in the little canal opposite the Zens' house. The post had a tin collar to protect the wood, and a few moments after each *vaporetto* passed down the Cannaregio, the wash would reach Umberto's boat and set it rubbing its gunwale against the collar, producing a series of metallic rasps.

"It was probably me moving around in here that you heard," Zen told her. "Now go back to bed before you catch cold."

"It didn't come from in here. It came from the other side. Across the canal. Just like that damned boat."

Zen took her by the arm, which felt alarmingly fragile. Widowed by the war, his mother had affronted the world alone on his behalf, wresting concessions from tradesmen and bureaucrats, labouring at menial jobs to eke out her pension, cooking, cleaning, sewing, mending, and making do, tirelessly and ingeniously hollowing out and shoring up a space for her son to grow up in. Small wonder, he thought, that the effort had reduced her to this pittance of a person, scared of noises and the dark, with no interest in anything but the television serials she watched, whose plots and characters were gradually becoming confused in her mind. Such motherhood as she had known was like those industrial jobs that leave workers crippled and broken, the only difference being that there was no one mothers could sue for damages.

Zen led her back into the musty bedroom she occupied at the back of the apartment, filled with the furniture she had brought with her from their home in Venice. The pieces were all elaborately carved from some wood as hard, dark, and heavy as iron. They covered every inch of wall space, blocking up the fire escape as well as most of the window, which she always kept tightly shuttered anyway.

"Are you going to stay up and watch the rest of that film?" she asked as he tucked her in.

"Yes, Mamma, don't worry, I'll be just in there. If you hear anything, it's only me."

"It didn't come from in there! Anyway, I told you who did it. The skinny one in the swimming costume."

"I know, Mamma," he murmured wearily. "That's what everyone thinks."

He wandered back to the living room just as two o'clock began to strike from the churches in the Vatican. Zen stood surveying the familiar faces locked up on the flickering screen. They were familiar not just to him but to everyone who had watched television or looked at the papers that autumn. For months the news had been dominated by the dramatic events and still more sensational implications of the Burolo affair.

In a way it was quite understandable that Zen's mother had confused the characters involved with the cast of a film she had seen. Indeed, it *was* a film that Zen was watching, but a film of a special kind, not intended for commercial release and only available to him as an officer of the Criminalpol section of the Ministry of the Interior in connection with the report he had been asked to prepare, summarising the case to date. He wasn't really supposed to take it home, but the Ministry didn't run to video machines for its employees, even those of Vice-Questorial rank. So what was he supposed to do, Zen had demanded in his ignorance of the nature of video tape, hold it up to the window, frame by frame?

He sat down on the sofa again, groped for the remote control unit, and pressed the play button, releasing the blurred figures to laugh, chat, and generally ham it up for the camera. They knew it was there, of course. Oscar Burolo made no secret of his mania for recording the high points of his life. On the contrary, every visitor to the billionaire's Sardinian hideaway had been impressed by the underground vault containing hundreds of video tapes and computer disks, all carefully shelved and indexed. Like all good libraries, Oscar's collection was constantly expanding. Indeed, shortly before his death a complete new section of shelving had been installed to accommodate the latest additions.

"But do you actually ever watch any of them?" the guest might ask.

"I don't need to watch them," Oscar would reply, smiling in a peculiar way. "It's enough to know that they're there."

If the six people relaxing at the water's edge were in any way uneasy about the prospect of having their antics preserved for posterity, they certainly showed no sign of it. An invitation to the Villa Burolo was so sought after that no one was going to quibble about the conditions. Quite apart from the experience itself, it was something to brag about at dinner parties for months to come. "You mean to say you've actually *been* there?" people would ask, their envy showing like an ill-adjusted slip. "Tell me, is it true that he has lions and tigers freely roaming the grounds and that the only way in is by helicopter?" Secure in the knowledge that no one was likely to contradict him, Oscar Burolo's exguest could freely choose whether to distort the facts ("I solemnly assure you, I who have been there and seen it with my own eyes, that Burolo has a staff of over thirty servants—or rather *slaves!*—that he bought, cash down, from the president of a certain African country . . .") or, in more sophisticated company, to suggest that the truth was actually stranger than the various lurid and vulgar fictions which had been circulating.

On the face of it, this degree of interest was itself almost the oddest feature of the business. Nothing could be more banal than for a rich Italian to buy himself a villa in Sardinia. Sardinia, of course, meant the Costa Smeralda on the northern coast of the island, which the Aga Khan had bought for a pittance from the local peasant farmers and turned into a holiday paradise for the superwealthy, a ministate which sprang into being every

summer for two months. Its citizens hailed from all parts
of the world and from all walks of life: film stars, indus-
trialists, sheiks, politicians, criminals, pop singers, bank-
ers. Their cosmopolitan enclave was protected by an
extremely efficient private police force, but its internal
regime was admirably democratic and egalitarian. Reli-
gious, political, and racial discrimination were unknown. The only requirement was money and lots of it.

As founder and owner of a construction company
whose rapid success was almost uncanny, there was no
question that Oscar Burolo satisfied that requirement.
But instead of meekly buying his way into the Costa like
everyone else, he did something unheard-of, something
so bizarre and outlandish that some people claimed afterwards that they had always thought it was ill-omened
from the start. For *his* Sardinian retreat, Oscar chose an
abandoned farmhouse halfway down the island's almost
uninhabited eastern coast, and not even on the sea, for
God's sake, but several kilometres inland!

Italians have no exaggerated respect for eccentric-
ity, and this kind of idiosyncrasy might very easily have
aroused nothing but ridicule and contempt. It was a
measure of the panache with which Oscar carried off
his whims that exactly the opposite was the case. The
full resources of Burolo Construction were brought to
bear on the humble farmhouse, which was swiftly altered out of all recognition. One by one, the arguments
against Oscar's choice were made to look small-minded
and unconvincing.

The security aspect, so important in an area notorious for kidnapping, was taken care of by hiring the top
firm in the country to make the villa intruder-proof, no
expense spared. Used to having to cut corners to make
security cost-effective, the consultant was delighted for
once to have an opportunity to design a system without
compromises. "If any intruder ever manages to get into
this place, I'll believe in ghosts," he assured his client
when the work was completed. Having bought peace of
mind with hard cash, Oscar then added a characteristic
touch by buying a pair of rather moth-eaten lions from a

bankrupt safari park outside Cagliari and turning them loose in the grounds, calculating that the resulting publicity would do as much as any amount of high technology to deter intruders.

But even Oscar couldn't change the fact that the villa was situated almost two hundred kilometres from the nearest airport and the glamorous nightspots of the Costa Smeralda, two hundred kilometres of tortuous and poorly maintained road where no electronic fences could protect him from kidnappers. Wasn't that a drawback? Well, it might be, Oscar retorted, for someone who still thought of personal transport in terms of cars. But Olbia and the Costa were only half that distance as the crow flew, and when the crow in question was capable of two hundred and twenty kilometres an hour . . . To clinch the argument, Oscar would bundle his guests into the crow—an Agusta helicopter—and pilot them personally to Palau or Porto Cervo for aperitifs.

As for swimming, since Oscar would not go to the coast like everyone else, the coast was made to come to him. A wide irregular hollow the size of a small lake was scooped out of the parched red soil behind the farm. This was lined with concrete, filled with water, and decorated with a sandy beach and wave-smoothed rocks dynamited and bulldozed out of the foreshore, barnacles and all. And the barnacles throve, because one of the biggest surprises awaiting Burolo's guests as they padded off for their first dip was that the water was salty. "Fresh from the Mediterranean," Oscar would explain proudly. "Pumped up here through five thousand four hundred and thirty seven metres of sixty centimetre duct, filtered for impurities, agitated by six asynchronous wave simulators and continuously monitored to maintain a constant level of salinity." Oscar liked using words like asynchronous and salinity and quoting squads of figures: it clinched the effect which the villa was already beginning to have on his listener. But he knew when to stop and at this point would usually slap his guest on the back—or, if it was a woman, place his hand familiarly at the base of her spine just above the buttocks—and say, "So what's missing, except for a lot of fish and crabs and lobsters? Mind you, we have those, too, but they know their place here—on a plate!''

Zen paused the video again as footsteps sounded in the street outside. A car door slammed shut. But instead of the expected sound of the car starting up and driving away, the footsteps returned the way they had come, ceasing somewhere close by.

He walked over to the window and opened the shutters. The wooden jalousies beyond the glass were closed, but segments of the scene outside were visible by looking down through the angled slats. Both sides of the street were packed with cars parked on the road, on either side of the trees lining it, and all over the pavement. Some distance from the house a red sedan was parked beyond all these, all by itself, facing toward the house. It appeared to be empty.

The scene was abruptly plunged into darkness as the streetlamp attached to the wall just below turned itself off. Something had gone wrong with its automatic switch, so that the lamp was continually fooled into thinking that its own light was that of the dawn and therefore turned itself off. Then, after some time, it would start to glow faintly again, gradually growing brighter and brighter until the whole cycle repeated itself. Zen closed the shutters and walked back to the sofa. Catching sight of his reflection in the large mirror above the fireplace, he paused, as though the person he saw there might hold the key to what was puzzling him. The prominent bones and tautness of the skin, especially around the eyes, gave his face a slightly exotic air, probably due to Slav or even Semitic blood somewhere in the family's Venetian past. It was a face that gave nothing away, yet seemed always to tremble on the brink of some expression that never quite appeared. His face had made Zen's reputation as an interrogator, for it was a perfect screen onto which others could project their own suspicions, fears, and apprehensions. Where other policemen confronted criminals, using the carrot or the stick according to the situation, Zen's subjects found themselves shut up with a man who barely seemed to exist, yet who mirrored back to them the innermost secrets of their hearts. They read their every fleeting emotion accurately imaged on those scrupulously blank features and knew that they were lost.

Like all the other furniture in the apartment, the mirror had come from the family house in Venice, now shut up and empty. It was old without being valuable, and the silvering was wearing off in places. One particularly large patch covered much of Zen's chest. It made him think of the last terrible scenes of the video he was watching, of Oscar Burolo reeling away from the shotgun blasts which had come from nowhere, passing through the elaborate electronic defences of his property as though they did not exist.

With a shiver, Zen deliberately stepped to one side, moving the stain of darkness away. There was something about the Burolo case which was different from any other he had ever been involved with. He had known cases which had obsessed him professionally, taking over his life until he was unable to sleep properly or to think about anything else, but this was far more disturbing. It was as though the aura of mystery and horror surrounding the killings had extended itself even to him, as though he too was somehow in danger from the faceless power which had ravaged the Villa Burolo. This was absurd, of course. The case was closed, an arrest had been made, and Zen's involvement with it was temporary, secondhand, and superficial. But despite that, the sensation of menace remained. The sound of footsteps was enough to make him rush to the window, and a car parked halfway down the street seemed to pose some threat.

The fact was that it was time to go to bed, long past it, in fact. He walked back to the sofa and picked up his crumpled pack of Nazionali cigarettes, considered briefly whether to have one more before turning in, decided against it, then lit up anyway. He yawned and glanced at his watch. A quarter past two. No wonder he was feeling so strange. Seen through the mists of sleeplessness, everything had the insubstantial, fluid quality of a dream. He picked up the remote control, pressed the play button, and tried to concentrate on the screen again.

You had to hand it to Oscar! No doubt the camera angle had been carefully chosen, but it was really very difficult to believe that this beach, these rocks, those splashing wavelets, were not part of a natural coastline but a swimming pool situated five kilometres inland. As for the group sitting around the table in the shadow of a huge green and blue parasol, toying with iced drinks, packs of cards, and magazines full of games and puzzles, it was fairly typical of those that might have been found at the villa on any given day during July and August that summer. Besides Oscar and his wife, there were just four guests: Burolo assiduously preserved the mystique of the villa by restricting the number of visitors, thus increasing their sense of being privileged intimates. His excuse was that the household was not able to cope with huge parties. Despite the tall tales of resident slave communities, Oscar's staff was in fact limited to an elderly caretaker and his wife, together with a young man who had come with the lions and also helped look after the garden. Oscar made much of being a self-made man with no wish for ostentatious display. "I am what I am," he declared, "a simple builder and nothing more." The truth was that he had realised that it was easier to dominate and manipulate small groups than large ones. The video made this very clear. In every scene, inside or out, it was the host himself who was invariably the focus of attention. Lounging on his personalised beach in silver shorts and a clashing pink and blue silk shirt, his head exaggerated in size as though by a caricaturist's pen, Oscar looked like the love child of the Michelin man and an overweight gorilla. One of his unsuccessful rivals had remarked that anyone who still doubted the theory of evolution obviously hadn't met Oscar Burolo. But it was a waste of time trying to be witty at Oscar's expense. He promptly took up the story, telling it himself with great relish, and concluding, "Which is why I've survived and

Roberto's gone to the wall, like the dinosaur he is!"
Oscar the ebullient, the irrepressible Oscar! Nothing
could touch him, or so it seemed.

Such was the spell cast by Burolo that it was only
by an effort of attention that one became aware of the
others present. The slightly saturnine man with thinning
grey hair and a wedge-shaped face sitting to Oscar's left
was a Sicilian architect named Vianello who had collabo-
rated with Burolo Construction on the plans for a new
electricity generating station at Rieti. Unfortunately their
offer had been rejected on technical grounds—a previously unheard-of eventuality—and the contract had
gone to another firm. Dottor Vianello was wearing an
immaculate pale cream cotton suit and a slightly
strained smile, possibly due to the fact that he was having to listen to Oscar's wife's account of an abortive
shopping expedition to Olbia. Rita Burolo had once
been an exceptionally attractive woman, and the sense
of power which this had given her had remained even
now that her charms were visibly wilting. Her inane
comments had commanded total attention for so long
that Rita had at last come to believe that she had more
to offer the world than her legs and breasts, which was
quite a consolation now that the latter were no longer
quite first-division material. Opposite her sat the wife of
the Sicilian architect, a diminutive pixie of a woman
with frightened eyes and a faint moustache. Maria Pia
Vianello gazed at the spectacle of her hostess in full
career with a kind of awestruck amazement, like a
schoolgirl with a crush on her teacher. Clearly *she*
would never dream of trying to dominate a gathering in
this way.

Despite these superficial dissimilarities, however,
the Vianellos and the Burolos were basically much of a
muchness. No longer young, but rich enough to keep
age at bay for a few years yet, the men ponderous with
professional *gravitas,* like those toy figurines which cannot be knocked over because they are loaded with lead,
the women exuding the sullen peevishness of those
who have been pampered with every luxury except

freedom and responsibility. The remaining couple were different.

Zen reversed the tape again briefly, hauling the swimmer up out of the water once more, and then froze the picture, studying the man who had dominated the news for the previous three months. Renato Favelloni's sharp, ferrety features and weak chest and limbs, coupled with lanky hair and an overready smile, gave him the air of a small-town playboy, by turns truculent and toadying, convinced of being God's gift to the world in general and women in particular, but quite prepared to lower himself to any dirty work in the interest of getting ahead. At first Zen had found it almost incomprehensible that such a man could have been the linchpin of the deals that were rumoured to have taken place between Oscar Burolo and the senior political figure who was referred to in the press as *l'onorevole,* the formula reputedly used by Burolo in his secret memoranda of their relationship. Only gradually had he come to understand that it was precisely Favelloni's blatant sleaziness which made him acceptable as a go-between. There are degrees even in the most cynical corruption and manipulation. By embodying the most despicable possible grade, Renato Favelloni made his clients feel relatively decent by comparison.

His wife, like Renato himself, was a good ten years younger than the other four people present, and exactly the kind of stunning bimbo that Rita Burolo must have been at the same age. This cannot have recommended Nadia Favelloni to Oscar's wife any more than the younger woman's habit of wandering around the place half-naked. Having reached the age at which women begin to employ clothing for purposes of concealment rather than display, Signora Burolo discreetly retained a flowing wrap of some material that was a good deal less transparent than it first appeared.

A sense of revulsion suddenly overcame Zen at the thought of what was shortly to happen to that pampered, veiled flesh. Vanity, lust, jealousy, boredom, bitchiness, beauty, wit—what did any of it matter? As

the doomed faces glanced flirtatiously at the camera,
wondering how they were coming across, Zen felt like
screaming at them, "Go away! Get out of that house
now!"

The Favellonis had done precisely that, of course,
which was one reason why everyone in Italy from the
magistrate investigating the case to the know-it-all in
your local bar agreed with Zen's mother that Renato
Favelloni was "the one who did it." With the seedy fixer
and his disturbingly bare-breasted wife out of the way,
the two maturer couples had settled down to a quiet
dinner in the villa's dining room, with its rough tiled
floor and huge trestle table which had originally graced
the refectory of a Franciscan monastery. The meal had
been eaten and coffee and liqueurs served when Oscar
once again switched on the camera to record the after-
dinner talk, dominated as always by his booming, em-
phatic voice, punctuated by blows of his hairy fist on
the tabletop.

Apart from a distant metallic crash whose source
and relevance were in dispute, the first sign of what was
about to happen appeared in Signora Vianello's nervous
eyes. The architect's wife was sitting next to their host,
who was in the middle of a bawdy tale concerning a
well-known TV presenter, a stripper turned member of
parliament who had appeared on his talk show, and
what they had reputedly got up to during the commercial break. Maria Pia Vianello had been listening with a
vague, blurry smile, as though she wasn't quite sure
whether it was proper for her to appear to understand.
Then her eyes were attracted by something on the other
side of the room, something which made such consider-
ations irrelevant. The vague smile abruptly vanished,
leaving her features completely blank.

No one else had noticed anything. The only sound
in the room was Oscar's voice. Whatever Signora Vianello had seen was on the move, and her eyes tracked it
across the room until Oscar saw it too. He broke off
in midsentence, threw his napkin on the table and
stood up.

"What do you want?"

There was no answer, no sound whatever. Oscar's wife and Dottor Vianello, who were sitting with their backs to the camera, looked round. Rita Burolo emitted a scream of terror. Vianello's expression did not change, except to harden slightly.

"What do you want?" Burolo repeated, his brows knitted in puzzlement and annoyance. Abruptly he pushed his chair aside and strode toward the intruder, staring masterfully downward as though to cow an unruly child. You could say what you liked, thought Zen, but the man had guts. Or was he just foolhardy, trying to show off to his guests, to preserve an image of bravado to the last? At all events, it was only in the final moment that any fear entered Oscar's eyes, and he flung up his hands in an instinctive attempt to protect his face.

A brutal eruption of noise swamped the soundtrack. Literally disintegrated by the blast, Oscar's hands disappeared, while bright red blotches appeared all over his face and neck like an instant infection. He reeled away, holding up the stumps of his wrists. Somehow he managed to recover his balance and turn back, only to receive the second discharge, which carried away half his chest and flung him against the corner of the dining table where he collapsed in a bloody heap at his wife's feet.

Rita Burolo scrambled desperately away from the corpse as Vianello dived under the table, a pistol appearing in his hand. The ratchet sound of a shotgun being reloaded by pump action mingled with two sharp light cracks from the architect's pistol. Then the soundtrack was bludgeoned twice more in quick succession. The first barrel scoured the space below the table, gouging splinters out of the wood, shattering plates and glasses, wounding Signora Vianello terribly in the legs, and reducing her husband to a nightmare figure crawling about on the floor like a tormented animal. The second caught Rita Burolo trying desperately to climb out of the window that opened out to the terrace. As she was further away than the others, the wounds she sustained were more dispersed, covering her in a spray as fine and evenly distributed as drizzle on a windscreen. With a despairing cry she fell through the window to the paving stones of the terrace, where she slowly bled to death.

Even though her legs were lacerated, Maria Pia Vianello somehow struggled to her feet. Despite her own diminutive stature, she too gave the impression of looking down at the intruder.

"Just a moment, please," she muttered over the dry, clinical sound of the gun being reloaded. "I'm afraid I'm not quite ready yet. I'm sorry."

The shot took her at close range, flaying her so fearfully that loops of intestine protruded through the wall of her abdomen in places. Then the second barrel spun her round. She clutched the wall briefly, then collapsed into a dishevelled heap, leaving a complex pattern of dark streaks on the whitewashed plaster.

It had taken less than twenty seconds to turn the room into an abattoir. Fifteen seconds later, the caretaker would appear, having run from the two-room service flat where he and his wife had been watching a variety show on television. Until then, apart from wine dripping from a broken bottle at the edge of the table and a swishing caused by the convulsive twitches of the dying Vianello's arm, there was no sound whatsoever. "If anyone ever manages to break into this place, I'll believe in ghosts," the security analyst had assured Oscar Burolo. Nevertheless, someone or something *had* got in, butchered the inhabitants, and then vanished without trace, all in less than a minute, and in the most perfect silence. Even in broad daylight and the company of others it was difficult to ignore this almost supernatural dimension of the killings. In the eerie doldrums of the night, all alone, it seemed almost impossible to believe that there could be a rational explanation for them.

The silence of the running tape was broken by a distant scraping sound. Zen felt his skin crawl and the hairs on his head stir. He reached for the remote control unit and stilled the video. The noise continued, a low persistent scraping. "Like old Umberto's boat," his mother had said.

Zen walked quietly across to the inner hallway of the apartment, opened the door to his mother's bedroom, and looked inside.

"Can you hear it?" a voice murmured in the darkness.

"Yes, Mamma."

"Oh, good. I thought it might be me imagining it. I'm not quite right in the head sometimes, you know."

He gazed toward the invisible bed. It was the first time that she had ever made such an admission. They were both silent for some time, but the noise did not recur.

"Where is it coming from?" he asked.

"The wardrobe."

"Which wardrobe?"

There were three of them in the room, filled with clothes that no one would ever wear again, carefully preserved from moths by liberal doses of napthalene, which gave the room its basic funereal odour.

"The big one," his mother replied.

The biggest wardrobe occupied the central third of the wall that opened onto the internal courtyard of the building. Its positioning had occasioned Zen some anxiety at the time, since it obstructed access to the fire escape, but the wardrobe was too big to fit anywhere else.

Zen walked over to the bed and straightened the counterpane and sheets. Then he patted the hand which emerged from the covers, all the obsolete paraphernalia of muscles and arteries disturbingly revealed by the parchmentlike skin.

"It was just a rat, Mamma."

The best way of dispelling her formless, childish fears was by giving her a specific unpleasantness to focus on.

"But it sounded like metal."

"The skirting's lined with zinc," he improvised. "To stop them gnawing through. I'll speak to Giuseppe in the morning and we'll get the exterminators in. You try and get some sleep now."

Back in the living room, he turned off the television and rewound the video tape, trying to dispel his vague sense of unease by thinking about the report which he had to write the next day. It was the lateness of the hour that made everything seem strange and threatening now, the time when—according to what Zen's uncle had once told him—a house belongs not to the person who happened to live there now, but to all those who have preceded him over the centuries. Tomorrow morning everything would have snapped back into proportion and the uncanny aspects of the Burolo case would seem mere freakish curiosities. The only real question was whether to mention them at all. It wasn't that he wanted or needed to conceal anything. For that matter he wouldn't have known where to begin, since he had no idea who the report was destined for. The problem was that there were certain aspects of the Burolo case which were very difficult to mention without laying himself open to the charge of being a credulous nincompoop. For example, the statement made by the seven-year-old daughter of Oscar Burolo's lawyer, who had visited the villa in late July. As a special treat, she had been allowed to stay up for dinner with the adults, and in the excitement of the moment she had sneaked some of her father's coffee, with the result that she couldn't sleep. It was a luminous summer night, and eventually the child left her room and set out to explore the house. According to her statement, in one of the rooms in the older part of the villa she saw a figure moving about. "At first I was pleased," she said. "I thought it was a child, and I was lonely for someone to play with. But then I remembered that there were no children at the villa. I got scared and ran back to my room."

Including things like that could easily make him the laughingstock of the department, while if he left them out he laid himself open to the charge of suppressing evidence. Fortunately it was no part of Zen's mandate to draw conclusions or offer opinions. All that was needed was a brief report describing the various lines of investigation which had been conducted by the police and the Carabinieri and outlining the evidence against the various suspects. A clerical chore, in short, to which he was bringing nothing but an ability to read between the lines of official documents, picking out the grain of what was not being said from the overwhelming chaff of what was. Watching the video had been the last stage in this procedure. There was nothing left to do except sit down and write the thing, and this he would do next morning, while it was all fresh in his mind. By the afternoon, the Burolo affair would have no more significance for him than for any other member of the public.

Once again, footsteps sounded in the street below. A few minutes later the silence was abruptly shattered as a car started up and accelerated away with a squeal of tyres. By the time Zen reached the window it had already passed far beyond the area of street visible through the closed jalousies. The sound of its engine gradually faded away, echoing and reverberating ever more distantly through the intersecting channels of the streets. The streetlight was in its waxing phase, and as the light gradually intensified, Zen saw that the red car which had been parked further along the street was no longer there. He closed the shutters, wondering why its presence or absence should be of any interest or concern to him. Finding no answer, he decided that it was time to go to bed.

Nearly over now. Everything's going, the doubts, the fears, the cares, the confusion, even the pain. All draining away of its own accord. There's nothing I need do, nothing more to be done.

When I saw him standing there, the gun in his hand, it was like seeing myself in a mirror. He had taken my part, emerging from nowhere, implacable, confident, unsurprised. He sounded impatient, taunting me with a strange name, threatening me. "There's no point in trying to hide," he said. "Let's get it over with." As usual, I did what I was told.

He cried out in rage and disbelief. Whatever he had been expecting, it wasn't that. Then something overwhelmed me, knocking me over, opening me up. I couldn't have resisted even if I'd wanted to. It wasn't like the first time, the man under the table wounding me with his pistol. All he gave me was pain. This was different. I knew at once that I was carrying a death.

It won't be long now. Already I feel light and insubstantial, as though I am dissolving. The darkness is on the move, billowing out to enshroud me, wind me in its endless folds. Everything is in flux. Solid rock gives way at my touch, the ground flows beneath me as though the river had returned to its courses, unexplored caverns burst open like fireworks as I advance. I am lost, I who know this place better than I know my own body!

WEDNESDAY: 0720 — 1230

As Zen closed the front door behind him, its hinges emitted their characteristic squeal, which was promptly echoed from the floor above. One of the tenants there kept a caged bird, which was apparently under the illusion that Zen's front door was a fellow inmate and responded to its mournful cry with encouraging chirps.

Zen clattered down the stairs two at a time, ignoring the ancient lift in its wrought-iron cage. Thank God for work, he thought, which gave him an unquestionable excuse to escape from his dark, cluttered apartment and the elderly woman who had taken it over to such an extent that he felt like a child again, with no rights or independent existence. What would happen when he no longer had this ready-made way of filling his days? The government had recently been making noises about the need to reduce the size of the bloated public sector. Early retirement for senior staff was one obvious option. Fortunately it was unlikely that anything more than talk would come of it. A government consisting of a coalition of five parties, each with an axe to grind and clients to keep happy, found it almost impossible to

pass legislation that was likely to prove mildly unpopu-
lar with anyone, never mind tackle the bureaucratic hy-
dra which kept almost a third of the working population
in guaranteed employment. Nevertheless, he would
have to retire one day. The thought of it continued to
haunt him like the prospect of some chronic illness.
How would he get through the day? What would he do?
His life had turned into a dead end.

Giuseppe, the janitor, was keeping a watchful eye
on the comings and goings from the window of his mez-
zanine flat. Zen didn't stop to mention the scraping
noises his mother had claimed to hear the night before.
In broad daylight the whole thing seemed as unreal as a
dream.

The streets were steeped in mild November sunlight and ringing with sounds. Gangs of noisy schoolchildren passed by, flaunting the personalities that would
be buried alive for the next five hours. The metallic
roars of shutters announced that the shops in the area
were opening for business. A staccato hammering and
the swishing of a paint sprayer issued from the open
windows of the basement workshops where craftsmen
performed mysterious operations on lengths of moulded
wood. But the traffic dominated: the uniform hum of
new cars, the idiosyncratic racket of the old, the throaty
gurgle of diesels, the angry buzzing of scooters and
three-wheeled vans, the buses' hollow roar, the chain-
saw sound of an unsilenced trail bike, the squeal of
brakes, the strident discord of horns in conflict.

At the corner of the block the newsagent was adding the final touches to the display of newspapers and
magazines draped around his stall in a complex overlap-
ping pattern. As usual, Zen paused to buy a paper, but
he did not even glance at the headlines. He felt good,
serene and carefree, released from whatever black
magic had gripped his soul the night before. There
would be time enough later to read about disasters and
scandals which had nothing whatever to do with him.

Across the street from the newsstand, at the corner
of the next block, was the cafe which Zen frequented,

largely because it had resisted the spreading blight of skimmed milk, which reduced the rich foam of a proper *cappuccino* to an insipid froth. The barman, whose face sported a luxuriant moustache to compensate for his glossily bald skull, greeted Zen with respectful warmth and turned away unbidden to prepare his coffee.

"Barbarians!" exclaimed a thickset man in a tweed suit, looking up from the newspaper spread out before him on the bar. "Maniacs! What's the sense of it all? What can they hope to achieve?"

Zen helped himself to a flaky brioche before broaching the chocolate-speckled foam on the *cappuccino* which Ernesto had placed before him. It was only after they had been meeting in the bar each morning for several years that Zen had finally discovered, thanks to an inflamed molar requiring urgent attention, that the indignant newspaper reader was the dentist whose name appeared on one of the two brass plates which Giuseppe burnished religiously every morning. He congratulated himself on having resisted the temptation to look at the paper. No doubt there had been some dramatic new revelation about the Burolo affair. Hardly a day went by without one. But while for the dentist such things were a form of entertainment, a pretext for a display of moral temperament, to Zen it was work, and he didn't start work for another half hour. Idly, he wondered what the other men in the bar would say if they knew that he was carrying a video tape showing the Burolo killings in every last horrific detail.

At the thought, he put his coffee cup down and patted his coat pocket, reassuring himself that the video cassette was still there. That was one mistake he certainly couldn't allow himself! There had already been one leak recently, when stills from the tape Burolo had made showing love scenes between his wife and the young lion-keeper had been published in a trashy scandal magazine. Such a magazine, or even one of the less scrupulous private TV stations, would be willing to pay a small fortune for a video of the killings themselves. The missing tape would immediately be traced to Zen, who had signed it out from Archives. Everyone would assume that Zen himself had sold the tape, and the denials of the magazine or TV station—if they bothered to deny it—would be discounted as part of the deal. Vincenzo Fabri had been waiting for months for just such an opportunity to present itself. He wouldn't let it go to waste!

Zen now knew that he had badly bungled his unexpected promotion from his previous menial duties to the ranks of the Ministry's prestigious Criminalpol division. This had been due to a widespread but mistaken idea of the work which this group did. The press, intoxicated by the allure of elite units, portrayed it as a unit of high-powered supercops who sped about the peninsula cracking cases which proved too difficult for the local officials. Zen, as he had ruefully reflected many times since, should have known better. He of all people should have realised that police work never took any account of individual abilities. It was a question of carrying out certain procedures, that was all. Occasionally these procedures resulted in crimes being solved, but that was incidental to their real purpose, which was to maintain or adjust the balance of power within the organisation itself. The result was a continual shuffling and fidgeting, a ceaseless and frenetic activity which was easy to mistake for purposeful action.

Nevertheless, it was a mistake which Zen should never have made and which had cost him dearly. When dispatched to Bari or Bergamo or wherever it might be, he had thrown himself wholeheartedly into the case, asking probing questions, dishing out criticism, reorganising the investigation, and generally stirring things up as much as possible. This was the quickest way to get results, he fondly imagined, not having realised that the results desired by the Ministry flowed automatically from his having been sent. He didn't have to lift a finger, in fact it was important that he didn't. Far from being the "007 from the Ministry," which the press liked to portray, Criminalpol personnel were comparable to inspectors of schools or airports. Their visits provided a chance for the Ministry to get a reasonably reliable picture of what was happening, a reminder to the local authorities that all power ultimately lay with Rome, and a signal to concerned pressure groups that something was being done. No one wanted Zen to solve the case he had been sent to look into. Not the local police, who would then be asked why they had failed to achieve similar results unaided, nor the Ministry, to whom any solution would just pose a fresh set of problems. All he needed to do to keep everyone happy was just to go through the motions.

Unfortunately by the time he finally realised this, Zen had already alienated most of his new colleagues. Admittedly he had started with a serious handicap owing to the manner of his appointment, which had been engineered by one of the suspects in the Miletti kidnapping case he had investigated in Perugia. Zen's subsequent promotion had naturally been regarded by many people as a form of payoff, which was bound to cause resentment. But this might eventually have been forgiven if it hadn't been for the newcomer's tactless display of energy together with the bad luck of his having made an enemy of one of the most articulate and popular men on the staff. Vincenzo Fabri had tried unsuccessfully on a number of occasions to use political influence to have himself promoted, and he couldn't forgive Zen for having succeeded where he had failed. Fabri provided a focus for the feelings of antipathy which Zen had aroused, which he kept alive with a succession of witty, malicious anecdotes that only came to Zen's ears when the damage had been done. And because Fabri's grudge was completely irrational, Zen knew that it was all the more likely to last.

He crumpled his paper napkin into a ball, tossed it into the rubbish bin, and went to pay the cashier sitting at a desk in the angle between the two doors of the cafe. The newspaper the dentist had been reading lay open on the bar, and Zen couldn't ignore the thunderous headline: THE RED BRIGADES RETURN. Scanning the article beneath, he learned that a judge had been gunned down at his home in Milan the night before.

So that was what the dentist's rhetorical questions had referred to. What indeed was the sense of it all? There had been a time when such mindless acts of terrorism, however shocking, had at least seemed epic gestures of undeniable significance. But that time had long passed, and reruns were not only as morally disgusting as the originals, but also dated and secondhand.

As he walked to the bus stop, Zen read about the shooting in his own paper. The murdered judge, one Bertolini, had been gunned down when returning home from work. His chauffeur, who had also been killed, had fired at the attackers and was thought to have wounded one of them. Bertolini was not a particularly important figure, nor did he appear to have had any connection with the trials of Red Brigades' activists. The impression was that he had been chosen because he represented a soft target, itself a humiliating comment on the decline in the power of the terrorists from the days when they had seemed able to strike at will.

Zen's eye drifted off to the smaller headlines further down the page. BURNED ALIVE FOR ADULTERY read one. The story described how a husband in Genova had caught his wife with another man, poured petrol over them both, and set them alight. He abruptly folded the paper up and tucked it under his arm. Not that he had anything to worry about on that score, of course. He should be so lucky!

As a bus approached the stop, the various figures who had been loitering in the vicinity marched out into the street to try their chances at the lottery of guessing where the rear doors would be when the bus stopped. Zen did reasonably well this morning, with the result that he was ruthlessly jostled from every side as the less fortunate tried to improve on their luck. Someone at his back used his elbow so enterprisingly that Zen turned round to protest, almost losing his place as a result. But in the end justice prevailed, and Zen managed to squeeze aboard just as the doors closed.

The events reported in the newspaper had already had their effect at the Viminale. The approaches leading up to the Ministry building were guarded by armoured personnel carriers with machine-gun turrets on the roof. The barriers were lowered and all vehicles were being carefully searched. Pedestrian access, up a flight of steps from the piazza, was through a fence of heavy metal screen railings whose gate was normally left open, but today each person was stopped in the cage and had to present his or her identification while being watched carefully by two guards wearing bulletproof vests and carrying submachine guns.

Having penetrated these security checks, Zen walked up to the third floor, where Criminalpol occupied a suite of rooms at the front of the building. The contrast with the windowless cell to which Zen had previously been confined could hardly have been more striking. Tasteful renovation, supplemented by a scattering of potted plants and antique engravings, had created a pleasant working ambience without the oppressive scale traditionally associated with government premises.

"Quite like the old days!" was Giorgio De Angelis's comment as Zen passed by. "The lads upstairs are loving it, of course. A few more like this and they'll be able to claw back all the special powers they've been stripped of since things quietened down."

De Angelis was a big, burly man with a hairline which had receded dramatically to reveal a large, shiny forehead of the type popularly associated with noble and unworldly intellects. What spoiled this impression was his bulbous nose, with nostrils of almost Negroid proportions from which hairs sprouted like plants that have found themselves a niche in crumbling masonry. He was from the town of Crotone, east of the Sila mountains in central Calabria. One of the odd facts still lodged in Zen's brain from school was that Crotone had been the home of Pythagoras. This perhaps explained why De Angelis reminded him of a cross between a Greek philosopher and a Barbary pirate, thus neatly summing up Zen's uncertainty about his character and motives.

"Frankly, I shouldn't be a bit surprised if they set up the whole thing," the Calabrian went on breezily. "Apparently the Red Brigades have denied responsibility. Anyway, this Bertolini had nothing to do with terrorism. Why pick on him?"

Zen took off his overcoat and went to hang it up. He would have liked to be able to like De Angelis, the only one of his new colleagues who had made any effort to be friendly. But this very fact, coupled with the politically provocative comments which De Angelis was given to making, aroused a suspicion in Zen's mind that the Calabrian had been deliberately assigned to sound him out and try and trap him into damaging confidences. Even given the mutual hostility between the criminal investigation personnel and their political colleagues upstairs, De Angelis's last remark had been totally out of line.

"Have you seen the papers?" De Angelis demanded. " 'The terrorists return.' 'Fear stalks the corridors of power.' Load of crap, if you ask me. The fucking Red Brigades don't go round spraying people with shotgun pellets. Nothing but the best hardware for our yuppie terrorists. M42s, Armalites, Kalashnikovs, state-of-the-art stuff. Shotguns are either old-style crime or DIY."

He looked at Zen, who was patting his overcoat with a frown.

"You lost something?"

Zen looked round distractedly. "What? Yes, I suppose so. But in that case it can hardly have been the Politicals either."

"How do you mean?"

Zen's hands searched each of the pockets of the overcoat at some length, returning empty.

"Well, they'd have used the right gun, presumably."

De Angelis looked puzzled. Then he understood, and whistled meaningfully.

"Oh, you mean . . . Listen Aurelio, I'd keep my voice down if you're going to say things like that."

Too late, Zen realised that he had walked into a trap.

"I didn't mean that they'd killed him," De Angelis explained, "only that they'd orchestrated the media response to his death. I mean, you surely don't believe . . ."

"No, of course not."

He turned away with a sickly smile. He had just given himself away in the worst possible fashion, voicing what everyone no doubt suspected but what no Ministry employee who wanted to succeed could afford to say out loud. But that didn't matter, not now. All that mattered was that the video cassette of the Burolo killings was missing from his pocket.

Zen walked through the gap in the Hessian-clad screens which divided off the space allotted to each official, slumped down behind his desk, and lit a cigarette. He recalled with horrible clarity what had happened as he boarded the bus. It was a classic pickpocket's technique, using heavy blows in a safe area like the back and shoulders to cover the light disturbance as a wallet or pocketbook was removed. The thief must have spotted the bulge in Zen's coat pocket and thought it looked promising.

Looking on the bright side, there was a good chance—well, a chance, anyway—that when the thief saw that he'd made a mistake, he would simply throw the tape away. Even if he was curious enough to watch it, the first scenes were not particularly interesting. Unless you happened to recognise Burolo and the others, it looked much like any other home video, a souvenir of someone's summer holiday. Everything depended on whether the thief realised that his mistake had netted him something worth more than all the wallets he could steal in a lifetime. He might, or he might not. The only sure thing was that Zen could do absolutely nothing to influence the outcome one way or the other.

He had expected writing the report to be a chore, but after what had just happened, it was a positive relief to pull the typewriter over, insert a sheet of paper, and immerse himself in work. The first section, summarising the scene-of-crime findings, went very fast. Owing to the evidence of the video recording and the caretaker's prompt arrival, there was no dispute about the method or timing of the killings. The murder weapon had not been recovered, but was assumed to have been the Remington shotgun that was missing from the collection Oscar kept in a rack next door to the dining room. The spent cartridges found at the scene were of the same make, type, and batch as those stored in the drawers beneath this rack. Unidentified fingerprints had been found on the rack and elsewhere in the house. The nature of the victims' wounds indicated that the shots had been angled upward, suggesting that the weapon had apparently been fired from the hip. At that range it was unnecessary to take precise aim, as the video all too vividly demonstrated.

The two pistol bullets fired by Vianello had been recovered, and one of them revealed traces of blood of a group matching stains found at a point consistent with the assassin's estimated position. A series of stains of the same blood group—which was also that of Oscar Burolo, Maria Pia Vianello, and Renato Favelloni—was found leading to the vault beneath the house where Oscar's collection of video tapes and computer discs were housed. When the villa was searched, this room was found to be in a state of complete disorder: the new section of shelving Oscar had recently installed had been thrown over, and video cassettes and floppy discs lay scattered everywhere. The fingerprints found on the gun rack were also present in profusion here.

Zen stopped typing to stub out his cigarette. From behind the Hessian screen he could hear male voices raised in dispute about the merits and demerits of the new Fiat hatchback. He recognised the voices of Vincenzo Fabri and another official called Bernardo Travaglini. Then a flicker of movement nearby caught his eye and he looked round to find Tania Biacis standing by his desk.

"Sorry?" he muttered.

"I didn't say anything."

"Oh."

He gazed at her helplessly, paralysed by his desire to reach out and touch her. These exchanges, full of non sequiturs and dead ends, were typical of their conversation. Presumably Tania just assumed that Zen was a bit scatterbrained and thought no more about it. He hoped so, anyway.

"This is for you."

She handed him an envelope from the batch of internal mail she was delivering.

"So what was it last night?" Zen asked. "The opera, the new Fellini?"

"The opera's on strike," she said after a momentary hesitation. "As for Federico, we gave up on him after that last one. Granted the man used to be a genius, but enough's enough. No, we went out to eat at this little place out in the country near Tivoli. Have you been there? It's all the rage at the moment. Enrico Montesano was there with the most peculiar woman I've ever seen in my life, if she *was* a woman. But you'd better hurry if you want to go. The food's going downhill already. In another week it'll be ruined."

Zen sat looking at her, hardly heeding what she said. Tall, large-boned and small-breasted, with brows that arched high above her deep brown eyes, prominent cheekbones, a strong neck, and a light down on her protruding upper lip, which was usually curved as if in suppressed amusement, Tania Biacis resembled a Byzantine madonna come down from her mosaic in some chilly apse, a madonna not of sorrow but of joy, of secret glee, who knew that the universe was actually the most tremendous joke and could hardly believe that everyone else was taking it seriously. Like himself, Tania was a Northerner, from a village in the Friuli region east of Udine. This had created an immediate bond between them, and as the days went by, Zen had learned of her interest in films, music, sailing, skiing, cookery, travel, and foreign languages. He also discovered that she was fourteen years younger than him and married.

"I don't care what your dealer told you," Vincenzo Fabri proclaimed loudly. "Until a gearbox has done a hundred thousand kilometres—under on-road conditions, not on some test track in Turin—not even Agnelli himself knows how it's going to hold up."

"What do I care?" retorted Travaglini. "With the discount I'm getting, I can drive it until the warranty runs out and still break even on the trade-in. That's a year's free motoring."

"Would you do me a favour?" Tania whispered hurriedly.

"Of course."

"You don't know what it is yet."

"It doesn't matter."

He saw nothing wild or extravagant in this claim, which represented the simple truth. But as she turned away with a disconcerted look, he realised that it had sounded all wrong, either too gushing or too casual.

"Forget it," she told him, disappearing through a gap in the screens like an actor leaving the stage.

Zen sat there taking in her absence with a sharp pain he'd forgotten about, the kind that comes with love you don't ask for or even necessarily want, but which finds you out. It was normal to suffer like this in one's youth, of course, but what had he done to deserve such a fate at his age?

He tore open the memorandum she had brought him.

FROM: DOGLIOTTI, ASSISTANT REGISTRAR, ARCHIVES.
TO: ZENO, VICE-QUESTORE, POLIZIA CRIMINALE.
SUBJECT: 46429 BUR 433/K/95 (VIDEO CASSETTE, ONE).
YOU ARE REQUESTED TO RETURN THE ABOVE ITEM AT YOUR EARLIEST CONVENIENCE SINCE IT IS _____

_____ .

In the blank space, someone had scrawled an illegible phrase.

Zen stuffed the memorandum into his pocket with

a weary sigh. He had been so concerned about the large-scale repercussions if the tape fell into the wrong hands that he had completely forgotten the immediate problems involved. The Ministry's copy of the Burolo video was of course just that, a copy, the original being retained by the magistrates in Nuoro. Technically speaking, its loss was no more than an inconvenience, but that didn't mean that Zen could just drop down to Archives and tell them what had happened. In theory, official files could only be taken out of the Ministry with a written exeat permit signed by the relevant departmental head. In practice no one took the slightest notice of this, but the moment anything went wrong, the letter of the law would be strictly applied.

Once again, Zen turned to the task in hand as an escape from these problems. The next section of the report was considerably less straightforward than the one he had just written. While the facts of the Burolo case were simple enough, the interpretations which could be placed on them were political dynamite. Zen's completed report would be stored in the Ministry's central database, accessible by anyone with the appropriate terminal and codeword, his views and conclusions electronically enshrined forever. At least he didn't have to deal with the dreaded glowing screens himself! The use of computers was spreading inexorably through the various law enforcement agencies, although the dream of a unified electronic data pool had faded with the discovery that the systems chosen by the Carabinieri and the police were incompatible both with each other and with the quite different system used by the judiciary. It was a sign of their elite status that those Criminalpol officials who wished to do so had been allowed to retain their battered manual Olivettis with the curvy fifties styling that was now fashionable again.

Zen lit another of the coarse-flavoured domestic Nazionali cigarettes, looked up at the rectangular tiles of the suspended ceiling for inspiration, then began to pound the keys again.

BECAUSE OF THE EXCEPTIONAL DIFFICULTY OF UNAUTHO-
RISED ACCESS TO THE VILLA, THE NUMBER OF SUSPECTS WAS EX-
TREMELY LIMITED. NEVERTHELESS, FIVE POSSIBILITIES HAVE AT
VARIOUS TIMES BEEN CONSIDERED WORTHY OF INVESTIGATION.
THE FIRST, CHRONOLOGICALLY, CONCERNS ALFONSO AND GIU-
SEPPINA BINI. BINI ACTED AS CARETAKER AND GENERAL HANDY-
MAN AT THE VILLA, WHILE HIS WIFE COOKED AND CLEANED.
BOTH HAD WORKED FOR BUROLO FOR OVER TEN YEARS. AT THE
TIME OF THE MURDERS, THE COUPLE CLAIM TO HAVE BEEN WATCH-
ING TELEVISION IN THEIR QUARTERS IN THE NORTH WING OF THE
PROPERTY. THIS IS SEPARATED FROM THE DINING ROOM BY THE
WIDTH OF THE WHOLE BUILDING, INCLUDING THE MASSIVE EXTE-
RIOR WALLS OF THE ORIGINAL FARMHOUSE. AS GIUSEPPINA BINI
IS SLIGHTLY DEAF, THE VOLUME OF THE TELEVISION WAS TURNED
QUITE HIGH. SUBSEQUENT TESTS CONFIRMED THE COUPLE'S STORY
THAT THE GUNSHOTS WERE AT FIRST ALMOST INAUDIBLE. IT WAS
ONLY WHEN THEY WERE REPEATED THAT ALFONSO WENT TO
INVESTIGATE.

THE EVIDENCE AGAINST THE BINIS NEVER AMOUNTED TO
MORE THAN THE FACT OF THEIR PRESENCE AT THE VILLA AT THE
RELEVANT TIME, BUT SINCE THE ONLY OTHER PEOPLE PRESENT
WERE ALL DEAD AND IT WAS APPARENTLY IMPOSSIBLE FOR ANY
INTRUDER TO HAVE ENTERED THE PROPERTY, IT IS UNDERSTAND-
ABLE THAT THE COUPLE CAME UNDER SUSPICION. HOWEVER, THE
CASE AGAINST THEM, WHICH ALREADY LACKED ANY CONCEIVABLE
VIABLE MOTIVE, WAS FURTHER WEAKENED BY THE DISCOVERY OF
THE VIDEO TAPE RECORDING ALFONSO BINI'S EVIDENTLY GENU-
INE SHOCK ON DISCOVERING THE BODIES AND BY THE FACT THAT
A METICULOUS SEARCH FAILED TO UNCOVER ANY TRACE OF THE
MURDER WEAPON AT THE VILLA, WHERE THE COUPLE HAD RE-
MAINED THROUGHOUT.

Zen paused to give his numbed fingers a chance to
recover. Next on his list was the vendetta theory, which
involved filling in the background about the attempted
kidnapping of Oscar Burolo. This had surprised no one,
except for the fact that the intended victim had gotten
away with nothing but a scratch on his shoulder. God-
damn it, people had murmured in tones of exasperated
admiration, how does he do it? Kidnapping was notori-

ously a way of life in Sardinia, and what had Burolo done but choose a property on the very edge of the Barbagia massif itself, the heartland of the kidnapping gangs and the location of the underground lairs where they hid their victims? He was *asking* for it!

And he duly got it. Fortunately for Oscar, the Lincoln Continental he had been driving at the time was a rather special model, built for the African president who figured in the fictitious slave story. Oscar did a lot of work in Africa, which he liked to describe as "a land of opportunity," rolling his eyes comically to suggest what kind of opportunities he had in mind. The president in question was unfortunately toppled from power just after taking delivery of the vehicle and just before Oscar could collect on the contract the president had signed for the construction of a new airport in the country's second-largest city, a job which had promised to be even more lucrative than most of those which Oscar was involved in.

Where other companies might reckon on a profit margin of twenty or thirty percent, regarding anything above that as an extraordinary windfall, the projects which Burolo Construction undertook seemed able to generate profits that were often in excess of the total original budget. Oscar had earned the sobriquet King Midas for his ability to turn the hardest rock, the most arid soil, and the foulest marshland into pure gold. In the case of the African airport, his bill had already soared to a sum amounting to almost four percent of the country's gross national product, but on this occasion Oscar was thus constrained to realism. Even if the new regime had been disposed to honour the commitments of the former president, it would have had considerable difficulty in doing so, since the latter had prudently diverted another considerable slice of the country's GNP to the Swiss bank account that was now financing his premature retirement. All this was very regrettable, but Oscar was a realist. He knew that while governments come and go, business goes on forever. So rather than stymie his chances of profitable intervention in the country's future by pointless litigation, he reluctantly agreed to accept a settlement which barely covered his expenses. To sweeten the pill, he asked for and was given the Lincoln Continental as well.

At the time, Oscar had seen the car as just another of the fancy gadgets with which he loved to surround himself, but it undoubtedly saved his life when the kidnappers tried to take him. He was driving back from the local village church when it happened. Much to most people's surprise, Oscar never missed Sunday Mass. Experience had taught him the importance of keeping on the right side of those in power, and compared with the kind of kickbacks, favours, and general dancing of attendance which some of his patrons expected, God seemed positively modest in His demands. It was true that you could never be absolutely certain that He was there, and if so, whether He was prepared to come up with the goods, but much the same could be said about most of the people in Rome, too. As long as all that was needed to stay in good with Him was taking communion every Sunday, Oscar thought it was well worth the effort. Unfortunately the local village church lacked a suitable landing place for the Agusta, so he had to drive.

As he rounded one of the many sharp bends that Sunday, Oscar found the road blocked by what appeared to be a minor accident. A car was lying on its side in the ditch, while the lorry which had apparently forced it off the road was slewed around broadside to the approaching limousine. Three men were kneeling beside a fourth who was lying facedown in the road.

As Oscar got out to help, the men turned toward him.

"Instantly, I *knew!*" he told countless listeners later. "Don't ask me how. I just knew!"

He leapt back into the car as the accident victim rolled to one side, revealing the rifles and shotguns on which he'd been lying. Several shots were fired, one of which wounded Oscar slightly in the shoulder. He didn't even notice. He threw the Lincoln into reverse and accelerated back up the road.

The kidnappers gave chase on foot, firing as they ran. But the African president, even more of a realist than Burolo himself, had specified armour-plating and bulletproof windows, and the kidnappers' shots rattled harmlessly away. When he reached the corner, Oscar reversed onto the shoulder to turn the car round. As he did so, the youngest of the four men sprinted forward, leaped onto the bonnet, pressed the muzzle of his rifle against the windscreen, and fired. The shot barely chipped the toughened glass, but for a second Oscar had stared death in the face. His reaction was to slam on the brakes, sending the man reeling onto the road, and then accelerate right over him.

By the time the police arrived at the scene there was nothing to see except a few tyre marks and a little blood mixed in with the loose gravel in the centre of the road. A few days later the funeral of a young shepherd named Antonio Melega took place in a mountain village some forty kilometres to the northwest. According to his grim-faced, taciturn relatives, he had been struck by a hit-and-run driver while walking home from his pastures.

The abortive kidnap made Oscar Burolo an instant hero among the island's villa-owning fraternity, eminently kidnappable every one. One enterprising shopkeeper did a brisk trade in T-shirts reading "Italians 1, Sardinians 0" until the local mayor protested. But although Burolo was quite happy to be lionised, in private he was a frightened man, haunted by the memory of that dull bump beneath the car and the man's muffled cry as the tons of armour-plating crushed the life out of him. He knew that by killing one of the kidnappers he had opened an account that would only be closed with his own death. Burolo had been born in the north, but his father had been from a little village in the province of Matera, and he had told his son about blood feuds and the terrible obligation of vendetta which could be placed on a man against his will, destroying him and everyone close to him because of something he had nothing to do with and of which he perhaps even disap-

proved. Young Oscar had been deeply impressed by
these stories. To his childish ear they had the ring of
absolute truth, matching as they did the violent and arbi-
trary rituals of the world he shared with other boys his
age. Just as he had known the kidnappers the moment
their eyes met, so now he knew they would not rest
until they had avenged the death of their colleague.

Faced with this knowledge, a lesser man might
have called it quits, sold off the villa—if he could find a
purchaser!—and taken his holidays elsewhere in the future. But Oscar's realism had its limits, and it ended
where his vanity began. Had it been a business deal,
where no one but himself and the other party would
have been any the wiser, he might have cut and run. But
he had invested all his self-esteem, to say nothing of
several billion lira, in the villa, and it would take more
than some bunch of small-time sheep-shaggers, as he
jeeringly referred to them, to see him off.

Nevertheless, someone *had* seen him off, and the
friends and relatives of the late Antonio Melega naturally
came under suspicion. Apart from the sheer ferocity of
the killings, some of the physical evidence seemed to
support this hypothesis. Sardinians, particularly those
from the poorer mountain areas, are the shortest of all
Mediterranean peoples. The fingerprints found on the
ejected shotgun cartridges at the scene of the murders
were exceptionally small—"like a child's," the Carabinieri's expert had remarked, an unfortunate phrase
which had provoked much mirth in the rival force. But
an adult gunman of small stature was another matter and
would also explain the low angle of fire which had previously been attributed to the gun being held at hip
level. Moreover, sheep rustlers would necessarily be
skilled in moving and acting soundlessly, hence the eerie silence which had so impressed everyone who had
seen the video tape.

UNFORTUNATELY, THERE WAS AN INSURMOUNTABLE PROB-
LEM ABOUT THIS ATTRACTIVE HYPOTHESIS, NAMELY THE QUESTION
OF ACCESS. THE DEFENSES OF THE VILLA BUROLO HAD BEEN

SPECIFICALLY DESIGNED TO PREVENT AN INCURSION OF PRECISELY
THIS KIND. IT IS TRUE THAT THE CONTROL ROOM ITSELF WAS NOT
MANNED AT THE TIME OF THE MURDERS, BUT THE SYSTEM WAS
DESIGNED TO SET OFF ALARMS ALL OVER THE VILLA IN THE EVENT
OF ANY INTRUSION. IN ORDER TO TEST THE EFFECTIVENESS OF
THESE ALARMS, A SPECIALIST ALPINE UNIT OF THE CARABINIERI
ATTEMPTED TO BREAK INTO THE VILLA BY A VARIETY OF MEANS,
INCLUDING THE USE OF PARACHUTES AND HANG GLIDERS. IN EV-
ERY CASE, THE ALARMS WERE ACTIVATED. ANY DIRECT ASSAULT
OF THE PREMISES, WHETHER BY LOCAL KIDNAPPERS OR ANY OTHER
GROUP, THUS HAD TO BE RULED OUT.

Placing an asterisk after *group,* Zen added a foot-
note at the bottom of the page.

SUBSEQUENT TO AN ASSESSMENT OF THE SITUATION UNDER-
TAKEN BY THIS DEPARTMENT IN LATE SEPTEMBER, DOTTOR VIN-
CENZO FABRI SUGGESTED THAT THE INTENDED VICTIM OF THE
KILLINGS MIGHT NOT HAVE BEEN OSCAR BUROLO, WHO WAS
UNARMED AND WHOSE DEMEANOUR THROUGHOUT THE VIDEO RE-
CORDING SHOWED HIM TO BE UNAFRAID OF THE INTRUDER, BUT
HIS GUEST EDOARDO VIANELLO. FABRI POINTED OUT THAT THE
FACT THAT THE ARCHITECT WAS CARRYING A PISTOL SHOWED
THAT HE FEARED FOR HIS SAFETY AND RAISED THE POSSIBILITY
THAT AN INVESTIGATION INTO VIANELLO'S PROFESSIONAL AFFAIRS
MIGHT REVEAL AN INVOLVEMENT WITH THE ORGANISED CRIME FOR
WHICH HIS NATIVE SICILY IS NOTORIOUS. TO OVERCOME THE
PROBLEM OF ACCESS, FABRI SUGGESTED THAT GIUSEPPINA BINI
WAS SECRETLY WORKING FOR THE MAFIA, DRAWING ATTENTION
TO THE FACT THAT IN 1861 HER MATERNAL GRANDFATHER HAD
BEEN BORN IN AGRIGENTO. FOR SOME REASON, HOWEVER, THIS
INGENIOUS THEORY FAILED TO ATTRACT THE SERIOUS ATTENTION
IT NO DOUBT MERITED.

Zen smiled sourly. It was rare for him to get an
opportunity to put one over on Vincenzo Fabri. What
the hell had the man been up to, he wondered, floating
this kind of wild and unsubstantiated rumour?

The next candidate on Zen's list came into the category of light relief.

FURIO PIZZONI WAS DETAINED ON HIS RETURN TO THE
VILLA ABOUT TWO HOURS AFTER THE KILLINGS HAD TAKEN PLACE.
WHEN QUESTIONED AS TO HIS EARLIER WHEREABOUTS, HE
CLAIMED TO HAVE SPENT THE EVENING IN A BAR IN THE LOCAL
VILLAGE. THIS ALIBI WAS SUBSEQUENTLY CONFIRMED BY THE
OWNER OF THE BAR AND SEVERAL CUSTOMERS. PIZZONI UNDOUBT-
EDLY HAD ACCESS TO THE REMOTE CONTROL DEVICE MENTIONED
BELOW (SEE FAVELLONI, RENATO), BUT GIVEN HIS ALIBI AND THE
ABSENCE OF ANY EVIDENT MOTIVE, INTEREST IN HIM SOON FADED,
ALTHOUGH IT WAS BRIEFLY REVIVED BY THE DISCOVERY OF VIDEO
TAPES SHOWING AMOROUS ENCOUNTERS BETWEEN HIM AND RITA
BUROLO.

Zen drew the last fragrant wisps of smoke from his
cigarette and crushed it out. After a moment's thought,
he decided against going into any more details. Even the
magazine which had paid so dearly for the photographs
made from one of those video tapes had drawn a discreet veil of verbiage over the exact nature of this little
love triangle. It was difficult to offer a tasteful account
of the fact that the murdered woman had been in the
habit of meeting Pizzoni by moonlight in the hut where
the lions slept during the day and rolling nude on the
straw bedaubed with their sweat and excrement while
the young man pleasured her in a variety of ways un-
dreamt of in the animal kingdom. For some people it
was still more difficult to accept that Oscar Burolo had
known about these orgies and had done nothing whatever about them, apart from rigging up a small video
camera in the rafters of the hut to record the scene for
his future delectation.

Suddenly Zen caught the sound of Tania's voice behind the screens.

"You promise?" She sounded anxious.

"But of course!" The heavy, monotonous voice was
that of an official called Romizi.

"Otherwise it'll mean a lot of trouble for me," Tania
stressed.

"Don't worry! I'll take care of it."

Zen slumped forward until his forehead touched

the cool metal casing of the typewriter. So she had found someone else to ask her favour of, after he had scared her away with his tactless impetuosity. He took a deep breath, expelled it as a long sigh, and began to pound the Olivetti's stubborn keys again.

GIVEN THE KILLER'S NEED OF SPECIALISED KNOWLEDGE TO OVERCOME THE VILLA'S SECURITY DEFENCES, IT WAS INEVITABLE THAT THE ONLY SURVIVING MEMBER OF OSCAR BUROLO'S IMMEDIATE FAMILY, HIS SON ENZO, SHOULD COME UNDER SUSPICION. RELATIONS BETWEEN ENZO AND HIS FATHER HAD REPORTEDLY BEEN STRAINED FOR SOME TIME, LARGELY OWING TO THE YOUNG MAN'S REFUSAL TO AGREE TO GIVE UP HIS ATTEMPT TO BECOME A PROFESSIONAL VIOLINIST IN FAVOUR OF A CAREER IN LAW OR MEDICINE. THAT AUGUST, ENZO BUROLO WAS ATTENDING A MUSIC SCHOOL IN AMERICA, AND ENQUIRIES BY THE FBI CONFIRMED THAT HE HAD BEEN IN THE BOSTON AREA DURING THE PERIOD IMMEDIATELY PRECEDING AND FOLLOWING THE MURDERS. THIS LINE OF INVESTIGATION WAS THEREFORE ALSO DROPPED.

Zen flexed his fingers, making the joints creak like old wood. He had now disposed of the suspects the judiciary had rejected. It only remained to discuss their eventual choice, currently awaiting trial in Nuoro prison. And here he had to tread very carefully indeed.

THE REMAINING POSSIBILITY CENTERED ON RENATO FAVELLONI. FAVELLONI HAD VISITED THE BUROLO PROPERTY ON MANY PREVIOUS OCCASIONS AND HAD BEEN STAYING THERE DURING THE PERIOD IMMEDIATELY PRIOR TO THE MURDERS. EARLY THAT EVENING HE AND HIS WIFE WERE FLOWN BY OSCAR BUROLO TO OLBIA AIRPORT TO CATCH ALISARDA FLIGHT IG113 TO ROME. ACCORDING TO NADIA FAVELLONI, SHORTLY BEFORE THE FLIGHT WAS CALLED, HER HUSBAND TOLD HER THAT HE HAD FORGOTTEN A VERY IMPORTANT DOCUMENT AT THE VILLA AND HAD TO RETURN TO GET IT. SHE WAS TO GO ON TO ROME WHILE HE WOULD TAKE A LATER FLIGHT. NADIA FAVELLONI DULY LEFT ON IG113, BUT AN EXAMINATION OF PASSENGER LISTS REVEALED THAT FAVELLONI HAD MADE NO BOOKING FOR A LATER FLIGHT. UNDER

QUESTIONING, FAVELLONI FIRST CLAIMED THAT HE HAD FLOWN TO MILAN INSTEAD. WHEN IT WAS POINTED OUT TO HIM THAT HIS NAME DID NOT APPEAR ON THE PASSENGER LIST OF THE MILAN FLIGHT EITHER, HE STATED THAT THE PURPOSE OF HIS TRIP HAD BEEN TO VISIT HIS MISTRESS. THIS WAS WHY HE HAD TOLD HIS WIFE THE FALSE STORY ABOUT LEAVING A DOCUMENT AT THE VILLA BUROLO AND WHY HE HAD BOOKED UNDER A FALSE NAME. HIS WIFE WAS SUSPICIOUS AND HAD ONCE HIRED A PRIVATE DETECTIVE TO CHECK ON HIS MOVEMENTS. HOWEVER, NONE OF THE STAFF OR PASSENGERS ON THE MILAN FLIGHT WAS ABLE TO IDENTIFY FAVELLONI, AND SINCE HIS MISTRESS'S TESTIMONY IS INADMISSIBLE, THERE IS NO PROOF THAT HE EVER LEFT SARDINIA ON THE NIGHT OF THE MURDERS.

THE KEY TO THE BUROLO CASE THROUGHOUT HAS BEEN THE QUESTION OF ACCESS. OSCAR BUROLO HAD PAID AN ENORMOUS SUM OF MONEY TO TURN HIS PROPERTY INTO A FORTRESS, YET THE MURDERER WAS ABLE TO ENTER AND LEAVE THE PROPERTY WITHOUT SETTING OFF ANY OF THE ALARMS, ALL WITHIN A FEW MINUTES. HOW WAS THIS POSSIBLE?

THE MOST LIKELY EXPLANATION REQUIRES SOME CONSIDERATION OF THE PROVISION MADE TO ENABLE THE INHABITANTS OF THE VILLA THEMSELVES TO COME AND GO. SINCE BUROLO REFUSED TO EMPLOY SECURITY GUARDS TO MAN THE GATES OR THE CONTROL ROOM, THIS HAD TO BE DONE AUTOMATICALLY, BY MEANS OF A REMOTE CONTROL UNIT, OR PROXIMITY DEVICE, SIMILAR TO THOSE USED FOR OPENING GARAGE DOORS. BUT WHILE MOST COMMERCIALLY AVAILABLE MODELS ARE OF LITTLE VALUE IN SECURITY TERMS SINCE THEIR CODES CAN EASILY BE DUPLICATED, THE SYSTEM AT THE VILLA BUROLO WAS VIRTUALLY UNBREAKABLE BECAUSE THE CODE CHANGED EVERY TIME IT WAS USED. ALONG WITH THE EXISTING CODE, WHICH CAUSED THE GATES TO OPEN, THE REMOTE-CONTROL UNIT TRANSMITTED A NEW RANDOMLY GENERATED CLUSTER REPLACING THE PREVIOUS CODE WHICH WOULD SERVE TO OPERATE THE MECHANISM AT THE NEXT OCCASION. SINCE EACH SIGNAL IS UNIQUE, IT IS IMPOSSIBLE FOR A WOULD-BE INTRUDER TO DUPLICATE IT. BUT ANYONE WHO HAD BEEN ADMITTED TO THE VILLA COULD EASILY REMOVE THE DEVICE AND USE IT TO REENTER THE PROPERTY WITHOUT TRIGGERING THE ALARMS.

So far, so good, thought Zen. Technical jargon about remote control devices was no problem. Where the Favelloni angle got sticky was when it came to dealing not with means and opportunity but with motive. It was widely assumed that the reason why Renato Favelloni had paid so many visits to the Villa Burolo that summer was that he was involved in negotiations between Oscar Burolo and the politician referred to as *l'onorevole,* whose influence had allegedly been instrumental in getting Burolo Construction its lucrative public-sector contracts. According to the rumours circulating in the press and elsewhere, the two men had recently fallen out, and Oscar had threatened to make public the records he kept detailing their mutually rewarding transactions over the years. Before he could carry out this threat, however, he and his guests had been gunned down, his documentary collection of video tapes and floppy discs ransacked, and *l'onorevole* spared any possible future embarrassment.

This was the aspect of the case which was presumably occupying the attention of the investigating magistrate, but Aurelio Zen, unprotected by the might and majesty of the judiciary, wanted to give the subject the widest possible berth. Fortunately he had a convenient excuse for doing so. Although these theories had been widely touted, because of the secrecy in which the prosecution case was prepared they remained mere theories, lacking any substantive backing whatsoever. Once Renato Favelloni was brought to trial—in a few weeks, perhaps—all this would very rapidly change, but until then no one could know the extent or gravity of the evidence against him. Thus all Zen needed to do was to plead ignorance.

As already stressed, the details of the case remain *sub judice,* but the fact that the charge is one of conspiracy to murder indicates that another person or persons are thought to be implicated. This might indeed have been inferred from the fact that Dottor Vianello's pistol shot apparently wounded the assassin, probably in

THE LEG, WHILE A MEDICAL EXAMINATION OF THE ACCUSED RE-
VEALED NO RECENT LESIONS. IN THIS HYPOTHESIS, RENATO
FAVELLONI WOULD HAVE REMOVED THE REMOTE-CONTROL DEVICE
FROM THE VILLA AND PASSED IT ON TO AN ACCOMPLICE, PROBA-
BLY A PROFESSIONAL GUNMAN, WHO USED IT TO ENTER VILLA
BUROLO AND LEAVE AGAIN, HAVING CARRIED OUT THE MURDERS.
IN A CASE LIKE THIS, ONE WOULD OF COURSE EXPECT A PROFES-
SIONAL KILLER TO USE HIS OWN WEAPON, PROBABLY WITH A
SILENCER. IT CAN BE ARGUED THAT THIS ANOMALY MERELY
STRENGTHENS THE CASE AGAINST FAVELLONI, INDICATING THAT
AN ATTEMPT WAS MADE TO DISGUISE THE FACT THAT THE CRIME
WAS A PREMEDITATED CONSPIRACY AGAINST THE LIFE OF OSCAR
BUROLO.

Zen knocked the pages into order and read through
what he had written, making a few corrections here and
there. Then he put the report into a cardboard folder
and carried it through the gap in the screens separating
his work area from that of Carlo Romizi.

"How's it going?" he remarked.

Romizi looked up from the railway timetable he
had been studying.

"Did you know that there's a train listed in here
that doesn't exist?"

In every organisation there is at least one person of
whom all his colleagues think, How on earth did he get
the job? In Criminalpol, that person was Carlo Romizi,
an Umbrian with a face like the man in the moon. Even
after some gruelling tour of duty, Romizi always looked
as fresh as a newly laid egg, and his expression of childlike astonishment never varied.

"No, I didn't know that," Zen replied.

"De Angelis just told me."

"Which one is it?"

"That's the whole point! They don't say. Every year
they invent a train which just goes from one bit of the
timetable to another. Each individual bit looks all right,
but if you put it all together you discover that the train
just goes round and round in circles, never getting anywhere. Apparently it started one year when they made a

mistake. Now they do it on purpose, as a sort of joke. I haven't found it yet, but it must be here. De Angelis told me about it."

Zen nodded noncommittally.

"What did la Biacis want?" he asked casually.

The effort of memory made Romizi frown.

"Oh, she was nagging me about some expense claim I put in. Apparently Moscati thinks that it was excessive. I mean excessively excessive. I said I'd send in a revised claim, only I forgot."

Youth is only a lightness of the heart, Zen thought as he walked away, as happy as a bird and all because Tania had not treated Romizi to her confidences after all.

In stark contrast to the Criminalpol suite, the administrative offices on the ground floor were designed in the old style, with massive desks drawn up in rows like tanks on parade. Tania was nowhere to be seen. One of her colleagues directed Zen to the accounts department, where he spent some time trying to attract the attention of a clerk who sat gazing into the middle distance, a telephone receiver hunched under each ear, repeating, "But of course!" and "But of course not!." Without looking up, he handed Zen a form marked Do Not Fold, Spindle Or Mutilate on which he had scribbled, Personnel? In the Personnel department on the fourth floor, Franco Ciliani revealed that the Biacis woman had just left after breaking his balls so comprehensively that he doubted whether they would ever recover.

"You know what her problem is?" Ciliani demanded rhetorically. "She's not getting enough. The thing with women is, if you don't fuck them silly every few days they lose all sense of proportion. We should drop her husband a line, remind him of his duties."

Apart from these words of wisdom, Ciliani was unable to help, but as Zen was walking disconsolately downstairs again, Tania suddenly materialised beside him.

"I've been looking for you everywhere," he said.

"Except the women's toilet, presumably."

"Ah."

He handed her the folder as they continued downstairs together.

"This is the report Moscati asked for. Can you get a couple of copies up there before lunch?"

"Of course!" Tania replied rather tartly. "That's what I'm here for."

"What's the matter? Did Ciliani say something to you?"

She shrugged. "No, he just gets on my nerves, that's all. It's not his fault. He reminds me of my husband."

This remark was so bizarre that Zen ignored it. Everything Tania had said so far suggested that she and her husband were blissfully happy together, a perfect couple.

As they reached the third floor landing, Zen reached over and took her arm.

"What was it you wanted me to do for you?"

She looked at him, then looked away.

"Nothing. It doesn't matter."

She didn't move, however, and he didn't let go of her arm. With his free hand he gestured toward the stairs. Whoever had designed the Ministry of the Interior had been a firm believer in the idea that an institution's prestige is directly proportional to the dimensions of its main staircase, which was built on a scale that seemed to demand heroic gestures and sumptuous costumes.

"Perhaps it would work better if we sang," Zen suggested with a slightly hysterical smile.

"Sang?" Tania repeated blankly.

He knew he should never have opened his mouth, but he was feeling light-headed because of her presence there beside him.

"This place reminds me of an opera. I mean, talking doesn't seem quite enough. You know what I mean?"

He released her, stretched out one arm, laid his other hand on his chest, and intoned, "What was it you wanted me to do for you?"

Tania's face softened into a smile.

"And what would I do?"

"You'd have an aria where you told me. About twenty times over."

They looked at each other for a moment. Then Tania scribbled something on a piece of paper.

"Ring this number at seven o'clock this evening. Say you're phoning from here and because of the murder of that judge there's an emergency on and I'm needed till midnight."

Zen took the paper from her.

"That's all?"

"That's all."

He nodded slowly, as though he understood, and turned away.

Blood everywhere, my blood. I'm collapsing like a sack of grain the rats have gnawed a hole in. No one will ever find me. No one but me knows about this place. I will have disappeared.

I made things disappear. People too, but that came later, and caused less stir. People drop dead all the time anyway. Things are more durable. A bowl or chair, a spade, a knife, can hang around a house so long that no one remembers where it came from. It seems that it's always been there. When it suddenly disappeared, everyone tried to hush up the scandal. "It must be somewhere! Don't worry, it'll turn up, just wait and see."

A crack had appeared in their world. And through it, for a moment, they felt the chill and caught a glimpse of the darkness that awaited them, too.

*   *   *

I've got together quite a collection, one way and another. What will become of it now, I wonder? Cups, pens, string, ribbon, playing cards, wallets, nails, clothing, tools, all piled up in the darkness like offerings to the indifferent god whose presence I sense at night in the space between the stars, featureless and vast.

Things don't just disappear for no reason. "There's a reason for everything," as old Tommaso likes to say, nodding that misshapen head of his that looks like a lump of rock left standing in a field for farmers to curse and plough around or else blow up. I'd like to blow it up, his wise old head. "What's the reason for this, then?" I'd ask as I pulled the trigger. Too late for that now.

Perhaps he would have understood at the last. Perhaps the others did, too. Perhaps the look on their faces was not just pain and terror, but understanding. At all events, the crack was there, the possibility of grace, thanks to me. Things are not what they seem. There's more to this place than meets the eye. I was living proof of that.

And they proved it too, dying.

WEDNESDAY: 2025 — 2205

"Is THIS GOING TO take much longer?" the taxi driver asked plaintively, twisting around to the back seat.

His passenger regarded him without enthusiasm.

"What do you care? You're getting paid, aren't you?"

The driver banged his palm on the steering wheel, making it ring dully.

"Eh, I hope so! But there's more to life than getting paid, you know. It's almost an hour we've been sitting here. I usually have a bite to eat around now. I mean, if you wanted me for the evening, you should have said so."

The street in which they were parked stretched straight ahead between the evenly spaced blocks of flats built on reinforced concrete stilts, the ground floor level consisting of a car park. In the nearest block, half of this space had been filled in to provide a few shops, all closed. Between two of them was a lit plate-glass frontage above which a blue neon sign read BAR.

"Well?" the driver demanded.

"All right. But don't take all night about it."

The driver clambered awkwardly out of the car, wheezing heavily. Years of high tension and low exercise seemed to have converted all his bone and muscle to flab.

"I'm talking about a snack, that's all!" he complained. "Even the fucking car won't go except you fill it up."

Hitching up his ample trousers, he waddled off past three metal rubbish skips overflowing with plastic bags and sacks. Zen watched him pick his way across the hummocks and gullies that looked like piles of frozen snow in the cheerless light of the ultramodern street-lamps.

Nothing else moved. No one was about. Apart from the bar, there was nothing in the vicinity to tempt the inhabitants out-of-doors after dark. The whole area had a provisional, partially finished look, as though the developer had lost interest halfway through the job. The reason was no doubt to be found in one of those get-out clauses which Burolo Construction's contracts had invariably included, allowing them to suck the lucrative marrow out of a project without having to tackle the boring bits.

Like the others, the block near which they were parked was brand new and looked as if it had been put together in about five minutes from prefabricated sections like a child's toy. Access to the four floors of flats was by rectangular stairwells which descended like lift shafts to the car park at ground level. The flat roof bristled with television aerials resembling the reeds which had flourished in this marshy land before the developers moved in.

Some of the windows were unshuttered, and from time to time figures appeared in these lighted panels, providing Zen with his only glimpse so far of the inhabitants of the zone. There was no way of knowing whether their shadowy gestures were of any relevance to his concerns or not. He had checked the list of residents posted outside each stairwell. The name Bevilacqua appeared opposite Flat 14, but the door to the stairs was locked and Zen hadn't gone as far as to try and gain entry to the block. It seemed to him that he'd gone quite far enough as it was!

Most of his afternoon had been spent trying to find a solution to the problem of the stolen video tape. A visit to an electronics shop had revealed the existence of complexities he had never guessed at, involving choices of type, brand, and length. In the end he'd selected one which had the practical advantage of being sold separately rather than in packs of three. It didn't really matter, he told himself. Either they would check or they wouldn't. If they did, they weren't going to feel any better disposed toward Zen because he had replaced the missing video with exactly the right kind of blank tape or even given them a Bugs Bunny cartoon in exchange.

Back at the Ministry, he walked down two flights of drably functional concrete stairs to the subbasement where the Archives department was housed. As he had foreseen, only one clerk was on duty at that time of day, so Zen's request to inspect the files relating to one of his old cases, selected at random, resulted in the desk being left unmanned for over five minutes. This was quite long enough for Zen to browse through the rubber stamp collection, find the one reading PROPERTY OF THE MINISTRY OF THE INTERIOR—Index No. _____, apply this to the labels on the face and spine of the video cassette, and then copy the index number from the memorandum he had been sent.

When the clerk returned with the file he had asked for, Zen spent a few minutes leafing through it for appearance's sake. The case was one that dated back almost twenty years to the time when Zen had been attached to the Questura in Milan. He scanned the pages with affection and nostalgia, savouring the contrast between the old-fashioned report forms and the keen flourish of his youthful handwriting. But as the details of the case began to emerge, these innocent pleasures were overshadowed by darker memories. Why had he asked for *this,* of all files?

The question was also the answer, for the Spadola case was not just another of the many investigations Zen had been involved with in the course of his career. It had been at once his first great triumph and his first great disillusionment.

After the war, when the fighting in Italy came to an end, many left-wing partisans were ready and willing to carry the armed struggle one stage further, to overthrow the government and set up a workers' state. Some had ideological reasons, others were just intoxicated by the thrills and glamour of making history and couldn't stomach the prospect of returning to a life of mundane, poorly paid work, even supposing there was work to be had. To such men, and Vasco Spadola was one, the decision of the Communist leader Togliatti to follow a path of reform rather than revolution represented a betrayal. Once it became clear that a national uprising of the Italian working class was not going to happen, Spadola and his comrades put their weapons and training to use in a sporadic campaign of bank raids and hold-ups which they tried to justify as acts of class warfare.

The success of these ventures soon caused considerable strains and stresses within the group. On one side were those led by Ugo and Carlo Trocchio, who still adhered to a doctrinaire political line, and on the other Spadola's followers, who were beginning to appreciate the possibilities of this kind of private enterprise. These problems were eventually resolved when the Trocchio brothers were shot dead in a cafe in the Milan suburb of Rho.

With their departure, the gang abandoned all pretence of waging a political struggle and concentrated instead on consolidating its grip on every aspect of the city's criminal life. High-risk bank raids were replaced by unspectacular percentage operations such as gambling, prostitution, drugs, and extortion. Spadola's involvement in these areas was well known to the police, but one aspect of his partisan training which he had not forgotten was how to structure an organisation in such a way that it could survive the penetration or capture of individual units. No matter how many of his operations were foiled or his associates arrested, Spadola himself was never implicated until the Tondelli affair.

Bruno Tondelli himself was not one of Milan's most savoury characters, but when he was done to death with a butcher's knife, it was still murder. The Tondellis had been engaged in a long-running territorial dispute with Spadola's men, which no doubt explained why Vasco found it expedient to disappear from sight immediately after the murder. Nevertheless, no one in the police would have wagered a piece of used chewing gum on their chances of pinning it on him.

Then one day Zen, who had been given the thankless task of investigating Tondelli's stabbing, received a message from an informer asking for a meeting. In order to protect them, informers' real names and addresses were kept in a locked file to which only a very few high-ranking officials had access. Everyone else referred to them by their code name. The man who telephoned Zen, known as "the nightingale," was one of the police's most trusted and reliable sources of information.

The meeting duly took place in a second class compartment of one of the *Ferrovia Nord* trains trundling up the line to Seveso. It was a foggy night in February. At one of the intermediate stations a man joined Zen in the prearranged compartment. Pale, balding, slight, and diffident, he might have been a filing clerk or a university professor. Vasco Spadola, he said, was hiding out in a farmhouse to the east of the city.

"I was there the night Tondelli got killed," the informer went on. "Spadola stabbed him with his own hand. 'This'll teach the whole litter of them a lesson,' he said."

"A lot of use that is to us if you won't testify," Zen retorted irritably.

The man gave him an arch look.

"Who said I wouldn't testify?"

And testify he duly did. Not only that, but when the police raided the farmhouse near the village of Melzo, they found not only Vasco Spadola but also a knife which proved to have traces of blood of the same group that had once flowed in Bruno Tondelli's veins.

Spadola was sentenced to life imprisonment and Aurelio Zen spent three days basking in glory. Then he learned from an envious colleague that the knife had been smeared with a sample of Tondelli's blood and planted at the scene by the police themselves, and that the reason why the nightingale had been prepared to come into court and testify that he had seen Spadola commit murder was that the Tondellis had paid him handsomely to do so.

Zen closed the file and handed it back to the clerk with the blank video cassette.

"Oh, by the way, if it isn't too much trouble, do you think you could manage to get my name right next time?" he asked sarcastically, flourishing the memorandum.

"What's wrong with it?" the clerk demanded, taking the substitute video without a second glance.

"My name happens to be Zen, not Zeno."

"Zen's not Italian."

"Quite right, it's Venetian. But since it's only three letters long, I'd have thought that even you lot would be capable of spelling it correctly. And while we're at it, what the hell does this say?"

He indicated the phrase scribbled in the blank space.

" '. . . since it is needed by another official,' " the clerk read aloud. "Maybe you need glasses."

Zen frowned, ignoring the comment.

"Who asked for it?"

The clerk sighed mightily, pulled open a filing cabinet and flicked through the cards.

"Fabri, Vincenzo."

Although it was still light as Zen left the Ministry to go home, he felt the presence of the superstitious fear that had haunted him the night before. This was more than just bad luck. It seemed like a plot, a deliberate and carefully laid scheme designed to humiliate him.

Why on earth should Vincenzo Fabri, of all people,

have put in a request for the Burolo video? He had nothing to do with the case, no legitimate reason for wishing to view the tape. And today, of all days! Whatever the reason, it was monstrously unfortunate. Not only would Zen's substitution of the blank tape immediately come to light, but it would do so through the offices of his sworn enemy. Whether or not this series of events was just a coincidence, Fabri wouldn't fail to capitalise on the numerous possibilities it offered for disgracing his rival.

Dinner was always the most difficult part of Zen's day. In the morning he could escape to work, and when he got home in the afternoon, Maria Grazia, the housekeeper, was there to dilute the situation with her bustling, loquacious presence. Later in the evening things got easier once again as his mother switched the lights off and settled down in front of the television, flipping from channel to channel as the whim took her, dipping into the various serials like someone dropping in on the neighbours for a few minutes of inconsequential chat. But first there was dinner to be got through.

Today, to make matters worse, his mother was having one of her deaf phases, when she was—or pretended to be—unable to hear anything that was said to her until it had been repeated three or four times at ever higher volume. Since their conversation had long been reduced to the lowest of common denominators, Zen found himself having to shout at the top of his voice remarks that were so meaningless it would have been an effort even to mumble them.

To Zen's intense relief, the television news made no reference to the discovery of exclusive video footage of the Burolo murders frame by gory frame. Indeed, for once the case was not even mentioned. The news was dominated by the shooting of Judge Giulio Bertolini and featured an emotional interview with the victim's widow, in the course of which she denounced the lack of protection given to her husband.

"Even when Giulio received threats, nothing whatever was done! We begged, we pleaded, we—"

"Your husband was warned that he would be killed?" the reporter interrupted eagerly.

Signora Bertolini made a gesture of qualification.

"Not in so many words, no. But there were tokens, signs, strange disturbing things. For example, an envelope was pushed through our letter box with nothing inside but a lot of tiny little metal balls, like caviare, only hard. And then Giulio's wallet was stolen, and later we found it in the living room, the papers and money all scattered about the floor. But when we informed the public prosecutor, he said there were no grounds for giving my husband an armed guard. And just a few days later he was gunned down, a helpless victim, betrayed by the very people who should . . ."

Zen glanced at his mother. So far neither of them had referred to the mysterious metallic scraping which had disturbed her the previous night and which he had dismissed as a rat in the skirting. He hoped Signora Bertolini's words did not make her think of another possible explanation which had occurred to him: that someone had been trying to break into the flat.

"Don't you like your soup?" he asked his mother, who was moodily pushing the vegetables and pasta around in her plate.

"What?"

"YOUR SOUP! AREN'T YOU GOING TO EAT IT?"

"It's got turnip in."

"What's wrong with that?"

"Turnips are for cattle, not people," his mother declared, her deafness miraculously improved.

"You ate them last time."

"What?"

Zen took a deep breath.

"PUT THEM TO ONE SIDE AND EAT THE REST!" he yelled, repeating word for word the formula she had once used with him.

"I'm not hungry," his mother retorted sulkily.

"That won't stop you eating half a box of chocolates while you watch TV."

"What?"

"NOTHING."

Zen pushed his plate away and lit a cigarette. From the television set, Signora Bertolini continued her confused and vapid accusations. Although he naturally sympathised with her, Zen also felt a sense of revulsion. It was becoming too convenient to blame the authorities for everything that happened. Soon the relatives of motorists killed on the *autostrada* would appear on television claiming that their deaths were due not to the fact that they had been doing two hundred kilometres an hour on the hard shoulder in the middle of a contraflow system, but to the criminal negligence of the highway authorities in not providing for the needs of people who were exercising their constitutional right to drive like maniacs.

At exactly one minute to seven Zen walked to the inner hallway where the phone was and dialled the number Tania had given him. A woman answered.

"Yes?"

"Good evening. I have a message for Signora Biacis."

"Who's this?"

The woman's voice was frugal and clipped, as though she had to pay for each word and resented the expense.

"The Ministry of the Interior."

Muffled squawks penetrated to the mouthpiece which the woman had covered with her hand while she talked to someone else.

"Who's this?" a man abruptly demanded.

"I'm calling from the Ministry," Zen recited. "I have a message for Signora Biacis."

"I'm her husband. What have you got to say?"

"You've no doubt heard about the recent terrorist outrage, Signor Biacis—"

"Bevilacqua, Mauro Bevilacqua," the man cut in.

Zen noted the name on the scratch pad by the phone. Evidently Tania Biacis, like many Italian married women, had retained her maiden name.

"As a result, all Ministerial staff have been placed

on an emergency alert. Your wife is liable for a half-shift this evening."

The man snorted angrily. "This has never happened before!"

"On the contrary, it has happened all too often."

"I mean she's never been called in at this time before!"

"Then she's been very lucky," Zen declared with finality and hung up.

That was all he'd needed to do, Zen thought as he sat in the taxi, waiting for the driver to return. It was all he'd been asked to do, it was all he had any right to do. But instead of returning to the living room and his mother's company, he'd lifted the phone again and called a taxi.

The address listed in the telephone directory after "Bevilacqua Mauro" did not exist on Zen's map of Rome. The taxi driver hadn't known where it was either, but after consultations with the dispatcher it had finally been located in one of the new suburbs on the eastern fringes of the city, beyond the *Grande Raccordo Anulare*.

Whether it was that the dispatcher's instructions had been unclear or that the driver had forgotten them, they had only found the street after a lengthy excursion through unsurfaced streets that briefly became country roads, pocked with potholes and ridged into steps where concrete-covered drainage pipes ran across the eroded surface. Until recently this had all been unfenced grazing land, the open *campagna* where sheep roamed amid striding aqueducts and squat round towers which now gave their name to the suburbs which had sprung into being as the capital, turned cancerous by money and power, began its pathological postwar growth. Laid out piecemeal as the area grew, the streets rambled aimlessly about, often ending abruptly in cul-de-sacs that forced the driver to make long and disorienting detours. Here was a zone of abusive development from the early sixties, a shanty town of troglodytic hutches run up by immigrants from the south, each surrounded by a patch of enclosed ground where chickens and donkeys roamed amid old lavatories and piles of abandoned pallets. Next came an older section of villas for the well-to-do, thick with pines and guard dogs, giving way abruptly to a huge cleared expanse of asphalt illuminated by gigantic searchlights trained down from steel masts, where a band of gypsies had set up home in caravans linked by canopies of plastic sheeting. After that there was a field with sheep grazing, and then the tower blocks began, fourteen storys high, spaced evenly across the landscape like the pieces in a board game for giants amid tracts of land that had been brutally assaulted and left to die. And finally they had found the development of walk-up apartments where Mauro Bevilacqua and Tania Biacis made their home.

Zen sank back in the seat, wondering why on earth he had come. As soon as the driver returned from his snack, he would go home. Tania must have left long ago, while the taxi was lost in this bewildering urban hinterland. Not that he had really intended to follow her, anyway. Putting together her comment about her husband that morning and then her request that Zen phone up with a fictitious reason for her to leave the house, it seemed pretty clear what she was up to. The last thing he wanted was proof of that. He had accepted the fact that Tania was happily and irrevocably married. He didn't now want to have to accept that, on the contrary, she was having an illicit affair, but not with him.

A silhouetted figure appeared at one of the windows of the nearby block. Zen imagined the scene viewed from that window: the deserted street, the parked car. It made him think of the night before, and suddenly he understood what he had found disturbing about the red car. Like the taxi, it had been about fifty metres from his house and on the opposite side of the street, the classic surveillance position. But he had not time to follow up the implications of this thought because at that moment a woman emerged from one of the stairwells of the apartment block.

She started to walk toward the taxi, then suddenly

stopped, turned, and hurried back the way she had come. At the same moment, as if on cue, the taxi driver reappeared from the bar and a swarthy man in his shirt-sleeves ran out into the car park underneath the apartment block, looking round wildly. The woman veered sharply to her left, making for the bar, but the man easily cut her off. They started to struggle, the man gripping her by the arms and trying to pull her back toward the door of the apartment.

Zen got out of the taxi and walked over to them, unfolding his identity card.

"Police!"

Locked in their clumsy tussle, the couple took no notice. Zen shook the man roughly by the shoulder.

"Let her go!"

The man swung round and aimed a wild punch at Zen, who dodged the blow with ease, seized the man by the collar and pulled him off balance, then shoved him backward, sending him reeling headlong to the ground.

"Right, what would you like to be arrested for?" he asked. "Assaulting a police officer—"

"You assaulted *me!*" the man interrupted indignantly as he got to his feet.

"—or interfering with this lady," Zen concluded.

The man laughed coarsely. He was short and slightly built, with a compensatory air of bluster and braggadocio which seemed to emanate from his neatly clipped moustache.

"Lady? What do you mean, lady? She's my wife! Understand? This is a family affair!"

Zen turned to Tania Biacis, who was looking at him in utter amazement.

"What happened, signor?"

"She was running away from her home and her duties!" her husband exclaimed. His arms were outstretched to an invisible audience.

"I . . . that taxi . . . I thought it was free," Tania said. She was evidently completely thrown by Zen's presence. "I was going to take it. Then I saw there was someone in it, so I was going to go to the bar to phone for one."

Mauro Bevilacqua glared at Zen.

"What the hell are you doing lurking about here, anyway? It's as bad as Russia, policemen on every street corner!"

"There happens to be a terrorist alert on," Zen told him coldly.

Tania turned triumphantly on her husband.

"You see! I told you!"

Having recovered her presence of mind, she appealed to Zen.

"I work at the Ministry of the Interior. I was called in for emergency duties this evening, but my husband wouldn't believe me. He wouldn't let me use the car. He said it was all a lie, a plot to get out of the house!"

Zen shook his head in disgust.

"So it's come to this! Here's your wife, signor, a key member of a dedicated team who are giving their all, night and day, to defend this country of ours from a gang of ruthless anarchists, and all you can do is to hurl puerile and scandalous accusations at her! You ought to be ashamed of yourself."

"It's none of your business!" Bevilacqua snapped.

"On the contrary," Zen warned him. "If I chose to make it my business, you'd be facing a prison sentence for assault."

He paused to let that sink in.

"Luckily for you, however, I have more important things to do. Just as your wife does. But to set your fears at rest, I'll accompany her personally to the Ministry. Will that satisfy you? Or perhaps you'd like me to summon an armed escort to make sure that she reaches her place of work safely?"

Mauro Bevilacqua flapped his arms up and down like a flightless bird trying vainly to take off.

"What I'd like! What I'd like! What I'd like is for her to start behaving like a wife should instead of gadding about on her own at this time of night!"

He swung round to face her.

"You should never have gone to work in the first place! I never wanted you to go."

"If you brought home a decent income from that stinking bank, I wouldn't have to!"

Mauro Bevilacqua looked at her with hatred in his eyes. "We'll settle this when you get home!" he spat out, turning on his heel.

Zen ushered Tania into the back of the taxi. He got into the front seat beside the driver.

"What *were* you doing there?" Tania asked after they had driven in silence for some time.

He did not reply. Now that their little farce had been played to its conclusion, all his confidence had left him. He felt constrained and ill at ease.

"You weren't really on a stakeout, were you?" she prompted.

Zen usually had no difficulty in thinking up plausible stories to conceal his real motives, but on this occasion he found himself at a loss. He couldn't tell Tania the truth and he wouldn't lie to her.

"Not an official one."

He glanced round at her. As they passed each streetlamp, its light moved across her in a steady stroking movement, revealing the contours of her face and body.

"You sounded very convincing," she said.

He shrugged. "If you're going to tell someone a pack of lies, there's no point in doing it half-heartedly."

With the help of Tania's directions, they quickly regained Via Casilina, and soon the city had closed in around them again. Zen felt as though he had returned to the earth from outer space.

"How can you stand living in that place?" he demanded.

As soon as he had spoken, he realised how rude the question sounded. But Tania seemed unoffended.

"That's what I ask myself every morning when I leave and every evening when I get back. The answer is simple. Money."

"You could always economise on your social life,

thought Zen sourly, cut out the fancy dinners and the season ticket to the opera and the weekends skiing and skindiving. He was rapidly going off Tania Biacis, he found. But he didn't say anything. Mauro Bevilacqua had been quite right. It was none of his business.

"So where to?" the driver asked as they neared Portomaggiore.

Zen said nothing. He wanted Tania to decide, and he wanted her to have all the time she needed to do so. Although Zen had aided and abetted her deception of her husband, he actually felt every bit as resentful of her behaviour as Mauro Bevilacqua himself, though of course Zen couldn't let it show. He was also aware that Tania would have to invent a different cover story for his consumption, since the one she had used with her husband clearly wouldn't do. He wanted it to be a good one, something convincing, something that would spare his feelings. He'd done the dirty work she'd requested. Now let her cover her tracks with him, too.

"Eh, oh, signor!" the driver exclaimed. "A bit of information, that's all I need. This car isn't a mule, you know. It won't go by itself. You have to turn the wheel. So, which way?"

Tania gave an embarrassed laugh.

"To tell you the truth, I just wanted to go to the cinema."

Well, it was better than saying outright that she was going to meet her lover, Zen supposed. But not much better. Not when she had been regaling him for months with her views of the latest films as they came out, flaunting the fact that she and her husband went to the cinema the way other people turned on the television.

To lie so crudely, so transparently, was tantamount to an insult. No wonder she sounded embarrassed. She couldn't have expected to be believed, not for a moment. She must have done it deliberately, as a way of getting the truth across to her faithful, stupid, besotted admirer. Well, it had worked! He'd understood, finally!

"Did you have any particular film in mind?" he enquired sarcastically.

"Anything at all."

She sounded dismissive, no doubt impatient with him, thinking that he'd missed the point. He'd soon put her right about that.

"Via Nazionale," he told the driver. Turning to Tania, he added, "I'm sure you'll be able to find what you want there. Whatever it happens to be."

As their eyes met, he had the uneasy feeling that he'd somehow misunderstood. But how could he? What other explanation was there?

"Please stop," Tania said to the driver.

"We're not there yet."

"It doesn't matter! Just stop."

The taxi cut across two lanes of traffic, unleashing a chorus of horns from behind. Tania handed the driver a ten thousand lire note.

"Deduct that from whatever he owes you."

She got out, slammed the door and walked away.

"Where now?" queried the driver.

"Same place you picked me up," Zen told him.

They drove down Via Nazionale and through Piazza Venezia. The driver jerked his thumb toward the white mass of the monument to Vittorio Emanuele.

"You know what I heard the other day? I had this city councilor in the back of the cab, and we were going past here. You know the Unknown Soldier they have buried up there? This councilor, he told me they were doing maintenance work a couple of years ago and they had to dig up the body. You know what they found? The poor bastard had been shot in the back! Must have been a deserter, they reckoned. Ran away during the battle and got shot by the military police. Isn't that the end? Fucking monument to military valour with the two sentries on guard all the time, and it turns out the poor fucker buried there was a deserter! Makes you think, eh?"

Zen agreed that such things did indeed make you think, but in fact his thoughts were elsewhere. The history of his relationships with women was passing in review before his eyes like the life of a drowning man.

And indeed Zen felt that he was drowning in a pool of black indifference and icy inertia. His failed marriage could be written off to experience: he and Luisella had married too early and for all the wrong reasons. That was a common enough story. It was what had happened since then that was so disturbing, or rather what had *not* happened. For Zen was acutely aware that in the fifteen years since his marriage broke up, he had failed to create a single lasting bond to take its place.

The final blow had been the departure of Ellen, the American divorcée he had been seeing on and off for over three years. The manner of her going had hurt as much as the fact. Ellen had made it clear that Zen had failed her in just about every conceivable way, and once he had got over his anger at being rejected, he found this hard to deny. The opportunity had been there for the taking, but he had hesitated and dithered and messed about, using his mother as an excuse, until things had come to a crisis. Then it had been a case of too much, too late, as he had blurted out an unconsidered offer of marriage which must have seemed like the final insult. It wasn't marriage for its own sake that Ellen had wanted but a sense of Zen's commitment to her. And he just hadn't been able to feel such a commitment.

It was no surprise, of course, at his age. With every year that passed, the number of things he really cared about decreased, and Zen soon convinced himself that his failure with Ellen had been an indication that love was fast coming to seem more trouble than it was worth. Why else should he have let the opportunity slip? And why did he never get around to answering the postcards and letters Ellen sent him from New York? The whole affair had been nothing but the self-delusion of an ageing man who couldn't accept that love, too, was something he must learn to give up gracefully.

Zen had just got all this nicely sorted out when Tania Biacis walked into his life. It was the first day of his new duties at the Ministry. Tania introduced herself as one of the administrative assistants and proceeded to explain the bureaucratic ins and outs of the department.

Zen nodded, smiled, grunted, and even managed to ask one or two relevant questions, but in fact he was on autopilot throughout, all his secondhand wisdom swept away by the living, breathing presence of this woman whom, to his delight and despair, he found that he desired in the old, familiar, raw, painful, hopeless way.

Unlike the Genoese couple who had been featured in the paper that morning, however, he and Tania ran no risk of being barbecued by an irate husband, for the simple reason that Mauro Bevilacqua had nothing whatever to feel jealous about, at least as far as Zen was concerned. True, he and Tania had become very friendly, but nothing precludes the possibility of passion as surely as friendliness. Those long casual chats which had once seemed so promising to Zen now depressed him more than anything else. It was almost as if Tania were treating him as a surrogate female friend, as though for her he was so utterly unsexed that she could talk to him forever without any risk of compromising herself.

Sometimes her tone became more personal, particularly when she talked about her father. He had been the village schoolteacher, an utterly impractical idealist who escaped into the mountains at every opportunity. Tania's name was not a diminutive of Stefania, as Zen had assumed, but of Tatania, her father having named her after Gramsci's sister-in-law, who stood by the Communist thinker throughout the eleven years of his imprisonment by the Fascists. But despite this degree of intimacy, Tania had never given Zen the slightest hint that she had any personal interest in him, while he had of course been careful not to reveal his own feelings. He quailed at the thought of Tania's reaction if she guessed the truth. It was clear from what she said that she and her husband lived a rich, full, exciting life. What on earth could Zen offer her that she could possibly want or need?

It was therefore a sickening blow to discover that Tania apparently *did* want or need things that her marriage didn't provide. Not only hadn't she thought of turning to him to provide them, but she had treated him as someone she could use and then lie to.

This was so painful that it triggered a mechanism which had been created back in the mists of Zen's childhood, when his father had disappeared into an anonymous grave somewhere in Russia. That loss still ached like an old fracture on a damp day, but at the time the pain had been too fierce to bear. To survive, Zen had withdrawn totally into the present, denying the past all reality, taking refuge in the here and now. That was his response to Tania's betrayal, and it was so successful that when they arrived and the taxi driver told him how much he owed, Zen thought the man was trying to cheat him.

"A hundred and twenty nine thousand lire for a short ride across the city!"

"What the hell are you talking about?" the driver retorted. "Two and a quarter hours you've had! I could have picked up three times the money doing short trips instead of freezing to death in some shitty suburb!"

Zen grudgingly counted out the notes. Well, that was the last amateur stakeout he'd be doing, he vowed, as the taxi roared away past a red sedan parked about fifty metres along the street on the other side.

The only people about were an elderly couple making their way at a snail's pace along the opposite pavement. Zen crossed over to the car, an Alfa Romeo with Rome registration plates. There were several deep scratches and dents in the bodywork and one of the hubcaps was missing, although the vehicle was quite new. Zen looked in through the dirty window. A packet of Marlboro cigarettes lay on one of the leather seats, which looked almost unused. The flooring was covered in cigarette butts and scorched with burn marks. The empty box of an Adriano Celentano tape lay in the tray behind the gear lever, the cassette itself protruding from the player.

He straightened up as footsteps approached, but it was only the elderly couple. They trudged past, the man several paces ahead of his wife. Neither of them looked at the other, although they kept up a desultory patter the whole time.

"Then we can . . ."

"Right."

"Or not. Who knows?"

"Well, anyway . . ."

Zen wrote down the registration number of the car and walked back to the house. Giuseppe was off duty, so the front door was closed and locked. The lift was on one of the upper floors. Zen pressed the light switch and set off up the stairs, taking the shallow marble steps two at a time. A rumble overhead was followed by a whining sound as the lift started down. A few moments later the lighted cubicle passed by, its single occupant revealed in fuzzy silhouette on the frosted glass.

By the time he reached the fourth floor, Zen was breathless. He paused briefly to recover before unlocking his front door. There was a clanking far below as the lift shuddered to a halt. Then the landing was abruptly plunged into darkness as the time switch expired. Zen groped his way to the door, opened it, and turned on the hall light. As he closed the door again, he noticed an envelope lying on the sideboard. He picked it up and walked along the passage, past the lugubrious cupboards, carved chests, and occasional tables for which no suitable occasion had ever presented itself. As he neared the living room, he heard the sound of voices raised in argument.

". . . never in a hundred years, never in a thousand, will I permit you to marry this man!"

"But Papa, I love Alfonso more than life itself!"

"Do not dare breathe his accursed name again! Tomorrow you leave for the convent, there to take vows more sacred and more binding than those with which you seek to dishonour our house."

"The convent! No, do not condemn me to a living death, dear Father . . ."

Zen pushed open the glass-panelled door. By the flickering light of the television he saw his mother asleep in her armchair. He crossed the darkened room and turned down the volume, silencing the voices but leaving the costumed figures to go through their melodramatic motions. Then he went to the window, opened the shutters, and peered out through the slats in the outer jalousies. The red sedan was no longer there.

He held the envelope so that it caught the light from the television. It seemed to be empty, although it was surprisingly heavy. His name was printed in block capitals, but there was no stamp or address. He wondered how it had come to be left on the sideboard. Normally post was put in the box in the hallway downstairs or left with Giuseppe. If a message was delivered to the door, Maria Grazia would have taken it into the living room.

He ripped the envelope open. It still seemed empty, but something inside made a scratching sound, and when he pulled the paper walls apart, he saw a quantity of tiny silvery balls clustered together at the very bottom. He let them roll out into his palm. In the flickering glimmer of the television they could have been almost anything: medicine, seeds, even cake decorations. But Zen knew they were none of these.

They were shotgun pellets.

The nights brought relief. At night I moved freely, I felt my strength returning. The others never venture out once darkness has fallen. Dissolved by darkness, the world is no longer theirs. They stay at home, lock their doors, and watch moving pictures made with light.

They are afraid of the dark. They are right to be afraid.

Beyond their locked doors and shuttered windows I came into my own, flitting effortlessly from place to place, appearing and disappearing at will, yielding to the darkness as though to the embraces of a secret lover. Until the lights came on, the inmates stirred, and the prison awoke to another day.

* * *

It was easy to find my way back here. I'd always come and gone as I liked. They never understood that. They never tried to understand. No one asked me anything. They told me things. They told me my imprisonment, as they called it, had been an accident, a mistake. "What you must have suffered!" they said. I'd lost my home and family, but they weren't satisfied with that. They wanted me to lose myself as well. What am I, but what the darkness made me? If that was a mistake, an accident, then so am I.

Sometimes the priest came. He had things to tell me, too, about a loving father, a tortured son, a virgin mother. Not like my family, I thought, the father who came home drunk and fucked his wife until she screamed, and she screamed again when the son was born, a pampered brat, arrogant and selfish, strutting about as though he owned the place, and all because of that thing dangling between his legs, barely the size of my little finger! But I kept my mouth shut. I didn't think the priest would want to know about them.

And who was I, when the family was together? The holy ghost, I suppose. The unholy ghost.

THURSDAY: 0755 — 1320

ALL THE TALK AT the cafe the next morning was of the overnight swoop by the police and Carabinieri on leftist sympathisers in Milan, Turin, and Genoa. "About time too," was the dentist's comment, but one of the craftsmen from the basement workshops disagreed.

"The real terrorists don't have anything to do with those *sinistrini*. It's just the cops trying to make a good impression. A week from now they'll all have been turned loose again and we'll be back where we started!"

The barman Ernesto and the dentist looked at Zen, who maintained a stony silence. The reason for this was neither professional reserve nor disapproval of the craftsman's cynical tone. Zen simply wasn't paying any attention to the conversation. He had problems of his own that were too pressing to allow him the luxury of discussing other people's problems which were quite literally closer to home.

Once again he had stayed up until the small hours of the morning, trying without success to find the missing link that would explain the events of the previous days. Not only hadn't he succeeded, he wasn't even sure that success was possible. The temptation to fit everything into a neat pattern, he knew, should be resisted. It might well be that two or more quite unrelated patterns were at work.

One thing was sure. During the three hours he had been absent from home the night before, someone had entered his flat and left an envelope filled with shotgun pellets on the sideboard in the hallway. Zen had locked the front door on leaving and it had still been locked on his return. Questioning his mother obliquely to avoid frightening her, he had confirmed that she had not let anyone in. The only other person with a key was Maria Grazia. Before leaving for work, Zen had interrogated her without result. The key was kept in her handbag, which hadn't been lost or stolen. Her family were all strict Catholics of the type who would have guilt pangs about picking up a hundred lire coin they found in the street. It was out of the question that any of them might have been bribed to pass on the key to a third party. Zen also questioned Giuseppe, who had duplicate keys to all the apartments. He was equally categorical in his denials, and given the fanatical vigilance with which he carried out his duties it seemed unlikely that the intruder could have gained access in this way.

Which left only the metallic scraping Zen's mother had reported hearing the night before. It had come from the other side of the room, she said, where the large wardrobe stood. It now seemed clear that the noise had been made by someone picking the lock of the door leading to the fire escape, only to find that it was blocked by the wardrobe which had been placed in front of it. Since this attempt had failed, the intruder had returned during Zen's absence the evening before and tried the riskier option of picking the lock of the front door.

Almost the most disturbing thing about the incident was what had *not* happened. Nothing had been stolen, nothing had been disarranged. Apart from the envelope, the intruder had left no sign whatever of his presence. He had come to leave a message, and perhaps the most important element of that message was that he had done nothing else. As a demonstration of power, of arrogant self-confidence, it made Zen think of the Villa Burolo killer. "I can come and go whenever I wish," was the implicit message. "This time I have chosen simply to deliver an envelope. Next time . . . who knows?"

Determined that there should not be a next time, Zen had made Maria Grazia swear by Santa Rita of Cascia, whose image she wore as a lucky charm, that she would bolt the front door after his departure and not leave the apartment until he returned.

"But what about the shopping?" she protested.

"I'll get something from the *tavola calda*," Zen snapped impatiently. "It's not important!"

Cowed by her employer's unaccustomed brusqueness, Maria Grazia timidly reminded him that she would have to leave by six o'clock at the latest in order to deal with her own family's needs.

"I'll be back by then," he replied. "Just don't leave the apartment unattended, not even for a moment. Understand? Keep the door bolted and don't open it except for me."

As soon as he got to work, Zen called the vehicle registration department and requested details of the red Alfa Romeo he had seen in the street the night before. It was a long shot, but there was something about the car that made him suspicious, although he wasn't quite clear what it was.

The information he received was not encouraging. The owner of the vehicle turned out to be one Rino Attilio Lusetti, with an address in the fashionable Pinciano area north of the Villa Borghese. A phone call to the Questura elicited the information that Lusetti had no criminal record. By now Zen knew that this was a wild-goose chase, but having nothing better to do, he looked up Lusetti in the telephone directory and rang the number. An uneducated female voice informed him that Dottor Lusetti was at the university. After a series of abortive phone calls to various departments of this institution, Zen eventually discovered that the car which had been parked near his house for the two previous nights was owned by the Professor of Philology in the Faculty of Humanities at the University of Rome.

Giorgio De Angelis wandered into Zen's cubicle while he was making the last of these calls.

"Problems?" he asked as Zen hung up.

Zen shrugged.

"Just a private matter. Someone keeps parking his car in front of my door."

"Give his windscreen a good coat of varnish," De Angelis advised. "Polyurethane's the best. Weather-proof, durable, opaque. An absolute bastard to get off."

Zen nodded.

"What's this you've been telling Romizi about a train that goes round in circles?"

De Angelis laughed raucously, throwing his head back and showing his teeth. Then he glanced round the screens to check that the official in question wasn't within earshot.

"That fucking Romizi! He'd believe anything. You know he loves anchovy paste? But he's a tight bastard, so he's always moaning about how much it costs. So I said to him, 'Listen, do you want to know how to make it yourself? You get a cat, right? You feed the cat on anchovies and olive oil, nothing else. What comes out the other end is anchovy paste.' "

"He didn't believe you, did he?"

"I don't know. I wouldn't be surprised if he gives it a try. I just wish I could be there. What I'd give to see him spreading cat shit on a cracker!"

As De Angelis burst out laughing again, a movement nearby attracted Zen's attention. He turned to find Vincenzo Fabri looking on at them through a gap in the screens. He was wearing a canary yellow pullover and a pale blue tie, with a maroon sports jacket and slacks and chunky hand-stitched shoes. Expensive leisurewear was Fabri's hallmark, matching his gestures, slow and calm, and his deep, melodious voice. "I'm so relaxed, so laid back," the look said. "Just a lazy old softy who wants an easy time."

Zen, who still wore a suit to work, felt by comparison like an old-fashioned ministerial *apparatchik,* a dull, dedicated workaholic. The irony was that Vincenzo Fabri was the most fiercely ambitious person Zen had come across in the whole of his career. His conversation was larded with references to country clubs, horses, tennis, sailing, and holidays in Brazil. Fabri wanted all that and more. He wanted villas and cars and yachts and clothes and women. Compared to the Oscar Burolos of the world, Fabri was a third-rater, of course. He wasn't interested in the real thing: power, influence, prestige. All he wanted were the trinkets and trappings, the toys and the bangles. But he wanted them so *badly!* Zen, who no longer wanted anything very much except Tania Biacis, didn't know whether to envy or despise Fabri for the childlike voracity of his desires.

"Giorgio!" Fabri called softly, beckoning to De Angelis. His expression was one of amused complicity, as though he wanted to share a secret with the only man in the world who could really appreciate it.

At the same moment, the phone on Zen's desk began to warble.

"Yes?"

"Is this, ah . . . that's to say, am I speaking to, ah, Dottor Aurelio Zen?"

Fabri, who had ignored Zen's presence until now, was staring at him insistently while he murmured something in De Angelis's ear.

"Speaking."

"Ah, this is, ah . . . that's to say, I'm calling from, ah, Palazzo Sisti."

The voice paused significantly. Zen grunted neutrally. He knew that he had heard of Palazzo Sisti, but he had no idea in what context.

"There's been some, ah . . . interest in the possibility of seeing whether it might be feasible to arrange . . ."

The rest of the sentence was lost on Zen as Tania

Biacis suddenly appeared beside him, saying something which was garbled by the obscure formulations of his caller. Zen covered the mouthpiece of the phone with one hand.

"Sorry?"

"Immediately," Tania said emphatically, as though she had already said it once too often. She looked tired and drawn and there were dark rings under her eyes.

"Are you all right?" Zen asked her.

"Me? What have I got to do with it?"

The phrase was delivered like a slap in the face. From the uncovered earpiece of the phone, the caller's voice squawked on like a radio program no one is listening to.

"So you'll do that, will you?" Tania insisted.

"See to what?"

"The video tape! They were extremely unpleasant about it. I said you'd call them back within the hour. I don't see why I should have to deal with it. It's got nothing whatever to do with me!"

She turned angrily away, pushing past De Angelis who was on his way back to his desk. He looked glum and preoccupied, his former high spirits quite doused. Fabri had disappeared again.

Zen uncovered the phone. "I'm sorry. I was interrupted."

"So that's agreed, is it?" the voice said. It was a question in form only.

"Well . . ."

"I'll expect you in about twenty minutes."

The line went dead.

Zen thought briefly about calling Archives, but what was the point? It was obvious what had happened. Fabri had told them that the tape of the Burolo killings was blank and they were urgently trying to contact Zen to find out what had happened to the original. This was no doubt the news that he had been gleefully passing on to De Angelis.

But how had Fabri found out so quickly that Zen

had been the previous borrower? Presumably Archives must have told him. Unless, of course . . .

Unless it had been the video tape and not a wallet or pocketbook that had been the thief's target all along. It would have been a simple matter for Fabri to find some pickpocket who would have been only too glad to do a favour for such an influential man. Once the tape was in his hands, Fabri had put in an urgent request for the tape at Archives, ensuring that Zen was officially compromised. Now he would no doubt sell the original to the highest bidder, thus making himself a small fortune and at the same time creating a scandal which might well lead to criminal charges being brought against his enemy. It was a masterpiece of unscrupulousness against which Zen was absolutely defenceless.

As he emerged from the portals of the Ministry and made his way down the steps and through the steel barrier under the eye of the armed sentries, Zen wondered if he was letting his imagination run away with him. In the warm hazy sunlight the whole thing suddenly seemed a bit farfetched. He lit a cigarette as he waited for the taxi he had ordered. He had decided against using an official car, since the caller had left him in some doubt as to whether or not this was an official visit. In fact, he had left him in doubt about almost everything, including his name. The only thing Zen knew for certain was that the call had come from Palazzo Sisti. The significance of this was still obscure to Zen, but the name was evidently familiar enough to the taxi driver, who switched on his meter without requesting further directions.

They drove down the shallow valley between the Viminal and Quirinal hills, leaving behind the broad utilitarian boulevards of the nineteenth century suburbs, across Piazza Venezia and into the cramped, crooked intestines of the ancient centre. Zen stared blankly out of the window, lost in troubled thoughts. Whatever the truth about the video tape, there was still the other threat hanging over him. The form of the message he had received the night before had been disturbing enough, but its content was even more so. According to Signora Bertolini, her husband had received threats before his death. "There were tokens, signs," she had said. "Once an envelope was pushed through our letter box with nothing inside but a lot of tiny little metal balls, like caviare, only hard."

It was no doubt symptomatic of their respective lifestyles that the contents of the envelope had made Zen think of cake decorations and Signor Bertolini of caviare, but there was little doubt that they had been the same. And a few days after receiving his message, Judge Giulio Bertolini had been killed by just such little metal balls, fired at high velocity from a shotgun.

Zen had no intention of letting his imagination run away with him to the extent of supposing that there was any direct connection between the two events. What he did suspect was that someone, probably Vincenzo Fabri, was trying to irritate him, to knock him off balance so that he would be too agitated to think clearly and perceive the real nature of the threat to him. No doubt Fabri's thief had first attempted to enter Zen's flat to steal the video, and having been foiled by the blocked emergency exit, had picked Zen's pocket in the bus queue the following morning. Then Fabri had seen the newscast in which the judge's widow spoke about the envelope, and with an opportunism typical of him he had seen a way to further ensure the success of his scheme by keeping Zen preoccupied with false alarms on another front.

The taxi wound slowly through the back streets just north of the Tiber, finally drawing up in a small piazza. By the standards of its period, Palazzo Sisti was modest in scale, but it made up for this by a wealth of architectural detail. The Sisti clan had clearly known their place in the complex hierarchy of sixteenth century Roman society, but had wished to demonstrate that despite this their taste and distinction was no whit inferior to that of the powerful Farnese or Barberini families. But neither their taste nor their modesty had availed them anything in the long run, and today their creation could well have been just another white elephant that had been divided up into flats and offices if it had not been for the two armed Carabinieri sitting in their jeep on the other side of the piazza and the large white banner stretched across the facade of the building, bearing the slogan A Fairer Alternative and the initials of one of the smaller political parties making up the government's majority in parliament.

Zen nodded slowly. Of course, that was where he had heard the name before. Palazzo Sisti was used by newscasters to refer to the party leadership, just as Piazza del Gesu indicated the Christian Democrats. This particular party had been much in the news recently, the reason being that prominent among its leaders was a certain ex-Minister of Public Works who was rumoured to have enjoyed a close and mutually profitable relationship with Oscar Burolo prior to the latter's untimely demise.

The entrance was as dark as a tunnel, wide and high enough to accommodate a carriage and team, lit only by a single dim lantern suspended from the curved ceiling. At the other end it opened into a small courtyard tightly packed with limousines whose drivers, dressed in neat cheap suits like funeral attendants, were standing around swopping gossip and polishing chrome.

A glass door to the left suddenly opened and an elderly man no bigger than a large dwarf scuttled out.

"Yes?" he called out brusquely.

A young woman carrying a large pile of files followed him out of the lodge.

"Well?" she demanded.

"I don't know!" the porter cried exasperatedly. "Understand? I don't know!"

"It's your job to know."

"Don't tell me what my job is!"

"Very well, *you* tell me!"

Zen walked over to them. "Excuse me."

They both turned to glare at him.

"Aurelio Zen, from the Ministry of the Interior."

The porter shrugged. "What about it?"

"I'm expected."

"Who by?"

"If I knew that, I wouldn't need to waste my time talking to a prick like you, would I?"

The woman burst into hoots of laughter. A phone started ringing shrilly in the lodge. Throwing them both a look of deep disgust, the porter went to answer it.

"Yes? Yes, dottore. Yes, dottore. No, he just got here. Very good, dottore. Right away."

Emerging from his lodge, the porter jerked his thumb at a flight of stairs opposite. "First floor. They're expecting you."

"And the Youth Section?" the young woman asked.

"How many times do I have to tell you, I don't know!"

The staircase was a genteel cascade of indolently curving marble which made the one at the Ministry look both vulgar and cheap. As Zen reached the first-floor landing, a figure he had taken to be a statue detached itself from the niche where it had been standing and walked toward him. The man had an air of having been assembled like Frankenstein's monster from a set of parts, each of which might have looked quite all right in another context but which didn't get along at all well together. He stopped some distance away, his gaze running over Zen's clothing.

"I'm not carrying one," Zen told him. "Never do, in fact."

The man looked at him as though he had spoken in a foreign language.

"You see, it's no use carrying a gun unless you're prepared to use it," Zen went on discursively. "If you're not, it just makes matters worse. It gives you a false sense of security and makes everyone else nervous. So you're better off without it, really."

The man turned away expressionlessly for a moment, then turned his back.

"This way."

He led Zen along a corridor which at first sight appeared to extend further than the length of the building. This illusion was explained when it became clear that the two men walking toward them were in fact their own reflections in the huge mirror that covered the end wall. The corridor was lit at intervals by tall windows that opened to the courtyard. Opposite each window a double door of polished walnut gleamed sweetly in the mellow light.

Zen's escort knocked at one of the doors and stood listening intently, holding the wrought silver handle.

"Come!" a distant voice instructed.

The room was long and relatively narrow. One wall was covered by an enormous tapestry so faded that it was impossible to make out anything except a general impression of a hunting scene. Facing this stood a glass-fronted bookcase where an array of massive tomes lay slumbering in a manner that suggested they had not been disturbed for some considerable time.

At the far end of the room, a young man was sitting at an antique desk in front of a window that reached all the way up to the distant ceiling. As Zen came in, he put down the sheaf of typed pages he had been perusing and walked round the desk, his hand held out in greeting.

"Good morning, dottore. So glad that you felt able to see your way clear to, ah . . ."

He was in his early thirties, slim and refined, with thin straight lips, delicate features, and eyes that goggled slightly, as though they were perpetually astonished by what they saw. His fastidious gestures and diffident manner gave him the air of a *fin de siècle* aesthete rather than a political animal.

He waved Zen toward a chair made of thin struts of some precious wood with a woven cane seat. It looked extremely valuable and horribly fragile. Zen lowered himself onto it apprehensively. The young man returned to the other side of the desk where he remained standing for a moment with hands outspread like a priest at the altar.

"First of all, dottore, let me express on behalf of . . . the interest and, ah . . . that's to say, the really quite extraordinary excitement aroused by your, ah . . .''

He picked up the pages he had been reading and let them fall back to the desk again as a knock resounded in the cavernous space behind.

"Come!" the young man enunciated.

A waiter appeared carrying a tray with two coffee cups.

"Ah, yes. I took the liberty of, ah . . .''

He waggled his forefinger at the two cups.

"And which one is . . . ?"

"With the red rim," the waiter told him.

The young man sighed expressively as the door closed again.

"Unfortunately, caffeine for me . . .''

Zen took the remaining cup of espresso and unwrapped the two lumps of sugar, studying the Interesting Facts About the World of Nature printed on the wrapper while he waited for his host to proceed.

"As you are no doubt aware, dottore, this has been a sad and difficult time for us. Naturally we already knew what your report makes abundantly clear, namely that the evidence against Renato Favelloni is both flimsy and entirely circumstantial. There is not the slightest question that his innocence would eventually be established by due process of law."

Zen noted the conditional as the coffee seared its way down his throat.

"But by then, alas, the damage will have been done!" the young man continued. "If mud is thrown as viciously as it has been and will be, some of it is bound to stick. Not just to Favelloni himself, but to all those who were in any way associated with him or who had occasion to, ah, call on his services at some time. This is the problem we face, dottore. I trust you will not judge me indiscreet if I add that it is one we were beginning to despair of solving. Imagine, then, the emotions elicited by your report! So much hope! So many interesting new perspectives! 'Light at the end of the tunnel,' as *l'onorevole* saw fit to put it."

Zen set his empty cup back in its saucer on the leather surface of the desk. "My report was merely a summary of the investigations carried out by others."

"Exactly! That was precisely its strength. If you had been one of our, ah, contacts at the Ministry, your findings would have excited considerably less interest. To be perfectly frank, we have been let down before by people who promised us this, that, and the other, and then couldn't deliver. Why, only a few days ago we asked our man there to obtain a copy of the video tape showing the tragic events at the Villa Burolo. A simple enough request, you would think, but even that proved beyond the powers of the individual in question. Nor was this the first time that he had disappointed us. So we felt it was time to bring in someone fresh, someone with the proper qualifications. Someone with a track record in this sort of work. And I must say that so far we have had no reason to regret our decision. Of course, the real test is still to come, but already we have been very favourably impressed by the way in which your report both exposed the inherent weaknesses of the case against Favelloni and revealed the existence of various equally possible scenarios which for purely political reasons have never been properly investigated."

The young man stood quite still for a moment, his slender fingers steepled as though in prayer.

"The task we now face is to ensure that we do not suffer as much damage from this innocent man being brought to trial and acquitted as we would do if he were really guilty. In a word, this show trial of Renato Favelloni—and by implication, *l'onorevole* himself—engineered by our enemies, must be blocked before it starts. Your report makes it perfectly clear that the evidence against Favelloni has been cobbled together from a mass of disjointed and unrelated fragments. Those same fragments, with a little initiative and enterprise, could be used to make an even more convincing case against one of the other suspects you mention."

Perched precariously on the low, fragile chair, Zen felt like a spectator in the front row of the stalls trying to make out what was happening on stage. The young man's expression seemed to suggest that the next move was up to Zen, but he was unwilling to make it until he had a clearer idea of what was involved.

"Do you mind if I smoke?" he asked finally.

The young man impatiently waved assent.

"Which of the other suspects did you have in mind?" Zen murmured casually as he lit up.

"Well, it seems to us that there are a number of avenues which might be explored with profit."

"For example?"

"Well, Burolo's son, for example."

"But he was in Boston at the time."

"He could have hired someone."

"He wouldn't have known how. Anyway, sons don't go around putting out contracts on their fathers because they want them to study law instead of music."

The young man acknowledged the point with a prolonged blink. "I agree that such a hypothesis would have needed a good deal of work before it became credible, but the possibility remains open. In fact, however, Enzo Burolo has close links with one of our allies in the government, so it would in any case have been inopportune to pursue the matter. I cited it merely as one example among many. Another, which appears to us considerably more fruitful, is the fellow Burolo employed to look after those absurd lions of his."

Zen breathed out a cloud of smoke.

"Pizzoni? He had an alibi too."

"Yes, he had an alibi. And what does that mean? That half a dozen of the local peasantry have been bribed or bullied to lie about seeing him in the bar that evening."

"Why should anyone want to protect Pizzoni? He was a nobody, an outsider."

The young man leaned forward across the desk. "Supposing that wasn't the case? Supposing I were to tell you that the man's real name was not Pizzoni but Padedda and that he was not from the Abruzzi, as his papers claim, but from Sardinia, from a village in the

Gennargentu mountains not far from Nuoro. What would you say to that?"

Zen flicked ash into a pewter bowl that might or might not have been intended for this purpose.

"Well, in the first instance I'd want to know why you haven't informed the authorities investigating the case."

The young man turned away to face the window. The tall panes of glass were covered with a thick patina of grime which reflected his features clearly. Zen saw him smile, as though at the fatuity of this comment.

"When one's opponent is cheating, only a fool continues to play by the rules," he recited quietly, as though quoting. "This piece of information came to light as a result of research carried out privately on our behalf. We know only too well what would happen if we communicated it to the judiciary. The magistrates have decided to charge Favelloni for reasons which have nothing to do with the facts of the case. They aren't going to review that decision unless some dramatic new development forces them to do so. Isolated, inconvenient facts which do not directly bear on the case they are preparing would simply be swept under the carpet."

He swung round to confront Zen.

"Rather than squander our advantage in this way, we propose to launch our own initiative, reopening the investigation that was so hastily slammed shut for ill-judged political reasons. And who better to conduct this operation than the man whose incisive and comprehensive review of the case has given us all fresh hope?"

Zen crushed out his cigarette, burning his fingertip on the hot ash.

"In my official capacity?"

"Absolutely, dottore! That's the whole point. Everything must be open and aboveboard."

"In that case, I would need a directive from my department."

"You'll get one, don't worry about that! Your orders will be communicated to you in the usual way through the usual channels. The purpose of this briefing is simply and purely to ensure that you understand the situation fully. From the moment you leave here today, you will have no further contact with us. You'll be posted to Sardinia as a matter of absolute routine. You will visit the scene of the crime, interview witnesses, interrogate suspects. As always, you will naturally have at your disposal the full facilities of the local force. In the course of your investigations you will discover concrete evidence demolishing the lion-keeper Pizzoni's alibi and linking him to the murder of Oscar Burolo. All this will take no more than a few days at most. You will then submit your findings to the judiciary in the normal way, while we for our part ensure that their implications are not lost on anyone concerned."

Zen stared across the room at a detail in the corner of the tapestry, showing a nymph taking refuge from the hunters in a grotto.

"Why me?"

The young man's finely manicured hands spread open in a gesture of benediction.

"As I said, dottore, you have a good track record. Once your accomplishments in the Miletti case had been brought to our attention, well, quite frankly, the facts spoke for themselves."

Zen gaped at him. "The Miletti case?"

"I'm sure you will recall that your methods attracted, ah, a certain amount of criticism at the time," the young man remarked with a touch of indulgent jocularity. "I believe that in certain quarters they were even condemned as irregular and improper. What no one could deny was that you got results! The conspiracy against the Miletti family was smashed at a single stroke by your arrest of that foreign woman. Their enemies were completely disconcerted, and by the time they reformed to cope with this unexpected development, the critical moment had passed and it was too late."

He came round the desk, towering above Zen.

"The parallel with the present case is obvious. Here, too, timing is of the essence. As I say, the truth would in any case emerge in due course, but not before the reputation of, ah, one of our most respected and influential leaders had been foully smeared. We have no intention of allowing that to happen, which is why we are entrusting you with this delicate and critical mission. In short, we're counting on you to apply in Sardinia the same methods which proved so effective in Perugia.''

Zen said nothing. After a few moments a slight crease appeared on the young man's brow.

"I need hardly add that a successful outcome to this affair is also in your own best interests. I'm sure you're only too well aware of how swiftly one's position in an organisation such as the Ministry can change, often without one even being aware of it. Your triumph in the Miletti case might easily be undermined by those who take, ah, a narrow-minded view of things. The size of the Criminalpol squad is constantly under review, and given the attrition rate among senior police officials in places such as Palermo, the possibility of transfers cannot be ruled out. On the other hand, success in the Burolo case would consolidate your position beyond question.''

He reached behind him and depressed a lever on the intercom.

"Lino? Dottor Zen is just leaving.''

Once again, Zen felt the pale, cool touch of the young man's hand.

"It really was most good of you to come, dottore. I trust that your work has not been . . . that's to say, that no serious disruption will make itself felt in . . .''

The appearance of the stocky Lino rescued them both from these incoherent politenesses. Like a man in a dream, Zen walked back through the dim vastness of the room to the walnut door, which Lino closed behind them as softly as the lid of an expensive coffin.

"This way.''

"That's very good,'' Zen remarked as they set off along the corridor. "Have they trained you to say anything else?''

Lino turned round, looking tough.

"You want your fucking teeth kicked in?"

"That depends on whether you want to be turned into low-grade dog food. Because that's what's liable to happen to anyone round here who fails to treat me with the proper respect."

"Bullshit!"

"On the contrary, chum. All I have to do is mention that I don't like your face and by tomorrow you won't *have* a face."

Lino sneered.

"You're crazy," he said without total conviction.

"That's not what *l'onorevole* thinks. Now beat it. I'll find my own way out."

For a moment Lino tried bravely to stare Zen out, but doubt had leaked into his eyes and he had to give up the attempt.

"Crazy!" he repeated, turning away with a contemptuous sniff.

Zen left the portal of Palazzo Sisti with a confident, unfaltering stride, a man with places to go to and people to see. The moment he was out of sight around the nearest corner, his manner changed out of all recognition. He might now have been taken for a member of one of the geriatric tourist groups that descended on Rome once the high season was over. So far from having an urgent goal in mind, he turned right and left at random, obeying impulses of which he wasn't even aware and which in any case were of no importance. All that mattered was to let the tension seep slowly out of his body, draining out through the soles of his feet as they traversed the grimy undulating cobbles, scattering pigeons and sending the feral cats scuttling for cover under parked cars.

Eventually he emerged into an open space which he recognised with pleasure as Piazza Campo dei Fiori, almost Venetian in its intimacy and hence one of Zen's favourite spots in Rome. The morning vegetable market created a gentle bustle of activity that was supremely restful. He made his way across the cobbles strewn with discarded leaves and stalks, past zinc bathtubs and buckets full of ashes from the wooden boxes burned earlier against the morning chill. Now the sun was high enough to flood most of the piazza with its light. The stall holders were still hard at work, washing and trimming salad greens under the communal tap. Elderly women in heavy dark overcoats with fur collars walked from stall to stall, looking doubtfully at the produce.

Zen walked over to a wine shop he knew, where he ordered a glass of *vino novello*. He leaned against the doorpost, smoking a cigarette and sipping the frothy young wine which had still been in the grapes when Oscar Burolo and his guests had been murdered. A gang of labourers working on a house nearby were shouting from one level of scaffolding to another in a dialect so dense that Zen could understand nothing except that God and the Virgin Mary were coming in for the usual steady stream of abuse. A neat, compact group of Japanese tourists passed by, accompanied by two burly Italian bodyguards. The female guide, clutching a furled pink umbrella, was giving a running commentary in which Zen was surprised to make out the name Giordano Bruno like a fish sighted underwater. She pointed with her umbrella to the centre of the square, where the statue of the philosopher stood on a plinth whose base was covered with the usual incomprehensible graffiti.

Nearby, an old woman bent double like a wooden doll hinged at the hips was feeding last night's spaghetti to a gang of mangy cats. Zen thought nostalgically of the cats of his native city, carved and living, obscure or monumental, the countless avatars of the Lion of the Republic itself. In Venice, cats were the familiars of the city, as much a part of it as the stones and the water, but the cats of Rome were just vermin to be periodically exterminated, as hideously pitiful as concentration camp survivors. It somehow seemed typical of the gulf which separated the two cities. For while Zen liked Campo dei Fiori, he could never forget that the statue at its centre commemorated a philosopher who had been burnt alive on that spot at just about the time that the gracious and exquisite Palazzo Sisti was taking shape a few hundred metres away.

Taking his empty glass back inside, Zen found himself drawn to the scene at the bar. One of the labourers, dressed in dusty blue overalls and a hat made from newspaper like an inverted toy boat, was knocking back a glass of the local white wine. Further along, two businessmen stood talking in low voices. On the bar before them stood their empty glasses, a saucer filled with nuts and cocktail biscuits, two folded newspapers, and a removable automobile cassette player.

Zen turned away. That was what had attracted his attention. But why? Nothing was more normal. No one left a cassette deck in their car any more. It was asking to have the windows smashed and the unit stolen.

It wasn't until Zen stepped into the band of shadow cast by the houses on the other side of the piazza that the point of the incident suddenly became clear to him. He *had* seen a cassette player in a parked car recently, in a brand-new luxury car parked in a secluded street late at night. Such negligence, coupled with the scratches and dents in the bodywork and the use of the floor as an ashtray, suggested a possibility that really should have occurred to him long before. Still, better late than never, he thought.

Or were there cases where that reassuring formula didn't hold, where late was just too late, and there were no second chances?

Back at the Ministry, Zen phoned the Questura and asked whether Professor Lusetti's red Alfa Romeo appeared on their list of stolen vehicles. Thanks to the recent computerisation of this department he had his answer within seconds. The car in question had been reported stolen ten days earlier.

He put the receiver down, then lifted it again and dialled another number. After some time the ringing tone was replaced by a robotic voice.

"Thank you for calling Paragon Security Consultants. The office is closed for lunch until three o'clock. If you wish to leave a message, please speak now."

"It's Aurelio, Gilberto. I was hoping to—"

"Aurelio! How are things?"

Zen stared at the receiver as though it had stung him.

"But . . . I thought that was a recorded message."

"That's what I wanted you to think. At least, not you, but any of the five thousand people I don't want to speak to at this moment."

"Why don't you get a real answering machine?"

"I have, but I can't use it just at the moment. One of my competitors has found a way to fake the electronic tone I can send down the line to have it play back the recorded messages to a distant phone. The result is that he downloaded a hundred million lire's worth of business as well as making me look like an idiot. Anyway, what can I do for you?"

"Well, I was hoping we could have a talk. I don't suppose you're free for lunch?"

"Today? Actually that's a bit . . . Well, I don't know. Come to think of it, that might work quite well. Yes! Listen, I'll see you at Licio's. Do you know where it is?"

"I'll find it."

Zen pressed down the receiver rest to get a dial tone, then rang his home and asked Maria Grazia if everything was all right.

"Everything's fine now," she assured him. "But this morning! Madonna, I was terrified!"

Zen tightened his grip on the receiver.

"What happened?"

"It was frightful, awful! The signor didn't notice anything, thanks be to God, but I was looking straight at the window when it happened!"

"When *what* happened?"

"Why, this man suddenly appeared!"

"Where?"

"At the window."

Zen took a deep breath.

"All right, now listen. I want you to describe him to

me as carefully as you can. All right? What did he look like?''

Maria Grazia made a reflective noise. "Well, let's see. He was young. Dark, quite tall. Handsome! Twenty years ago, maybe, I'd have—''

"What did he do?''

"Do? Nothing! He just disappeared. I went over and had a look. Sure enough, there he was, in one of those cages. He was trying to fix it but he couldn't. In the end they had to take it off the wall and put up a new one.''

"A new *what*, for the love of Christ?''

Stunned by this blasphemy, the housekeeper murmured, "Why, the streetlamp! The one that was forever turning itself on and off. But when I saw him floating there in midair I got such a shock! I didn't know what to think! It looked like an apparition, only I don't know if you can have apparitions of men. It always seems to be women, doesn't it? One of my cousins claimed she saw Santa Rita once, but it turned out she made it all up. She'd got the idea from an article in *Gente* about these little girls who . . .''

Zen repeated his earlier instructions about keeping the front door bolted and not leaving his mother alone, then hung up.

On his way downstairs, he met Giorgio De Angelis coming up. The Calabrian looked morose.

"Anything the matter?'' Zen asked him.

De Angelis glanced quickly up and down the stairs, then gripped Zen's arm impulsively.

"If you're into anything you shouldn't be, get out fast!''

He let go of Zen's arm and continued on his way.

"What do you mean?'' Zen called after him.

De Angelis just kept on walking. Zen hurried up the steps after him.

"Why did you say that?'' he demanded breathlessly.

The Calabrian paused, allowing him to catch him up.

"What's going on?'' Zen demanded.

De Angelis shook his head slowly.

"I don't know, Aurelio. I don't want to know. But whatever it is, stop doing it, or don't start."

"What are you talking about?"

De Angelis again looked up and down the stairs.

"Fabri came to see me this morning. He advised me to keep away from you. When I asked why, he said that you were being measured for the drop."

The two men looked at one another in silence.

"Thank you," Zen murmured almost inaudibly.

De Angelis nodded fractionally. Then he continued up the steps while Zen turned to begin the long walk down.

I never used to dream. Like saying, I never used to go mad. The others do it every night, jerking and tossing, sweating like pigs, groaning and crying out. "I had a terrible dream last night! I dreamt I'd killed someone and they were coming to arrest me and they'd guessed where I was hiding! It was horrible, so real!" You'd think that might teach them something about this world of theirs that also seems "so real!"

Then one night it happened to me. In the dream I was like the others, living in the light, fearing the dark. I had done something wrong, I never knew what, killed someone perhaps. As a punishment, they locked me up in the darkness. Not my darkness, gentle and consoling, but a cold dank airless pit, a narrow tube of stone like a dry well. The executioner was my father. He rammed me down, arms bound to my sides, and capped the tomb with huge blocks of masonry. I lay tightly wedged, the stones pressing in on me from every side. In front of my eyes was a chink through which I could just see the outside world where people passed by about their business, unaware of my terrible plight. Air seeped in through the hole, but not enough, not enough air! I was slowly suffocating, smothered beneath that intolerable dead weight of rock. I screamed and screamed, but no sound penetrated to the people outside. They passed by, smiling and nodding and chatting to each other, just as though nothing was happening!

It was only a dream, of course.

THURSDAY: 1340 — 1655

"So what's the problem, Aurelio? A little trip to Sardinia, all expenses paid. I should be so lucky! But once you're in business for yourself you learn that the boss works harder than . . ."

"I've already explained the problem, Gilberto! Christ, what's the matter with you today?"

It was the question that Zen had been asking himself ever since arriving at the restaurant. Finding his friend free for lunch at such short notice had seemed a stroke of luck which might help Zen gain control of the avalanche of events which had overrun his life.

Gilberto Nieddu, an excolleague who now ran an industrial counterespionage firm, was the person Zen was closest to. Serious, determined, and utterly reliable, there was an air of strength and density about him, as though all his volatility had been distilled away. Whatever he did, he did in earnest. Zen hadn't, of course, expected Gilberto to produce instant solutions, but he had counted on him to listen attentively and then bring a calm, objective view to bear on the problems. As a

Sardinian himself, his advice and knowledge might make all the difference.

But Gilberto was not his usual self today. Distracted and preoccupied, continually glancing over his shoulder, he paid little attention to Zen's account of his visit to Palazzo Sisti and its implications.

"Relax, Aurelio! Enjoy yourself. I'll bet you haven't been here that often, eh?"

This was true enough. In fact Zen had never been to Licio's, a legendary name among Roman luxury restaurants. The entrance was in a small street near the Pantheon. You could easily pass by without noticing it. Apart from a discreet brass plate beside the door, there was no indication of the nature of the business carried on there. No menu was displayed, no exaggerated claims made for the quality of the cooking or the cellar.

Inside you were met by Licio himself, a eunuchlike figure whose expression of transcendental serenity never varied. It was only once you were seated that the unique attraction of Licio's became clear. Thanks to the disposition of the tables in widely separated niches concealed from each other by painted screens and potted plants, you had the illusion that your party was the only group there. The prices at Licio's were roughly double the going rate for the class of cuisine on offer, but this was only logical since there were only half as many tables. In any case, the clientele came almost exclusively from the business and political worlds, and they were happy to pay whatever Licio wished to ask in return for the privilege of being able to discuss sensitive matters in a normal tone of voice with no risk of being either overheard or deafened by their neighbours. Hence the place's unique cachet: you went to other restaurants to see and be seen; at Licio's you paid more to pass unnoticed.

But on the rare occasions when Zen spent this kind of money on a meal, he went to places where the food rather than the ambience was the attraction, so Gilberto Nieddu's remark had been accurate enough. But that didn't make Zen feel any happier about the slightly patronising tone in which it had been made. Matters were not improved when Gilberto patted his arm familiarly and whispered, "Don't worry! This one's on me."

Zen made one final attempt to get his friend to appreciate the gravity of the situation.

"Look, I'll spell it out for you. They're asking me to frame someone. Do you understand? I'm to go to Sardinia and fake some bit of evidence, come up with a surprise witness, anything. They don't care what I do or how I do it as long as it gets the charges against Favelloni withdrawn or at least puts the trial date back several months."

Gilberto nodded vaguely. He was still glancing compulsively around the restaurant.

"This could be your big chance, Aurelio," he murmured, checking his watch yet again.

"Gilberto, we are talking here about sending an innocent person to prison for twenty years, to say nothing of allowing a man who has gunned down four people in cold blood to walk free. Quite apart from the moral aspect, that is seriously *illegal.*"

The Sardinian shrugged. "So don't do it. Phone in sick or something."

"For fuck's sake, this is not just another job! I've been *recommended* to these people! They've been told that I'm an unscrupulous self-seeker, that I cooked the books in the Miletti case and wouldn't think twice about doing so again. They've briefed me, they've cut me in. I know what they're planning to do and how they're planning to do it. If I try and get out of it now, they're not just going to say, 'Fine, suit yourself, we'll find someone else.' They already hinted that if I didn't play along I could expect to become another statistic in somewhere like Palermo. Down there you can get a contract hit done for a few million lire. There are even people who'll do it for free, just to make a name for themselves! And no one's going to notice if another cop goes missing. Are you listening to any of this?"

"Ah, finally!" Gilberto cried aloud. "A big client, Aurelio, very big," he hissed in an undertone to Zen. "If we swing this one, I can take a year off to listen to your problems. Just play along, follow my lead.''

He sprang to his feet to greet a stocky, balding man with an air of immense self-satisfaction who was being guided to their table by the unctuous Licio.

"Commendatore! Good morning, welcome, how are you? Permit me to present Vice-Questore Aurelio Zen. Aurelio, Dottor Dario Ochetto of SIFAS Enterprises." Lowering his voice suggestively, Gilberto added, "Dottor Zen works directly for the Ministry of the Interior."

Zen felt like walking out, but he knew he couldn't do it. His friendship with Gilberto was too important for him to risk losing it by a show of pique. The fact that Gilberto had probably counted on just this reaction didn't make Zen feel any happier about listening to the totally fictitious account of Paragon Security's dealings with the Ministry of the Interior which Gilberto used as a warm-up before presenting his sales pitch. Meanwhile Zen ate his way through the food that was placed before them and drank rather more wine than he would normally have done. Occasionally Gilberto turned in his direction and said, "Right, Aurelio?" Fortunately, neither he nor Ochetto seemed to expect a reply.

Zen found it impossible to tell whether Ochetto was impressed, favourably or otherwise, by this farce, but as soon as he had departed, amid scenes of enthusiastic hand-shaking, Gilberto exploded in jubilation and summoned the waiter to bring over a bottle of their best malt whisky.

"It's in the bag, Aurelio!" he exclaimed triumphantly. "An exclusive contract to install and maintain antibugging equipment at all their offices throughout the country, and at five times the going rate because what isn't in the contract is the work they want done on the competition."

Zen sipped the whisky, which reminded him of a tar-based patent medicine with which his mother had used to dose him liberally on the slightest pretext.

"What kind of work?"

Nieddu gave him a sly look. "Well, what do you think?"

"I don't think anything," Zen retorted aggressively. "Why don't you answer the question?"

Nieddu threw up his hands in mock surrender. "Oh! What is this, an interrogation?"

"You've gone into the bugging business?" Zen demanded.

"Have you got any objection?"

"I certainly have! I object to be tricked into appearing to sanction illegal activities when I haven't even been told what they are, much less asked whether I mind being dragged in! Jesus Christ almighty, Gilberto, I don't fucking well *need* this! Not any time, and especially not now."

Gilberto Nieddu gestured for calm, moving his hands smoothly through the air as though stroking silk.

"This lunch has been arranged for weeks, Aurelio. I didn't ask you to come along. On the contrary, *you* phoned *me* at the last moment. I would normally have said I was busy, but because you sounded so desperate I went out of my way to see you. But I had to explain your presence to Ochetto, otherwise he'd have been suspicious. This way, he'll just think I was trying to impress him with my contacts at the Ministry. It worked beautifully. You were very convincing. And don't worry about repercussions. He's already forgotten you exist."

Zen smiled wanly as he dug a Nazionale out of his rapidly collapsing pack. *You were very convincing.* Tania had said the same thing the night before, and it had apparently been Zen's convincing performance in the Miletti case which had recommended him to Palazzo Sisti. Everyone who used him for their own purposes seemed very satisfied with the results.

"So you're in the shit again, eh?" continued Nieddu, lighting a cigar and settling back in his chair. "What's it all about this time?"

Zen pushed his glass about on the tablecloth stained with traces of the various courses they had consumed. He no longer had any desire to share his troubles with the Sardinian.

"Oh, nothing. I'm probably just imagining it."

Nieddu eyed his friend through a screen of richly fragrant smoke.

"It's time you got out of the police, Aurelio. What's the point of slogging away like this at your age, putting your life on the line? Leave that to the young ambitious pricks who still think they're immortal. Let's face it, it's a mug's game. There's nothing in it unless you're crooked, and even then it's just small change really."

He clicked his fingers to summon the bill.

"You know, I never had any idea what was going on in the world until I went into business. I simply never realised what life was about. I mean, they don't teach you this stuff at school. What you have to grasp is, *it's all there for the taking!* Somebody's going to get it. If it isn't you, it'll be someone else."

He sipped his whisky and drew at his cigar.

"All these cases you get so excited about, the Burolos and all the rest of it, do you know what that amounts to? Traffic accidents, that's all. If you have roads and cars, a certain number of people are going to get killed and injured. Those people attract a lot of attention, but they're really just a tiny percentage of the number who arrive safely without any fuss or bother. It's the same in business, Aurelio. The system's there, people are going to use it. The only question is whether you want to spend your time cleaning up after other people's pile-ups or driving off where you want to go. Fancy a cognac or something?"

It was after three o'clock when the two men emerged, blinking, into the afternoon sunlight. They shook hands and parted amicably enough, but as Zen walked away, he felt as though a door had slammed shut behind him.

People changed, that was the inconvenient thing one always forgot. It was years now since Gilberto had left the police department in disgust at the way Zen had been treated over the Moro affair, but Zen still saw him as a loyal colleague, formed in the same professional mould, sharing the same perceptions and prejudices. But Gilberto Nieddu was no longer an expoliceman, but a prosperous and successful businessman, and his views and attitudes had changed accordingly.

On a day-to-day level this had been no more apparent than the movement of a clock's hands. It had taken this crisis to reveal the distance that now separated the two men. The Sardinian still wished Zen well, of course, and would help him if he could. But he found it increasingly difficult to take Aurelio's problems very seriously. To him they seemed trivial, irrelevant, and self-inflicted. What was the point of getting into trouble and taking risks with no prospect of profit at the end of it all?

Gilberto's attitude made it impossible for Zen to ask him for help, yet help was what he desperately needed for the project that was beginning to form in his mind. If he couldn't get it through official channels or friendly contacts, then there was only one other possibility.

The first sighting was just north of Piazza Venezia. After the calm of the narrow streets from which most traffic was banned, the renewed contact with the brutal realities of Rome life was even more traumatic than usual. I'm getting too old, Zen thought as he hovered indecisively at the kerb. My reactions are slowing, I'm losing my nerve, my confidence. So he was reassured to see that a tough-looking young man in a leather jacket and jeans was apparently just as reluctant to take the plunge. In the end, indeed, it was Zen who was the first to step out boldly into the traffic, trusting that the drivers would choose not to exercise their power to kill or maim him.

It was marginally less reassuring to catch sight of the same young man just a few minutes later in Piazza di Campidoglio. Zen had taken this route because it avoided the maelstrom of Piazza Venezia, although it meant climbing the long steep flights of steps up the Capitoline hill. Nevertheless, when he paused for breath by the plinth where a statue of his namesake had stood until recently succumbing to air pollution, there was the young man in the leather jacket, about twenty metres behind, bending down to adjust his shoelaces.

Zen swung left and walked down past the Mamertine prison to Via dei Fori Imperiali. He paused to light a cigarette. Twenty metres back, Leather Jacket was lounging against a railing, admiring the view. As Zen replaced his cigarettes, a piece of paper fluttered from his pocket to the ground. He continued on his way, counting his strides. When he reached twenty, he looked round again. The young man in the leather jacket was bending to pick up the paper Zen had dropped.

The only thing he would learn from it was that Zen had spent twelve hundred lire in a wine shop in Piazza Campo dei Fiori that morning. Zen, on the other hand, had learnt two things: the man was following him, and he wasn't very good at it. Without breaking his pace, he continued along the broad boulevard toward the Colisseum. This, or rather the underground station of the same name, had been his destination from the start, but he would have to lose the tail first. The men he was planning to visit had a code of etiquette as complex and inflexible as any member of Rome's vestigial aristocracy and would take a particularly poor view of anyone arriving with an unidentified guest in tow.

Without knowing who Leather Jacket was working for, it was difficult to choose the best way of disposing of him. If he was a solo operator, the easiest thing would be to have him arrested on some pretext. This would also be quick—a phone call would bring a patrol car in minutes—and Zen was already concerned about getting back to the house before six o'clock when Maria Grazia went home. But if Leather Jacket was part of an organisation, then this solution would sacrifice Zen's long-term advantage by showing the tail that he had been burned. He would simply be replaced by someone unknown to Zen and quite possibly someone more experienced and harder to spot. Zen therefore reluctantly decided to go for the most difficult option, that of losing the young man without him realising what had happened. It was not until the last moment, as he was actually passing the entrance, that he realised that the perfect territory for this purpose was conveniently at hand.

In the ticket office, three men in shirtsleeves were engaged in a heated argument about Craxi's line on combatting inflation. Zen flashed his police identity card at them and then at the woman perched on a stool at the entrance, a two-way radio in one hand and a paperback novel in the other. Without looking around to see if Leather Jacket was following, he walked through the gateway and into the Forum.

To his untutored eye, the scene before him resembled nothing so much as a building site. All that was missing were the tall green cranes clustered together in groups like extraterrestrial invaders. But this project had evidently only just passed the foundation level, and only then in a fragmentary and irregular way. Some areas were still pitted and troughed, awaiting the installation of drainage and wiring, while in others a few pillars and columns provided a tantalising hint of the building to come. Elsewhere whole sections of the massive brick structures—factories? warehouses?—which had formerly occupied the area had still not been completely demolished.

For the moment, work seemed to have ground to a halt. No dump trucks or concrete pourers moved along the rough track running the length of the site. Perhaps some snag had arisen over the financing, Zen thought whimsically. Perhaps the government had been reshuffled yet again, and the new minister was reluctant to authorise further expenditure on a project which had already overrun its estimated cost by several hundred percent—or was at least holding out for some financial inducement on a scale similar to that which had induced his predecessor to sign the contract in the first place.

A Carabinieri helicopter was thrashing about overhead like a shark circling for the kill. Zen tossed away his cigarette and strolled along a path in the patchy grass between the ruins. A fine dust covered everything, beaten into the air by passing feet from the bone-dry soil. The sun crouched low in a cloudless sky, its weak rays absorbed and reflected by the marble and brick on every side. Overhead the helicopter swept past periodically, watchful, alien, remote. Halfway up the path, which veered to the right and started to climb the Palatine hill, Zen paused to survey the scene. At this time of year there were only a few tourists about. Among them was a young man in a leather jacket and jeans. Oddly enough, he was once again having problems with his laces.

Zen resumed his walk with a fastidious smile. If Leather Jacket thought that bending down to tie up your shoes made you invisible, then he shouldn't prove too difficult to unload. In fact he felt slightly piqued that such a third-rate operative had been considered adequate for the task of shadowing him. Evidently he couldn't even inspire respect from his enemies.

The path ran up a shallow valley between masses of ancient brickwork emerging from the grass like weathered rocky outcroppings. The signs and fences installed by the authorities had imposed some superficial order on the hill's chaotic topography, but this simply made its endless anomalies all the more bizarre and incomprehensible. Nothing here was what it appeared to be, having been recycled and cannibalised so many times that its original name and function were often unclear even to experts. Although no archeologist, Zen was intimately familiar with the many layered complexities of the Palatine, thanks to the Angela Barilli affair.

The daughter of a leading Rome jeweller, eighteen-year-old Angela had been kidnapped in 1975. After months of negotiations and a bungled payoff, the kidnappers had broken off contact. In desperation, the Barilli family had turned to the supernatural, engaging a clairvoyant from Turin who claimed to have led the police to three other kidnap victims. The medium duly informed Angela's mother that her daughter was being held in an underground cell somewhere in the vast net-

work of rooms and passages on the lower floors of the
Imperial palace at the heart of the Palatine.

Unlikely as this seemed, the political clout wielded
by the family was enough to ensure that Zen, who was
directing the investigation, had to waste three days or-
ganising a painstaking search of the area. The Barilli
girl's corpse was in fact discovered the following year
in a shallow concrete pit beneath a garage in the
Primavalle suburb where she had been held during her
ordeal, but Zen had never forgotten the three days he
had spent exploring the honeycomb of caverns, tunnels,
cisterns, and cellars that lay beneath the surface of the
Palatine. It was an area so rich in possibilities that Zen
could simply disappear into the mathematics, leaving
his follower to solve an equation with too many vari-
ables.

Reaching the plateau at the top of the hill, Zen
turned left behind the high stone wall which closed off
a large rectangle of ground surrounding a church and
waited for Leather Jacket to catch up. There was no one
about, and the only sound was the distant buzzing of the
helicopter. It had now moved further to the east, circling over the group of hospitals near San Giovanni in
Laterano. No doubt an important criminal was being
transferred from Regina Coeli prison for treatment, with
the helicopter acting as an eye in the sky against any
attempt to snatch him.

Footsteps approached quickly, almost at a run. At
the last moment, Zen stepped out from behind the wall.

"Sorry!"

"Excuse me!"

The collision had only been slight, but the young
man in the leather jacket looked deeply startled, as Zen
had intended he should be. Close up, his sheen of
toughness fell apart like an actress's glamour on the
wrong side of the footlights. Despite a virile stubble no
doubt due to shaving last thing at night, his skin looked
babyish and his eyes were weak and evasive.

"It always happens!" Zen remarked.

The man stared at him, mystified.

"When there's no one about, I mean," Zen explained. "Have you noticed? You can walk right through the Stazione Termini at rush hour and never touch anyone, but go for a stroll up here and you end up walking straight into the only other person about!"

The man muttered something inconclusive and turned away. Zen set off in the opposite direction. Not only would the encounter have shaken Leather Jacket, but it would now be impossible for him to pass off any future contacts as mere coincidence. That constraint would force him to hang back in order to keep well out of sight, thus giving Zen the margin he needed.

He made his way through a maze of gravelled paths winding among sections of ruined brick wall several metres thick. Lumps of marble lay scattered about like discarded playthings. Isolated stone pines rose from the ruins, their rough straight trunks cantilevering out at the top to support the broad green canopy. Here and there, excavations had scraped away the soil to expose a fraction of the hidden landscape beneath the surface. Fenced off and covered with sloping roofs of corrugated plastic sheeting, they looked like the primitive shelters of some future tribe, bringing the long history of this ancient hill full circle in the eternal darkness of a nuclear winter.

A line of pines divided this area from a formal garden with alleys flanked by close-clipped hedges. Screened by the dense thickets of evergreen trees and shrubs, Zen was able to move quickly along the paved path leading to a parterre with gravel walks, a dilapidated pavilion and terrace overlooking the Forum. A fountain dripped, bright dabs of orange fruit peeped through the greenery, and paths led away in every direction. In the centre, a flight of steps led down into a subterranean corridor running back the way he had come. Dimly lit by lunettes let into the wall just below the arched ceiling, the passage seemed to extend itself as Zen hurried along it. The walls, rough, pitted plaster, were hung with cobwebs as large and thick as handkerchiefs which fluttered in the cool draught.

The passage ended in another flight of steps leading up into the middle of the maze of brickwork and gravel paths which Zen had passed through earlier. Keeping under cover of the fragments of wall, he worked his way toward the massive ruins of the Imperial palace itself. The gate was just where he remembered it, barring off a niche giving access to a yard used for storing odds and ends of unidentified marble. It was supposed to be locked, but one of the things that Zen had learned in the course of his abortive search for Angela Barilli was that it was left open during the day because the staff used it as a shortcut. Ignoring the sign reading NO ADMISSION TO UNAUTHORISED PERSONS, Zen walked through the yard to a passage at the back. To the left, a modern doorway led into a museum. Zen turned the other way, down an ancient metal staircase descending into the bowels of the hill.

At first the staircase burrowed through a channel cut into the solid brickwork of the palace. As Zen walked down, the light diminished above, while simultaneously the darkness beneath began to glow. Then, without warning, he suddenly emerged into a vast underground space in which the staircase was suspended vertiginously, bolted to the brickwork. The other walls were immeasurably distant, mere banks of shadow, presences hinted at by the light seeping in far below, obscuring the ground like thick mist. Zen clutched the handrail, overwhelmed by vertigo. Everything had been turned on its head: the ground above, the light below.

Step by step, he made his way down the zigzag staircase through layers of cavernous gloom. The floor was a bare expanse of beaten earth illuminated by light streaming in through large rectangular openings giving on to the sunken courtyard at the heart of the palace. Zen walked across it, glancing up at the metal railings high above, where a trio of tourists stood reading aloud from a guidebook. A rectangular opening in the brickwork opposite led into a dark passage which passed through a number of sombre gutted spaces and then a huge enclosed arena consisting of rows of truncated columns flanking a large grassy area.

He sat down on one of the broken columns, out of sight of the path above, and lit a cigarette. At the base of the column lay a large pine cone, its scales splayed back like the pads of a great cat's paw. The air was still, the light pale and mild, as though it too were antique. The matchstick figures displayed on Zen's digital watch continued their elaborate ballet, but the resulting patterns seemed to have lost all meaning. The only real measure of time was the slow disappearance of the cigarette smouldering between Zen's fingers and the equally deliberate progress of his thoughts.

Who could Leather Jacket be working for? Until now Zen had assumed that he must be connected with the break-in at his flat and the envelope full of shotgun pellets which had been left there, but after some consideration he now rejected this idea. Leather Jacket simply didn't look nasty enough to have a hand in the attempt to scare Zen by copying the bizarre warnings sent to Judge Giulio Bertolini before his death. He didn't *care* enough. It wasn't a personal vendetta he was involved in, Zen was sure of that. He was in it for the money, a cut-rate employee hired by the hour to keep track of Zen's movements. But who had hired him? The longer Zen thought about it, the more significant it seemed that Leather Jacket had put in his first appearance shortly after Zen's interview at Palazzo Sisti.

The only surprising feature of this solution was that they should have chosen such a low-grade operative to do the job, but this was no doubt explained by the fact that Lino was in charge of that department. They might even prefer Zen to know that they were keeping tabs on him. He was their man now, after all. Why shouldn't they keep him under surveillance? What reason had they to trust him, after all?

It was only when he had asked himself this question that Zen realised that it wasn't rhetorical. *Once your accomplishments in the Miletti case had been brought to our attention,* the young man had told him, *the facts spoke for themselves.* But who had brought those accomplishments to their attention in the first place? Presumably one of the contacts at the Ministry the young man had mentioned earlier. *We have been let down before by people who promised us this, that, and the other, and then couldn't deliver. Why, only a few days ago we asked our man there to obtain a copy of the video tape showing the tragic events at the Villa Burolo. A simple enough request, you would think, but even that proved beyond the powers of the individual in question. Nor was this the first time that he had disappointed us.*

Zen looked up with a start. The sheer stone walls of the arenas appeared to have crept closer, hemming him in. Only the day before he had asked himself why Vincenzo Fabri had gone out on a limb with his harebrained notion about Burolo not being the murderer's intended victim, that the killings had actually been a Mafia hit on the architect Vianello. The answer, of course, was that this had been a bungled attempt to divert suspicion from Renato Favelloni. Fabri's mission to Sardinia had only nominally been undertaken on behalf of Criminal-pol. His real client had been *l'onorevole.*

And he'd blown it! That was why Fabri had not been offered the chance to exploit the new evidence about the lion-keeper Furio Pizzoni's real identity. It was too good a chance for Palazzo Sisti to risk wasting on someone in whom they no longer had any faith. Instead, they had plumped for Zen, whose record "spoke for itself." Only it hadn't, of course. Someone had spoken for it first. Someone had brought Zen's "accomplishments in the Miletti case" to the attention of Palazzo Sisti and suggested that this unscrupulous manipulator of evidence and witnesses might be just the right man to bring the Burolo imbroglio to a satisfactory conclusion. And that someone, it was now clear, could only be the Party's man at the Ministry, Vincenzo Fabri himself.

Zen lit another cigarette from the butt of the first, a habit he normally despised. But normality was rapidly losing its grip on his life. Vincenzo Fabri had recommended Zen to his masters as the white knight who could save Renato Favelloni from prison and *l'onorevole* from disgrace. By doing so, he had not only given his bitterest enemy a chance to succeed, but to do so on the very ground where he himself had recently suffered a humiliating failure. Why would he do a thing like that?

The only possible answer was that Fabri knew damn well that Zen was not going to succeed. So, far from doing his enemy a good turn, Fabri had placed him in a trap with only two exits, each potentially fatal. If Zen failed to satisfy Palazzo Sisti, they would have him transferred to a city where his life could be terminated without attracting attention. If on the other hand he did what was necessary to get the Favelloni trial postponed, Fabri would tip off the judiciary and have Zen arrested for conspiracy to pervert the course of justice. Whatever happened, Zen was bound to lose. If his new friends didn't get him, his old enemy would.

By now the sun had disappeared behind the grove of pines whose foliage was just visible above the far end of the sunken stadium. At once the air revealed its inner coldness, the chill at its heart. It was time to go. Leather Jacket would most likely have given up the search by now and be waiting near the entrance on Via dei Fori Imperiali.

Zen got to his feet and started to pick his way through the jumble of ruins opposite. A brick staircase and a circuitous path scuffed through the grass brought him out on a track flanked by pines leading down to the exit on Via di San Gregorio. The odours of summer, pine sap and dried shit, lingered faintly in the undergrowth. There was no sign of Leather Jacket, but in any case Zen no longer greatly cared about him. Being tailed was the least of his worries now, and as for that matter, so was the missing video tape. To think that just that morning he had worked out an elaborate theory to explain the fact that Fabri had put in a request for it. The reason for this was now clear: Palazzo Sisti had told him to get hold of a copy. As for the theft, it must indeed have been the work of a pickpocket, as Zen had originally supposed.

Vincenzo Fabri had bigger and better schemes in mind than pilfered videos. Had he not warned De Angelis that very morning to keep away from Zen because he was being measured for the drop? The exact nature of that drop now seemed terrifyingly clear.

I was always biddable, a born follower. Like those ducklings we had, a fox killed the mother and they would follow whoever was wearing the green rubber boots that were the first thing they saw on opening their eyes. If the boots had been able to walk by themselves, they would have followed the boots, or a bit of rubbish blown past by the wind, whatever happened to be there when the darkness cracked open. Even the fox that killed their mother.

I can see him now, standing there, the light at his back, and all the forces of the light. "Come with me," he said. I can't, I told him, I mustn't. It seemed that all this had happened before. Where do they come from, these memories and dreams? They must belong to someone else. There was nothing before the darkness. How could there be? We come from darkness and to darkness we return. There is nothing else.

*   *   *

"It's all right," he said, "I'm a policeman. Come with me." I did what he told me. He would have taken me anyway, by force.

The light burned so much I had to close my eyes. When I opened them, there were men everywhere, rushing about, shouting at each other, crowding in, their eyes swishing to and fro like scythes. They took it in turns to pour their lies into me, filling me with unease. Everything that had happened had been a mistake. I'd done nothing wrong, it was all a mistake, a scandal, a tragic and shocking crime. When I tried to say something, my voice astonished me, a raven's croak passing through my body, nothing to do with me. After that I kept silent. There was no point in trying to resist. They were too strong, their desires too urgent. Sooner or later, I knew, they would have their way with me.

In the end they tired and let me go. You're free, they said. Like the follower I was, I believed them. I thought I could go back as though nothing had happened, as though it had all been a dream!

THURSDAY: 1720 — 1910

By the time the grubby blue and grey Metropolitana train emerged above ground at the Piramide stop, it was getting dark. Zen walked up the broad dim steps beneath a Fascist mural depicting the army, the family, and the workers, and out into the street.

The city's sparrows were in the grip of the madness that seized them at the changing of the light, turning the trees into loudspeakers broadcasting their gibberish, then swarming up out of the foliage to circle about in the dusky air like scraps of windborne rubbish. In the piazza below, gleaming tramlines crisscrossed in intricate patterns leading off in every direction, only to finish abruptly a few metres further on under a coat of tarmac or running headlong into a traffic divider.

Instead of making a detour to the traffic lights on Via Ostiense, Zen walked straight out into the vehicles converging on the piazza from every direction. Maybe that was where the sparrows got the idea, he thought. Maybe their frenzied swarming was just an attempt to imitate the behaviour patterns of the dominant life-form. But tonight the traffic didn't bother him. He was as invulnerable to accidents as a prisoner under sentence of death. Respecting his doomed self-assurance, the traffic flowed around him, casting him ashore on the far side of the piazza at the foot of the marble pyramid.

The most direct route to where he was going lay through Porta San Paolo and along Via Marmorata. But now that he was nearly there, Zen's fears about being followed had revived, so instead of the busy main road he took the smaller and quieter street flanked by the city walls on one side and dull apartment blocks on the other. Apart from a few prostitutes setting up their pitches in the strip of grass and shrubs between the street and the wall, there was no one about. He turned right through the arches opened in the wall and then left, circling the bulky mound which gave its name to the Testaccio district. At the base of the hill stood a line of squat, jerry-built huts guarded by savage dogs. Here metal was worked and spray-painted, engines mended, bodywork repaired, serial numbers altered. During Zen's time at the Questura, this had been one of the most important areas in the city for recycling stolen vehicles.

The other main business of the district had been killing, but that had ceased with the closure of the slaughterhouse complex that lay between the Testaccio hill and the river. Any killing that went on now was related to the part-time activities of some of the inhabitants, of which the trade in secondhand cars was only the most notable example. As for the abattoir, it was now a mecca for aspirant yuppies like Vincenzo Fabri who thronged to the former killing floors in their Mercedes and BMWs to acquire the art of sitting on a horse. Opposite, a few exclusive nightclubs had sprung up to attract those of the city's gilded youth who liked to go slumming in safety.

Skirting the oxblood-red walls of the slaughterhouse, Zen walked on into the grid of streets beyond. Although no more lovely than the suburb where Tania and her husband lived, the Testaccio was quite different. It had a history, for one thing: two thousand years of it, dating back to the time when the area was the port of Rome and the hill in its midst had gradually been built up from fragments of amphorae broken in transit or handling. The four-square, turn-of-the-century tenements which now lined the streets were merely the latest expression of its essentially gritty, no-nonsense character. The merest change in the economic climate would be enough to sweep away the outer suburbs as though they had never existed, but the Testaccio would be there forever, lodged in Rome's throat like a bone.

Night had fallen. The street was sparsely lit by lamps suspended on cables strung across from one apartment block to another. Rows of jalousies painted a dull institutional green punctuated the expanses of bare walling. In an area where cars were a medium of exchange rather than a symbol of disposable income, it was still possible to park in an orderly fashion at an angle to the kerb, leaving the pavements free for pedestrians. Zen walked steadily along, neither hurrying nor loitering, showing no particular interest in his surroundings. This was enemy territory, and he had particular reasons not to want to draw attention to himself. After crossing two streets running at right angles, he caught sight of his destination, a block of shops and businesses comprising a butcher, a barber, a grocery, and a paint wholesaler. Between the barber and the butcher lay the Rally Bar.

It had been years since Zen had set foot there, but as soon as he walked in he saw that nothing had changed. The walls and the high ceiling were painted in the same terminal shade of brown and decorated with large photographs of motor-racing scenes and the Juventus football team and posters illustrating the various ice creams available from the large freezer at the end of the bar. Two bare neon strips suspended by chains from the ceiling dispensed a frigid, even glare reflected back by the indestructible slabs of highly polished aggregate on the floor. Above the bar hung a tear-off calendar distributed by an automobile spare parts company featuring a colour photograph of a peacock, framed permits from

the city council, a price list, a notice declaring the establishment's legal closing day to be Wednesday, advertise-
ments for various brands of *amaro* and beer, and a
drawing of a tramp inscribed, He always gave discounts
and credit to everyone.

The three men talking in low voices at the bar fell
silent as Zen entered. He walked up to them, pushing
against their silent stares as though into a strong wind.

"A glass of beer."

The barman, gaunt and lantern-jawed, plucked a
bottle of beer from the fridge, levered the cap off the
bottle, and dumped half the beer into a glass still dripping from the draining board. The glass was thick and
scored with scratches. At the bottom, a few centimetres
of beer lay inaccessible beneath a layer of bubbles as
thick and white as shaving foam.

The barman picked up a copy of the *Gazzetta dello
Sport*. The other customers gazed up over their empty
coffee cups at the bottles of half-drunk spirits and cor-
dials stacked on the glass shelving. Above the bar, in
pride of place, stood a clock whose dial consisted of a
china plate painted with a list showing the amount of
time the proprietor was allegedly prepared to spend on
tax collectors, rich aged relatives, door-to-door sales-
men, sexy housewives, and the like. Plainclothes policemen on unofficial business were not mentioned.

Zen carefully poured the rest of the beer into the
glass, dousing the bubbles. He drank half of it and then
lit a cigarette.

"Fausto been in tonight?"

The second hand described almost a complete
revolution of the china plate before the barman swiv-
elled smoothly to face Zen.

"What?"

Zen looked him in the eye. He said nothing. Eventually the barman turned away again and picked up his
newspaper. The second hand of the clock moved from
"mothers-in-law" through "the blonde next door" and
back to its starting place.

"This beer tastes like piss," Zen said.

The pink newspaper slowly descended.

"And what do you expect me to do about it?" the barman demanded menacingly.

"Give me another one."

The barman rocked backward and forward on his feet for a moment. Then he snapped open the heavy wooden door of the fridge, fished out another bottle, decapitated it, and banged it down on the zinc counter. Zen took the bottle and his glass and sat down at one of the three small round metal tables covered in blue and red plastic wickerwork.

As if they had been waiting for this, the two other customers suddenly came to life. One of them fed some coins into the video game machine, which responded with a deafening burst of electronic screams and shots. The other man strode over to Zen's table. He had slicked-back dark hair and ears that stood out from his skull like a pair of gesturing hands. There was a large soggy bruise on his forehead, his nose was broken, and his cheek had recently been slit from top to bottom. Wary of the fearful things that had happened to the rest of his face, the man's eyes cowered in deep, heavy-lidded sockets.

"All right if I sit down?" he asked, doing so.

On the video screen, a gaunt grim detective in a trenchcoat stalked a nocturnal city street. Menacing figures wielding guns appeared at windows or popped out from behind walls. If the detective shot them accurately, they collapsed in a pool of blood and a number of points was added to the score, but if he missed, then there was a female scream and a glimpse of the busty half-naked victim.

"I couldn't help overhearing what you said," Zen's new companion remarked.

Zen stubbed out his cigarette in a smoked-glass ashtray printed with the name, address and telephone number of a wholesale meat supplier. *All home-killed produce,* read the slogan. *Bulk orders our specialty.*

"I'm a friend of Fausto," the man went on. "Unfortunately he's out of town at the moment. Perhaps I could help."

Zen moved the ashtray about on the table as though it were a counter in a game and he hadn't quite decided on his move. "That would depend on what I wanted," he said.

"And on who you are."

So that the attractions of the video game should not be lost on those unable to see the screen, the manufacturers had thoughtfully provided it with a range of sound effects which were repeated at regular intervals. One in particular, a mocking little motif like an electronic sneer, invariably caused the player to blaspheme and slap the side of the machine with his palm. At length he turned away in disgust, crossed over to the bar, and slapped down a banknote.

"Gimme five," he said.

The barman laid down his pink sports paper, massively unmoved by the shattering events referred to in the headline: *JUVE, WHAT A LETDOWN!!! ROMA, WHAT A LETOFF!!!*. He tossed the coins on the stainless steel surface. A moment later the video player was lost to the world again, his buttocks twisting and swivelling as though copulating with the machine.

"I'm also a friend of Fausto's," said Zen.

The man raised his eyebrows. "Strange we haven't met before."

"Fausto has a lot of friends. A lot of enemies, too. Maybe that's why he's out of town."

"He didn't tell me."

"That's no way to treat a friend," Zen remarked.

The barman tossed his newspaper aside and stepped down from the raised wooden stage from which he lorded it over the customers. An oddly insignificant figure now, diminished by more than just height, he moved restlessly about, straightening chairs and tables and polishing ashtrays.

"Anyway, if I run into Fausto, I'll let him know you were asking for him," the man said. "What did you say your name was?"

Zen wrote his telephone number on a piece of paper and handed it to the man. "Tell him to ring me this evening."

"Why would he want to do that?"

"For the same reason he's out of town. For his health, for his future, for his peace of mind."

He got up and started to walk to the door.

"Hey, what about the beers?" the barman called.

Zen jerked his thumb at the table.

"My friend's buying," he said.

He walked down the street without looking back. Once he had rounded the corner, he stopped in a patch of shadow cast by a large delivery van, keeping an eye on the door of the Rally Bar. A cloying odour emanated from the van, the odour of blood, of death. It had its own smell, quite distinct from all others. Zen recalled a visit he had made to another abattoir in the course of an investigation into an extortion racket, maybe even the Spadola case. He had watched the animals being prodded and kicked to their deaths, squealing piteously, showing the whites of their eyes. Men in blue overalls and red rubber aprons went about the killing in an atmosphere of rough, good-natured camaraderie, and at lunchtime went home to their wives and children and ate fried back muscles and veins and intestine and stomach lining.

A figure emerged from the bar and started to walk straight toward him. Zen backed into the shadows, keeping in the lee of the van, then ran quickly into the courtyard of a nearby apartment block. Palms and small evergreen shrubs surrounded a dripping communal tap. The courtyard was separated from the street by a wall topped with high iron railings. Zen took shelter immediately inside, behind the wall, ready to follow the man once he had passed by.

But he didn't pass by. The footsteps came closer and closer, and then he was there, no more than a metre away. He walked past Zen without seeing him, crossed the courtyard, and disappeared into one of the doorways. Zen followed.

Inside the door, a narrow marble staircase with a heavy wooden banister on wrought-iron supports ran up to a landing. The man was already out of sight. Zen stopped still, listening to the footsteps in the stairwell above. One, two, three, four, five, six, seven, eight, then a brief pause as he reached the landing. This pattern was repeated twice. Then there was a faint knocking, repeated after some time. The murmur of voices was cut off by the sound of a door closing.

Zen ran up the stairs to the second floor. As on the other landings, there were two flats, one to the left and the other facing the stairs. There were numbers on the doors, but no names. Zen continued halfway up the next flight of steps, where he stopped, waiting for the man to emerge again.

The voice of a television newscaster was blaring away in one of the apartments nearby. ". . . investigation appears to have ground to halt. The authorities have denied that a fresh wave of arrests is imminent. The secretary of the Radical Party today called for alternatives to the terrorist hypothesis to be considered, pointing out that Judge Bertolini never presided in political . . ."

A door opened on the floor above and women's voices drowned out the rest of the sentence.

"Bye, then!"

"Bye! I'll make the pasta, but don't forget the artichokes, eh?"

"Don't worry. Some thrushes too, if Gabriele has any luck."

"A bit of good wine wouldn't come amiss either."

"That goes without saying."

"And remind Stefania to bring a pudding. You know what she's like!"

The door closed. An elderly woman appeared on the stairs. She was wearing a long coat of some heavy, dark, dowdy-looking material, trimmed with cheap fur at the collar, and wore a woollen scarf over her shoulders. She paused to take in Zen, leaning against the wall.

"No more puff, eh?" she cackled.

Zen nodded ruefully. "It's my heart. I have to be careful."

"Quite right! You can't be too careful. Not that it makes any difference in the end. My sister's brother-in-law, that's by her second marriage, to someone from Ancona, although now they live here in Rome because he got a job with the radio, her husband I mean, he does the sound for the football matches."

"The brother-in-law?"

"Eh, no, the husband! The brother-in-law doesn't do anything, that's what I'm telling you, he just dropped dead one day. And do you know the funny thing?"

There was the sound of a door opening on the second floor. Zen glanced round the angle of staircase. In the doorway facing the steps the man from the Rally Bar stood nodding and muttering something to someone inside the flat.

"The funny thing is," the woman went on, "that very evening he had to go to Turin to see his cousin's twin girls who'd been born the weekend before, and the train, the one he'd been going to take, you know what happened? It came off the rails, just outside Bologna. And there was another train coming the other way that would have run straight into the wreckage, except that it was late so they had time to stop it. Otherwise it would have been a terrible disaster with hundreds and hundreds of people killed, including poor Carlo, who was dead already, as I said. It all goes to show that when your time comes, there's nothing you can do about it."

The door below had closed and the man's footsteps could be heard faintly descending the steps and echoing in the courtyard outside. The old woman cackled again and hobbled downstairs past Zen. As soon as she had gone, he walked down to the landing and knocked on the door in an authoritative way.

There was a scurry of steps inside.

"Who is it?" piped a childish voice.

"Gas Board. We've got a suspected leak in the building, got to check all the apartments."

The door opened a crack, secured by a chain. There seemed to be no one there.

"Let me see your identification."

Looking much lower down the opening, Zen finally spotted a small face and two eyes fixed unblinkingly on him. He got out his police identity card and dropped it through the centimetre-wide crack.

"Show this to your father."

The eyes regarded him doubtfully. The girl couldn't have been more than about seven or eight years old. She tried to shut the door, but Zen had planted his foot in it.

The child turned away, the card held between her index finger and thumb like something dangerous or disgusting. After some time a still younger girl appeared, keeping well away from the door but watching Zen with an air of fascination.

Zen smiled at her. "Hello, there."

"Have you come to kill my daddy?" she asked brightly.

Before Zen could reply, the child was shooed away by a man's voice.

"Good evening, Fausto," called Zen. "It's been a long time."

A figure scarcely larger than the children's appeared round the rim of the door.

"Dottore!" breathed a hushed voice. "What an honour. What a pleasure. You're alone?"

"Alone."

"You'll have to move your foot. I can't get the chain undone."

"I just want to ask you a small favour, Fausto. Maybe I can do you one in return."

"Just move your fucking foot!"

Zen did so. There was a metallic rattle and in a single movement the door opened, a hand pulled Zen inside and the door closed again.

"Please forgive my language, dottore. I'm a bit nervous at the moment."

Fausto was a small, wiry man with the extreme skinniness that betrays an undernourished childhood.

His face was marked by a scar which split his upper lip. He claimed that he'd got it in a knife fight, but Zen thought it was more likely the result of a bungled operation for a cleft palate.

In compensation for the rigours of his childhood, Fausto had survived the passing years with remarkably little sign of ageing. That he had survived at all was a minor miracle, given the number of men he had betrayed. The recruitment of Fausto Arcuti had led directly to one of the great successes of Zen's years at the Questura in Rome, the smashing of the kidnap and extortion ring organised by a playboy named Francesco Fortuzzi. Arcuti had worked from inside the gang, continuing to supply information right up until the last moment. Then when the police swooped, he had been allowed to slip through the net along with various other minor figures who had never realised that they owed their escape to the fact that Zen was covering Fausto's tracks. The long-term prospects for informers were bleak. Once a man had sold his soul to the authorities, they could always threaten to expose him if he refused to collaborate again, and the risks of such collaboration grew with every successful prosecution. Sooner or later the criminal milieu figured out where the leaks were coming from. Against all the odds, however, Arcuti had survived.

"Come in!" he said, leading Zen inside. "What a pleasure! And so unexpected! Maria, bring us something to drink. You other kids, get the fuck out of here."

The apartment consisted of two small, smelly rooms crudely lit by exposed high-wattage bulbs. Forlorn pieces of ill-assorted furniture stood scattered about like refugees in transit. The walls were bedecked with images of the Virgin, the Bleeding Heart of Jesus, and various saints. Over the television hung a large three-dimensional picture of the crucifixion. As you moved your head, Christ's eyes opened and closed and blood seeped from his wounds.

"Sit down, dottore, sit down!" Arcuti exclaimed, clearing the sofa of toys and clothes. "Sorry about the mess. The wife's out at work all day, so we never seem to get things sorted out."

The eldest girl carried in a bottle of *amaro* and two glasses.

"I'd prefer to take you out to the bar," Arcuti said, pouring them each a drink, "but the way things are . . ."

"I've just come from there," Zen told him.

"I suppose you followed Mario?"

"If that's his name. The one with the Mickey Mouse ears."

Arcuti nodded wearily. "Half-smart, that's Mario. It's okay when they're clever and it's okay when they're stupid. It's the ones in between that kill you."

"So what's the problem?" Zen murmured, sipping his drink.

Arcuti sighed. "It's this Parrucci business. It's got us all spooked."

"Parrucci?" frowned Zen. The name meant nothing to him.

"You probably haven't heard about it. There's no reason why you should have, he wasn't working for you. In fact, he wasn't working for anyone, that's what makes it worse. He'd given it all up years ago. Of course in this business you never really retire, but Parrucci had been out of it for so long he must have thought he was safe. No one even knew he'd been in the game until it happened."

The informer drained his glass in a single gulp and poured himself another.

"We found out because of the way they did it. So we asked around, and it turned out that Parrucci had been one of the top informers up north, years ago. But he'd put all that behind him. Wanted to settle down and bring up his kids normally. That's why they picked him, I reckon."

"How do you mean?"

"Well, if they knock off someone who's still active, it looks like a personal vendetta. People who are not involved don't take much notice. But something like this is a warning to everyone. Once you inform, you're marked for life. We'll come for you, even if it takes years. That's what they're saying."

Zen lit a cigarette. He knew he was smoking too much, but this was not the time to worry about it.

"What did they do to him?" he asked.

Arcuti shook his head. "I don't even want to think about it."

He sat staring at the carpet for some time, balanced on the forward edge of the threadbare armchair. Then he grabbed a cigarette from the packet lying open beside him and lit up, glaring defiantly at Zen.

"You really want to know? All right, I'll tell you. In dialect, if a man is full of energy and drive, they say he has fire in his belly. That's a good thing, unless you have too much, unless you break the rules and start playing the game on your own account. What they used to do with traitors, down south, was to get a big iron cooking pot and build a charcoal fire inside. Then they stretched the poor bastard out on his back, tied him up, set the pot on his stomach, and then used the bellows until the metal got red-hot. Eventually the pot burnt its way down into the man's stomach under its own weight. It could take hours, depending on how much they used the bellows."

"That's what they did to Parrucci?"

"Not exactly. That's the traditional method, but you know how it is these days, people can't be bothered. Parrucci they kidnapped from his house and took him out to the country, out near Viterbo somewhere. They broke into a weekend cottage, stripped him naked, laid him out flat across the electric cooker with his wrists and ankles roped together, and then turned on the hot plates."

"Jesus."

Arcuti knocked back the second glass of *amaro* amid frantic puffs at his cigarette.

"Now do you see why I'm nervous, dottore? Because I could be the next name on the list!"

"How do you know there'll be any more?"

"Because no one's claimed responsibility. Usually when something like this happens, you find out who did it and why. They make damn sure you know! That's the whole point. But this time no one's saying anything. The only reason for that is that the job isn't finished yet."

Zen glanced at his watch. To his dismay, he found that it was almost ten to six. At six o'clock Maria Grazia would leave to go home, and from then on Zen's mother would be alone in the apartment.

Fausto Arcuti had noticed his visitor's gesture.

"Anyway, that's enough of my problems. What can I do for you, dottore?"

"It's a question of borrowing a car for a few days, Fausto."

"Any particular sort of car?"

"Something fairly classy, if you can. But the main thing is, it needs to be registered in Switzerland."

"Actually registered?"

Zen corrected himself. "It needs to have Swiss number plates."

Arcuti drew the final puff of smoke from his cigarette and let it drown in the dregs of *amaro*.

"This car, you want to borrow it for how long?"

"Let's say the inside of a week."

"And afterwards, will it be, er, compromised in any way?"

Zen gave him a pained look. "Fausto, if I wanted to do anything illegal, I'd use a police car."

Arcuti conceded a thin smile. "And how soon do you need it?"

"Tomorrow ideally, but I don't suppose there's any chance of that."

The informer shrugged.

"Why ever not, dottore? You're doing business with the Italy that works! I may be shut up in this lousy, rotten, stinking hole, but I still have my contacts."

He produced the piece of paper Zen had given the man called Mario.

"I can contact you at this number?"

"In the evening. During the day I'm at the Ministry."

"Which department?"

"Criminalpol."

Arcuti whistled. "Congratulations! Well, if I have any luck I'll phone you in the morning. I won't give any name. I'll just say that I wanted to confirm our lunch date. There'll be a message for you at the bar here."

"Thanks, Fausto. In return, I'll see what I can do to shed some light on this Parrucci business."

"I'd appreciate it, dottore. It's not just for me, though that's not exactly the way I'd choose to go. But the girls, it's wrong for them to have to grow up like this."

Zen walked away past the shuttered and gated market toward the bustle of activity on Via Marmorata. He was well satisfied with the way things had gone. Fausto Arcuti's lifestyle might appear unimpressive, but as a broker for favours and information he was second to none. Moreover, Zen knew that he would want to make up for the poor figure he had cut, cowering in fear of his life in a squalid flat.

Zen's main preoccupation now was to get home with as little delay as possible. He was in luck, for no sooner had he turned on to the main traffic artery than a taxi stopped just in front of him. The family which emerged from it seemed numerous enough to fill a bus, never mind a taxi, and still the matriarch in charge kept pulling them out like a conjuror producing rabbits from a hat. At length the supply was exhausted, however, and after an acrimonious squabble about extras, discounts, and tips, they all trooped away. In solitary splendour Zen climbed into the cab, which was as hot and smelly as a football team's changing room, and had himself driven home.

To his relief, the red Alfa Romeo was nowhere to be seen. The lift was ready and waiting, for once, and Zen rode it up to the fourth floor. The experiences of the day had left him utterly drained.

He saw it immediately as he opened the front door,

a narrow black strip as thin as a razor blade and seemingly endless. It continued all the way along the hallway, gleaming where the light from the living room reflected off its surface. He bent down and picked it up. It felt cold, smooth, and slippery.

He walked slowly down the hallway, gathering in the shiny strip as he went. As he passed the glass-panelled door to the living room, music welled up from the television as though to signify his relief at finding his mother alive and well, her eyes glued to the play of light and shadow on the screen. Then he looked past her, uncomprehending, disbelieving. The gleaming strip ran riot over the entire room, heaped in coils on the sofa and chairs, running around the legs of the chairs, draped over the table. In its midst lay a small rectangular box with tape sprouting from slits in either end. Zen picked it up. *Ministry of the Interior,* he read, *Index No 46429 BUR 433/K/95.*

"What's the matter with you tonight?" his mother snapped. "I asked you to bring me my camomile tea ages ago and you didn't even bother to answer."

Zen got slowly to his feet, staring at her.

"But Mamma, I've only just got home."

"Don't be ridiculous! Do you think I didn't see you? I may be old, but I'm not so old I don't recognise my own son! Besides, who else would be here once Maria Grazia's gone home, eh?"

A cold shiver ran through Zen's body.

"I'm sorry, Mamma."

"You didn't even have the common decency to reply when I spoke to you! You always bring me my camomile tea before *Dynasty* starts, you know that. But tonight you were too busy cluttering the place up with that ribbon or string or whatever it is."

"I'll fetch it right away," Zen mumbled.

But he didn't do so, for at that moment he heard a sound from the hallway and remembered that he had left the front door standing wide open.

Among the furniture stored in the hallway was a wardrobe inset with long rectangular mirrors which reflected an image of the front door onto the glass panel of the living room door. Thus even before he set foot in the hallway, Zen could see that the entrance to the apartment was now blocked by a figure thrown into silhouette by the landing light. The next moment this switched itself off, plunging everything into obscurity.

"Aurelio?" said a voice from the darkness.

Zen's breathing started again. He groped for the switch and turned on the light.

"Gilberto," he croaked. "Come in. Close the door."

What is the worst, the most obscene and loathsome thing that one person can do to another? Go on, rack your brains! Let your invention run riot! (I often used to talk to myself like this as I scuttled about.) Well? Is that all? I can think of far worse things than that! I've done *far worse things than that*. But let's not restrict ourselves to your hand-me-down imaginations. Because whatever you or I or anyone else can think up, no matter how hideous or improbable, one thing is sure. It has happened. Not just once but time and time again.

This prison is also a torture house. No one cares what goes on here.

You know Vasco, the blacksmith? Everyone still calls him the blacksmith, though he repairs cars now. What do you think of him? A steady sort, a bit obstinate, gives himself airs? As I was passing his workshop *one morning I saw him pick up his three-year-old daughter by the hair, hold her dangling there a while, then let her fall to the floor. A moment later he was back to work, moulding some metal tubing while the child wept in a heap on the ground, her little world in pieces all around her. I wanted to comfort her, to tell her how lucky she had been. All her daddy had done was pull her hair. He could have done other things. He could have used the blowtorch on her. He could have buried her alive in the pit beneath the cars. He could have done anything.*

He could have done anything.

FRIDAY: 1115 — 1420

WHILE THE ARCHIVES SECTION presented a slightly more animated appearance during office hours than on Zen's previous visit, it could by no means have been described as a hive of activity. True, there were now about a dozen clerks on duty, but this manning level had evidently been dictated by some notional bureaucratic quota rather than the actual demands of the job, which was being carried on almost entirely by one man. He had a neurotically intense expression, compulsive, jerky movements, and the guilty air of someone concealing a shameful secret.

Unlike the others, he couldn't just sit back and read the paper or chat all morning. If there was work to be done, he just couldn't help doing it! It was this that made him a figure of fun in his colleagues' eyes. They watched him scurry about, collecting and dispatching the files which had been ordered, sorting and reshelving those which had been returned, cataloguing and indexing new material, typing replies to demands and queries. Their looks were derisory, openly contemptuous. They despised him for his weakness, as he did himself for that matter. Poor fellow! What could you do with people like that? Still, he had his uses.

As on his previous visit, Zen asked to consult the file on the Vasco Spadola case. While it was being fetched, he called to the clerk who had been on duty the last time he had been there.

The man looked up from the crossword puzzle he was completing.

"You want to speak to me?" he demanded, with the incredulous tone of a surgeon interrupted whilst performing an open-heart operation.

Zen shook his head. "You want to speak to me. At least, so I've been told. Something about a video tape."

An anticipatory smile dawned on the clerk's lips.

"Ah, so it was you, was it? Yes, I remember now!"

The other clerks had all fallen silent and were watching with curiosity. Their colleague strode languidly over to the counter where Zen was standing.

"Yes, I'm afraid there's been a slight problem with that tape, dottore."

"Really?"

"Yes, really."

"And what might it be?"

"Well it *might* be almost anything," the clerk returned wittily. "But what it *is*, quite simply, is that the tape you gave us back is not the same tape that you took out."

"What do you mean, not the same?"

"I mean it's not the same. It's blank. Clear? There's nothing on it."

"But . . . but . . . ." Zen stammered.

"Also, the tapes we use here are specially made up for us and are not available commercially, whereas what you handed in is an ordinary BASF ferrous oxide cassette obtainable at any dealer."

"But that's absurd! You must have muddled them up somehow."

At that moment, the other clerk interrupted to hand Zen the file he had requested. But his colleague had no intention of letting Zen get away with his clumsy attempt to shift the blame for what had happened.

"No, dottore! That's not the problem. The problem is that the tape you brought back is a blank. Raw plastic."

Zen fiddled nervously with the Spadola file.

"What exactly are you accusing me of?" he blustered.

The clerk gestured loftily. "I'm not accusing anyone of anything, dottore. Naturally, everyone knows how easy it is to push the wrong button on one of those machines and wipe out the previous recording . . ."

"I'm sure I didn't do that."

"I *know* you didn't," the clerk replied with a steely smile that revealed the trap Zen had almost fallen into. "Our tapes are all copy-protected, so that's impossible. Besides, as I said, the brand was different. So a substitution must have taken place. The question is, where is the original?"

There was a crash as the Spadola file fell to the floor, spilling documents everywhere. As Zen bent down to pick them up, the assembled clerks signalled their colleague's triumph with a round of laughter.

Zen straightened up, holding a video cassette.

"46429 BUR 433/K/95," he read from the label. "Isn't that the one you've been making so much fuss about?"

"Where did that come from?" the clerk demanded.

"It was inside the file."

Without another word, he went back to picking up the scattered documents. The clerk snatched the tape and bustled off, muttering angrily about checking its authenticity.

Zen wasn't worried about that, having played it through the night before after he and Gilberto spent the best part of an hour rewinding the damn thing into the cassette by hand. His mother had gone to bed by then, still blissfully ignorant that a stranger had entered the apartment while she had been watching television.

Zen himself was still in shock from what had happened, and it was left to Gilberto to bring up the question of what was to become of his mother during his absence in Sardinia, now that their home was demonstrably under threat. In the end, Gilberto insisted that she stay with him and his wife until Zen returned.

"Quite impossible!" Zen had replied. His mother hadn't left the apartment for years. She would be lost without the familiar surroundings that replicated the family home in Venice. Anyway, she was practically senile much of the time. It was very difficult even for him to communicate with her or understand what she wanted, and it didn't help that she often forgot that her Venetian dialect was incomprehensible to other people. She could be demanding, irrational, bad-tempered, and devious. Rosella Nieddu already had her hands full looking after her own family. It would be an intolerable imposition for her to have to take on a moody old woman, contemptuous and distrustful of strangers, someone who in her heart of hearts believed that the civilised world ended at Mestre.

But Gilberto had brushed these objections aside.

"So what *are* you going to do with her, Aurelio? Because she can't stay here."

Zen had no answer to that.

And so it came about that early the following morning an ambulance rolled up to the front door of Zen's house. The attendants brought a mobile bed up to the apartment, placed Zen's mother on it, and took her downstairs in the lift before sweeping off, siren whooping and lights flashing, to the General Hospital. Thirty seconds later, siren stilled and flasher turned off, the ambulance quietly emerged on the other side of the hospital complex and drove to the modern apartment block where the Nieddus lived.

Throughout her ordeal the old lady had hardly spoken a word, though her eyes and the way she clutched her son's hand showed clearly how shocked she was. Zen had explained that there was something wrong with their apartment, something connected with the noises she had heard, and that it was necessary for them

both to move out for a few days while it was put right. It
made no difference what he said. His mother sat rigidly
as the ambulance men wheeled her into the neat and
tidy bedroom which Rosella Nieddu had prepared for
her, having shooed out the two youngest children to
join their elder siblings next door. Zen thanked Rosella
with a warmth that elicited a hug and a kiss he found
oddly disturbing. Gilberto's wife was a very attractive
woman, and the contact had made Zen realise that he
had neglected that side of his life for too long.

The Archives clerks had gone back to their desks,
now that the fun was over. Zen gathered up the papers
relating to the Spadola case and started to put them into
some sort of order while he awaited confirmation that
the video tape he had produced from his pocket after
dropping the file was indeed the genuine article.

Suddenly his hands ceased their mechanical activity. Zen scanned the smudgy carbon-copied document
he was holding, looking for the name which had leapt
off the page at him.

. . . INFORMED THAT SPADOLA WAS IN HIDING AT A
FARMHOUSE NEAR THE VILLAGE OF MELZO. AT 0400 HOURS ON
JULY 16TH PERSONNEL OF THE SQUADRA MOBILE UNDER THE
DIRECTION OF ISPETTORE AURELIO ZEN ENTERED THE HOUSE AND
ARRESTED SPADOLA. AN EXTENSIVE SEARCH OF THE PREMISES RE-
VEALED VARIOUS ITEMS OF MATERIAL EVIDENCE (SEE APPENDIX
A), IN PARTICULAR A KNIFE WHICH PROVED TO BE MARKED WITH
TRACES OF BLOOD CONSISTENT WITH THOSE OF THE VICTIM.
SPADOLA CONTINUED TO DENY ALL INVOLVEMENT IN THE AFFAIR,
EVEN AFTER THE DAMNING NATURE OF THE EVIDENCE HAD BEEN
EXPLAINED TO HIM. AT THE JUDICIAL CONFRONTATION WITH PAR-
RUCCI, THE ACCUSED UTTERED VIOLENT THREATS AGAINST THE
WITNESS . . .

Once again, Zen felt the superstitious chill that had
come over him that night after viewing the Burolo
video. Parrucci! The informer whose gruesome death
had thrown Fausto Arcuti into a state of mortal terror! It
seemed quite uncanny that the same man should have

figured in the file which Zen had asked to see two days earlier as part of his strategem for substituting the blank video tape.

But he had no more time to consider the matter, for at that moment the clerk reappeared, video cassette in hand.

"It's the right one," he confirmed grudgingly. "So where did the other come from, I'd like to know?"

Zen shrugged. "I'd say that's pretty obvious. When I brought the tape back the other day, you got it muddled up with the file I asked to consult at the same time. When you couldn't find it, you started to panic because you knew that it had been handed back and that you would be responsible. So you substituted a blank tape, hoping that no one would notice. Unfortunately, one of my colleagues had asked to see the tape, and he immediately discovered that—"

"That's a lie!" the man shouted.

Snatching the Spadola file from Zen, he abruptly went on to the attack.

"Look at this mess you've made! It would be no wonder if things sometimes *did* get confused around here with people like you wandering in and upsetting everything. Leave it, leave it! You're just making a worse muddle. These documents must be filed in chronological order. Look, this judicial review shouldn't be here. It must come at the end."

"Let me see that!"

The form was stiff and heavy, imitation parchment. The text, set in antique type and printed in the blackest of inks, was as dense and lapidary as Latin, clogged with odd abbreviations and foreshortenings, totally impenetrable. But there was no need to read it to understand the import of the document. It was enough to scan the brief phrases inserted by hand in the spaces left blank by the printer.

29TH APRIL 1964 . . . MILAN . . . SPADOLA, VASCO ERNESTO . . . CULPABLE HOMICIDE . . . LIFE IMPRIS-

ONMENT . . . INVESTIGATING MAGISTRATE GIULIO
BERTOLINI . . .

It was enough to scan the spaces, read the messages, make the connections. That was enough, thought
Zen. But he had failed to do it, and now it might be too
late.

Back at his desk in the Criminalpol offices, which
were deserted that morning, Zen phoned the Ministry of
Justice and enquired about the penal status of Vasco
Ernesto Spadola, who had been sentenced to life imprisonment in Milan on 29 April 1964. A remote and disembodied voice announced that he would be rung back
with the information in due course.

Zen lit a cigarette and wandered over to the window, looking down at the forecourt of the Ministry with
its pines and shrubbery flanking the sweep of steps leading down to the huge shallow bath of the fountain in
Piazza del Viminal. Although the implications of the
facts he had just stumbled on were anything but cheer-
ing, he felt relieved to find that there was at least a
rational explanation for the things that had been going
on. It had not been just an uncanny coincidence that
Zen had happened to ask for the Spadola file the day
that he had read about the killing of Judge Bertolini. At
some level below his conscious thoughts he must have
recalled the one occasion on which his path and that of
the murdered judge had crossed. As for Parrucci, the
reason why the name had meant nothing to Zen was
that he knew the informer only by his code name "the
nightingale." When Parrucci agreed to testify against
Spadola, his name had of course been revealed, but by
that time Zen's involvement with the case was at an
end.

A thin Roman haze softened the November sunlight, giving it an almost summery languor. At a window
on the other side of the piazza a woman was hanging
out bedding to air on the balcony. A three-wheeled Ape
van was unloading cases of mineral water outside the
bar below, while on the steps of the Ministry itself three

chauffeurs were having an animated discussion involving sharp decisive stabs of the index finger, exaggerated shrugs and waves of dismissal, cupped palms pleading for sanity, and attention-claiming grabs at each other's sleeves. Zen only gradually became aware of an interference with these sharply etched scenes, a movement seemingly on the other side of the glass where the ghostly figure of Tania Biacis was shimmering toward him in midair.

"I've been looking for you all morning."

He turned to face the original of the reflection. She was looking at him with a slightly playful air, as though she knew that he would be wondering what she meant. But Zen had no heart for such tricks.

"I was down in Archives, sorting out that video tape business. Where is everyone, anyway?"

A distant phone began to ring.

"Don't go!" Zen called as he hurried back to his desk. He snatched up the phone.

"Yes?"

"Good morning, dottore," a voice whispered confidentially. It sounded like some tiny creature curled up in the receiver itself. "Just calling to remind you of our lunch appointment. I hope you can still make it."

"Lunch? Who is this?"

There was long silence.

"We talked last night," the voice remarked pointedly.

Belatedly, Zen remembered his arrangement with Fausto Arcuti.

"Oh, right! Good. Fine. Thanks. I'll be there."

He put the receiver down and turned. Tania Biacis was standing close behind him and his movement brought them into contact for a moment. Zen's arm skimmed her breast, their hands jangled briefly together like bells.

"Oh, there you are!" he cried. "Where's everyone gone to?"

It was as though he regretted being alone with her!

"They're at a briefing. The chief wants to see you."

"Immediately?"

"When else?"

He frowned. The Ministry of Justice might phone back at any minute, and as it was Friday the staff would go off duty for the weekend in half an hour. He *had* to have that information.

"Would you do me a favour?" he asked.

The words were exactly the ones she had used to him two days earlier. It was clear from her expression that she remembered.

"Of course," she replied, with a faint smile that grew wider as he responded, "You don't know what it is yet."

"You decided before I told you what I wanted," she pointed out.

"But I had reasons which you may not have."

Tania sighed. "I don't know what you must think of me," she said despondently.

"Don't you? Don't you really?"

They looked at each other in silence for some time.

"So what is it you want?" she asked eventually.

Zen looked at her in some embarrassment. Now that his request had become the subject of so much flirtatious persiflage, it would be ridiculous to admit that he had only wanted her to field a phone call for him.

"I can't tell you here," he said. "It's a bit complicated, and . . . well, there're various reasons. Look, I don't suppose you could have lunch with me?"

It was a delaying tactic. He was counting on her to refuse.

"But you've already got a lunch engagement," she frowned.

It took him a little while to understand.

"Oh, the phone call! No, that's . . . that's for another day."

Tania inspected her fingernails for a moment. Then she reached out and lightly, deliberately, scratched the back of his hand. The skin turned white and then red, as though burned.

"I have to be home by three," she told him. She sounded like an adolescent arranging a date.

Zen was about to reply when the phone rang again.

"Ministry of Justice, Records Section, calling with reference to your enquiry re Spadola, Vasco Ernesto."

"Yes?"

"The subject was released from Asinara Prison on October 7th of this year."

Zen's response was a silence so profound that even the disembodied voice unbent sufficiently to add, "Hello? Anyone there?"

"Thank you. That's all."

He hung up and turned back to Tania Biacis.

"Shall we meet downstairs, then?" he suggested casually, as though they'd been lunching together for years. She nodded.

"Now please go and see what Moscati wants before he takes it out on me."

Lorenzo Moscati, head of Criminalpol, was a short stout man with smooth, rounded features which looked as though they were being flattened out by an invisible stocking mask.

"Eh, finally!" he exclaimed when Zen appeared. "I've been able to round up everyone except you. Where did you get to? Never mind, no point in you attending the briefing anyway. All about security for the *camorra* trial in Naples next week. But that won't concern you because you're off to Sardinia, you lucky dog! That report you did on the Burolo case was well received, very well received indeed. Now we want you to go and put flesh on the bones, as it were. You leave on Monday. See Ciliani for details of flights and so on."

Zen nodded. "While I'm here, there's something else I'd like to discuss," he said.

Moscati consulted his watch. "Is it urgent?"

"You could say that. I think someone's trying to kill me."

Moscati glanced at his subordinate to check that he'd heard right, then again to see if Zen was joking.

"What makes you think that?"

Zen paused, wondering where to begin.

"Strange things have been happening to me recently. Someone's picked the lock to my apartment and broken in while I'm not there. But instead of taking anything, they leave things instead."

"What sort of things?"

"First an envelope full of shotgun pellets. Then something which had been stolen from me at the bus stop a couple of days earlier."

"What?"

Zen hesitated. He obviously couldn't tell Moscati about the theft of the Ministry's video.

"A book I was carrying in my pocket. I assumed some thief thought it was my wallet. But last night I got home to find my apartment covered in paper. The book had been torn apart page by page and scattered all over the floor."

"Sounds like some prankster with a twisted sense of humour," Moscati remarked dismissively. "I wouldn't . . ."

"That's what I thought, at first." Zen didn't mention that his principal suspect had been Vincenzo Fabri. "Then I remembered that the widow of that judge who was shot said that exactly the same things had happened to her husband just before he was murdered. Meanwhile, someone has been watching my apartment from a stolen Alfa Romeo recently, and yesterday I was followed halfway across the city. Nevertheless, it didn't seem to add up to anything until I heard that an informer named Parrucci had been found roasted to death near Viterbo. Parrucci was the key witness in a murder investigation case I handled twenty years ago when I was working in Milan. The investigating magistrate in that case was Giulio Bertolini."

All trace of impatience had vanished from Moscati's manner. He was following Zen's words avidly.

"A gangster named Vasco Spadola was convicted of the murder and sentenced to life imprisonment. He was released from prison about a month ago. Since then both the judge who prepared the case and the man who gave evidence against Spadola have been killed. It doesn't seem too farfetched to conclude that the police officer who conducted the investigation is next on his list.''

A strange light burned in Lorenzo Moscati's eyes. ''So it's *not* political, after all!''

''The killing of Bertolini? No, it was straight revenge, a personal vendetta. You see, the evidence against Spadola was faked and Parrucci's testimony paid for by the victim's family. Presumably Bertolini didn't know that, but . . .''

''Do you realise what this means?'' Moscati enthused. ''The Politicals have been holding up this Bertolini affair as proof that terrorism isn't finished after all and so they still need big budgets and lots of manpower. If we can show that it's not political at all, they'll never live it down! That bastard Cataneo won't dare show his face in public for a month!''

Zen nodded wearily as he understood the reasons for his superior's sudden interest in the affair.

''Meanwhile my life is in danger,'' Zen reminded him. ''Two men have been killed and I'm number three. I want protection.''

Moscati grasped Zen's right arm just above the elbow, as though giving him a transfusion of courage and confidence.

''Don't worry, you'll get it! The very best. A crack squad has been set up to handle just this sort of situation. All handpicked men, weapons experts, highly skilled, using the very finest and most modern equipment. With them looking after you, you'll be as safe as the President of the Republic himself.''

Zen raised his eyebrows. This sounded too good to be true. ''When will this become effective?''

Moscati held up his hands in a plea for patience and understanding.

''Naturally there are a lot of calls on their time at the moment. In the wake of the Bertolini killing, everyone's a bit anxious. It'll be a question of reviewing the situation on an on-going basis, assessing the threat as it develops and then allocating the available resources accordingly.''

Zen nodded. It *had* been too good to be true.

"But in the meantime you'll put a man outside my house?''

Moscati gestured regretfully.

"It's out of my hands, Zen. Now this new squad exists, all applications for protection have to be routed through them. It's so they can draw up a map of potential threats at any given time, then put it on the computer and see if any overall patterns emerge. Or so they claim. If you ask me, they're just protecting their territory. Either way my hands are tied, unfortunately. If I start allocating men to protection duties, they'll cry foul and we'll never hear the end of it.''

Zen nodded and turned to leave. From a bureaucratic point of view, the logic of Moscati's position was flawless. He knew only too well that it would be a sheer waste of time to point out any discrepancy between that logic and common sense.

As the working day for state employees came to an end, doors could be heard opening all over the Ministry. The corridors began to hum with voices which, amplified by the resonant acoustic, rapidly became a babble, a tumult prefiguring the crowds surging invisibly toward the hallway where Zen stood waiting. Within a minute they were everywhere. The enormous staircase was barely able to contain the human throng eager to get home, have lunch and relax, or else hasten to their clandestine afternoon jobs in the booming black economy—"the Italy that works" as Fausto Arcuti had joked.

Ever since Tania Biacis had accepted his invitation to lunch, Zen had been racking his brains over the choice of restaurant. Given her wide and sophisticated experience of eating out in Rome, this was not something to be taken lightly. The only places he knew personally these days were those close to the Ministry and therefore regularly patronised by its staff, and it would clearly be unwise to go there. Quite apart from the risk of compromising Tania, Zen didn't want to have to deal with winks, nudges, or loaded questions from his colleagues. Again, it was important to get the class of establishment right. Nothing cheap or seedy, of course, but neither anything so grand or pretentious that it might make her feel that he was trying the crude, old, I'm-spending-a-lot-of-money-on-you-so-you'll-have-to-come-across approach. Finally, there were the practicalities to consider. If Tania had to be home by three, it had to be somewhere in the centre, where by this time most of the better restaurants might well be full. Every possibility that occurred to Zen failed one of these tests. He was still at a loss when Tania appeared.

"So, where are we going?" she demanded.

She sounded tense and snappy, as though she was already regretting having agreed to come. Zen panicked. He should never have confused his fantasies with reality like this. The situation was all wrong. It would end in disaster and humiliation.

"There's a place in Piazza Navona," he found himself saying as he led the way out into the pale sunlight. "It's crowded with tourists in summer, but at this time of year . . ."

He didn't add that the last time he was there had been with Ellen.

Outside the Ministry, Zen hailed a taxi. The brief journey did nothing to alleviate his fears that a major fiasco was in the offing. He and Tania sat as far apart as possible, exchanging brief banalities like a married couple after a row.

The taxi dropped them by the small fountain at the south end of the piazza. As they walked out into its superb amplitude, two kids sped past on a moped, one standing on the pillion and grasping the driver's shoulders. The noise scattered the flock of pigeons, which rose like a single being and went winging around the obelisk rising above the central fountain, while a second flock of shadows mimicked their progress across the grey stones below. The breeze caught the water spurting out of cleavages in the fountain, winnowing it out in an aerosol of fine droplets where a fragmentary rainbow briefly shimmered. Just for a moment Zen thought that everything was going to be all right after all. Then he caught sight of the restaurant, shuttered and bolted, the chairs and tables piled high, and knew that he'd been right the first time. *Chiuso per turno* read a sign in the window.

Tania Biacis looked at her watch. "It's getting late."

Zen nodded. "Perhaps we'd better leave it till another time."

He knew that there would be no other time.

Tania stared intently at the facade of the palazzo opposite, as though trying to decipher a message written in the whorls and curlicues of stone.

"Your place isn't very far away, is it? We could pick up something from a *rosticceria* and take it back there, that's if you don't mind. The food's not that important. What we really want to do is talk, isn't it?"

She made it sound so natural and sensible that Zen was almost unsurprised.

"Well, if that's . . . all right."

"All right?"

"I mean, it's all right with me."

"With me, too. Otherwise I wouldn't have suggested it."

"Then it's all right."

"It looks like it," she said with a slightly ironic smile.

"How do you know where I live?" Zen asked as they walked up the piazza.

"I looked you up in the phone book. I thought you'd be the only one, but there are about a dozen of you in Rome. Are the others relatives?"

Zen shook his head absently. He was wondering whether Vasco Spadola had employed the same simple method to track him down.

In a *rosticceria* just north of the piazza they bought two of the egg-shaped rice croquettes called telephone wires, because when you pull them apart the ball of melted mozzarella in the middle separates into long curving strands, and a double portion of the only main dish left, a rabbit stew. Then they walked on, out of the clutches of the old city and across the river. Zen paused to draw Tania's attention to the view downstream toward the island, the serried plane trees lining the stone-faced embankment, the river below as smooth and still as a darker vein in polished marble. While she was looking, he looked over his shoulder again. This time there was no doubt.

They moved on toward the wildly exuberant facade which might have been a grand opera house or the palace of a mad king, but was in fact the law courts. Here they paused until the traffic lights brought the cars to a reluctant, grudging halt, then crossed the Lungotevere and turned right alongside the law courts.

"Wait a minute," Zen told Tania as they passed the corner.

A few moments later a young man in a denim suit trimmed with a sheepskin collar appeared, striding quickly along. Zen stepped in front of him, flourishing his identity card.

"Police! Your papers!"

The man gawked at him open-mouthed.

"I haven't done anything!"

"I didn't say you had."

The man took out his wallet and produced a battered identity card in the name of Roberto Augusto Dentice. In the photograph, he looked younger, timid and studious. Zen plucked the wallet out of his hand.

"You've got no right to do that!" the man protested.

Ignoring him, Zen riffled through the compartments of the wallet, inspecting papers and photographs. Among them was a permit issued by the Rome Questura authorising Roberto Augusto Dentice to practice as a private detective within the limits of the province of Rome.

"All right, what's going on?" Zen demanded.

"What do you mean?"

"Someone's hired you to follow me. Who and why?"

"I don't know what you're talking about. I was just going for a walk."

"And I suppose you were just going for a walk yesterday, when you followed me all the way from that restaurant to the Palatine? You really like walking, don't you? You should join the Club Alpino."

On the main road behind them, a chorus of horns sounded out like the siren of a great ocean liner.

"What are you talking about?" the man said. "I was at home all day yesterday."

Zen's instinct was to arrest the man on some pretext and shut him up in a room with one of the heavier-handed officials. But he no longer worked at the Questura where such facilities were available, and besides, Tania was waiting.

"All right," he said in a voice laden with quiet menace. "Let me explain what I'm talking about. This job you're doing, whatever it may be, ends here. If I so much as catch sight of you again, even casually, on a bus or in a bar, anywhere at all, then this permit of yours will be withdrawn and I'll make damn sure that you never get another. Do we understand each other?"

These tactics proved unexpectedly successful. Faced with violence and menaces, the man might have remained defiant, but at the threat of unemployment his resistance suddenly collapsed.

"No one told me you were a cop!" he complained.

"What *did* they tell you?"

"Just to follow you after work."

"How did you report?"

"He phoned me in the evening. And he paid cash. I don't know who he is, honest to God!"

Zen handed back the man's wallet and papers and turned away without another word.

"What was all that about?" Tania asked as they resumed their walk.

"My mistake. I thought he looked like someone wanted for questioning in the Bertolini killing."

That was the second time that afternoon that he

had broken his rule about not lying to Tania, Zen reflected. No doubt it had been an unrealistic ideal in the first place.

It felt odd to be walking home with the woman who had occupied so much of his thoughts recently, to pass the cafe at the corner in her company, to walk into the entrance hall together under Giuseppe's eagle eye, travel up in the lift to the fourth floor, unlock the front door, admit her to his home, his other life. He was acutely aware that for the first time in years his mother was not there. Freed from the grid of rules and regulations her presence imposed, the apartment seemed larger and less cluttered than usual, full of possibilities. Zen felt a momentary stab of guilt, as though he had manoeuvred her transfer to the Nieddus just so that he could bring Tania here! It was strangely exciting, like being an adolescent again, and he found himself speculating on what might happen after lunch. Rather to his surprise, Zen found that he could quite easily imagine going to bed with Tania. Without any voyeuristic thrill, he visualised the two of them lying in the big brass bed he had occupied alone for so long. Naked, Tania looked thinner and taller than ever, but that didn't matter. She looked like she belonged there.

Zen put these thoughts out of his mind. Life rarely turns out the way you imagine it is going to, he reasoned, so the more likely it seemed that he and Tania might end up in bed together, the less likely it would happen.

Maria Grazia had been told to stay away for the time being, and since Zen had no idea where she kept the everyday cutlery and crockery, he and Tania foraged around in the kitchen and the sideboard in the dining room, assembling china, silverware, and crystal Zen had last seen about twelve years previously at a dinner to celebrate his wedding anniversary. Unintimidated by these formal splendours, they ate the rice croquettes with their fingers, mopped up the stew with yesterday's bread, and drank a lukewarm bottle of pinot spumante

which had been standing on a shelf in the living room
since the Christmas before last. Tania ate hungrily and
without the slightest self-consciousness. When they finally set aside their little piles of rabbit bones, she announced, "That's the best meal I've had in ages."

Zen pushed the fruit bowl in her direction. "I find
that hard to believe."

She gave him a surprised glance.

"Given the life you lead," he explained.

"Oh, that!"

She skinned a tangerine and started dividing it into
segments.

"Look, there's something we'd better clear up,"
she said. "You see, I didn't quite tell you the truth."

He thought of them sitting together in the speeding
taxi, the bands of light outlining the swell of her breasts,
the line of her thigh.

"I know," he said.

It was her turn to look surprised.

"Was it that obvious?"

"Oh, come on!" he exclaimed. "Did you honestly
think I'd believe that you went to all that trouble, getting me to fake a phone call from work and all the rest
of it, just so that you could go out to the cinema? I mean
you don't have to explain. I don't care what you were
doing. And even supposing I did, it's none of my business."

Tania was gazing at him with dawning comprehen-
sion.

"But that *was* what I was doing! Just that! It was all
the other times that were lies, when I told you about the
films I'd seen, and going to the opera and the theatre
and all the rest of it."

Tears swelled in her eyes. She looked away.

"That's why I got so embarrassed in the taxi, when
you asked where I was going. It wasn't that I had a
guilty secret, at least not the kind you thought! It was
just that my pathetic little deception had been found out
and I felt so ashamed of myself!

"It all started when you mentioned some film I'd read about in the paper. That's all I ever *did* do, read about it. So I thought it would be fun to pretend that I'd seen it. Then I started doing it with other things, building a whole fantasy life that I shared with you every morning at work. It was never real, Aurelio, none of it! On the contrary! We never go anywhere, never do anything. All Mauro wants to do is sit at home with his mother and his sister and any cousins or aunts or uncles who happen to be around.

"The irony of it is that that's one thing that attracted me to Mauro in the first place, the fact that he came with a ready-made family. My own parents are dead, as you know, and my only brother emigrated to Australia years ago. Well, I've got myself a family now all right, and *what* a family! Do you know what his mother calls me? 'The tall cunt.' I've heard them discussing me behind my back. 'Why did you want to marry that tall cunt?' she asks him. They think I can't understand their miserable dialect. 'It's your own fault,' she says. 'You should never have married a foreigner. Wife and herd from your own backyard.' This is the way they talk! This is the way they think!"

She broke off.

"What is it, Aurelio?"

He had got to his feet, listening. He went to the window and looked out. Then he turned and walked quickly toward the inner hallway, closing the door behind him. He lifted the phone and dialled 113, the police emergency number. Keeping his voice low so that Tania would not hear, Zen gave his name, address, and rank.

"There's a stolen vehicle in the street outside my house. A red Alfa Romeo, registration number Roma 84693 P. Get a car here immediately, arrest the occupant, and charge him with theft. Approach with caution, however. He may be armed."

"Very good, dottore."

As Zen replaced the phone, he heard a sound from

the living room. No, it was more distant, beyond the living room. From the hallway.

His heart began to beat very fast. Slowly, deliberately, he walked through the doorway and past the television, brushing his fingertips along the back of his mother's chair. How could he have been so stupid, so thoughtless and selfish? To imagine that no harm could come to him in the daylight but only after dark, like a child! To put a person he loved at risk by bringing her to a place he knew to be under deadly threat. They'd been watching the house. They'd seen Tania and him enter, and they'd had plenty of time to prepare their move. Now they had come for him.

As he approached the glass-panelled door that opened into the hallway, there was a loud click, followed by the characteristic squeal as the front door opened. On the floor above, the canary chirped plaintively in response.

The scene reflected on the glass door was almost a replica of the one the night before. But this time Zen knew that he had not left the door open, and the dark figure walking toward him along the hallway did not call his name in a familiar voice, and it was carrying a shotgun.

"What's going on, Aurelio?"

Tania was standing on the threshold of the inner hallway, looking anxiously at him. Zen waved her away, but she took no notice. Outside in the streets a siren rose and fell, gradually emerging from the urban backdrop as it rapidly neared the house. The gunman, now halfway along the hall, paused. The siren wound down to a low growl, directly outside the house.

Zen jumped as something touched his shoulder. He whirled round, staring wildly at Tania's hand. She was close behind him, gazing at him with an expression of affectionate concern. He looked at the reflection of the hallway on the surface of the glass door. The figure had vanished. Zen grabbed Tania suddenly, holding her tightly, gasping for breath, trembling all over.

Then he abruptly thrust her away again.

"I'm sorry! I'm sorry!" he exclaimed repeatedly. "I didn't mean to! I couldn't help it!"

After a moment she came back to him of her own accord and took him in her arms.

"It's all right," she told him. "It's all right."

I didn't mean to do it. I was just paying a visit, like before. They shouldn't have tried to shut me out though, or else done it properly. As it was, I just pushed and twisted until the whole thing came crashing down. But it made me angry. They shouldn't have done that.

I thought the noise might bring them running, but they were as deaf and blind as usual. To get my own back, I decided to make the gun disappear. I'm no stranger to guns. My father was famous for his marksmanship. After Sunday lunch, when the animals had been corralled and lassoed, wrestled to the ground like baby giants, and dosed with medicine or branded, the men would hurl beer bottles up into the air to fire at. Drunk as he was, the sweet grease of the piglet they had roasted before the fire still glistening on his lips and chin, my father could always hit the target and make the valley ring with the sound of breaking glass.

"There's nothing to it!" he used to joke. *"You just pull the trigger and the gun does the rest."*

As I lifted it from the rack, I heard someone laugh in the next room. It was sleek and fat and arrogant, his laugh, like one of the young men lounging in the street, fingering their cocks like a pocket full of money. That was when I decided to show myself. That would stop the laughter. That would give them something to think about.

After that, things happened without consulting me. A man came at me. A woman ran. I worked the trigger again and again.

Father was quite right. The gun did the rest.

Sardinia

SATURDAY: 0505 — 1250

A CHILL, TANGY WIND, laden with salt and darkness, whined and blustered about the ship, testing for weaknesses. By contrast, the sea was calm. Its shiny black surface merged imperceptibly into the darkness all around, ridged into folds, tucks, and creases, heaving and tilting in the moonlight. The choppy waves slapping the metal plates below seemed to have no effect on the motion of the ship itself, which lay still as though it were already roped to the quay.

A man stood grasping the metal rail thick with innumerable coats of paint, staring out into the night as keenly as an officer of the watch. The unbuttoned overcoat flapping about like a cloak gave him an illusory air of corpulence, but when the wind failed for a moment, he was revealed as quite slender for his height. Beneath the overcoat he was wearing a rumpled suit. A tie of nondescript hue was plastered to his shirt by the wind in a lazy curve like a question mark. His face was lean and smooth with an aquiline nose and slate-blue eyes whose gaze was as disconcertingly direct as a child's. His hair, its basic undistinguished brown now flecked with silvery-grey highlights at the temples, was naturally curly, and the wind tossed it back and forth like the frantic wavelets in the storm scene on a Greek vase. The man himself, for that matter, might well have been the model for one of the figures in such a scene, grasping a trident, a fishing-net, or wrestling with some fabulous sea-beast, a monster from the deep.

A few hundred metres astern of the ship, the full moon reflected up at him from the sea's unstable surface. It was deep here, off the eastern coast of the island, where the mountains plunged down to meet the sea and then kept going. Zen stood breathing in the wild air and scanning the horizon for some hint of their landfall. But there was nothing to betray the presence of the coast, unless it was the fact that the darkness ahead seemed even more unyielding, solid and impenetrable. The steward had knocked on the cabin door to wake him twenty minutes earlier, claiming that their arrival was imminent. Emerging on deck, Zen had expected lights, bustling activity, a first view of his destination. But there was nothing. The ship might have been becalmed in midocean.

He didn't care. He felt weightless, anonymous, stripped of all superfluous baggage. Rome was already inconceivably distant. Sardinia lay somewhere ahead, unknown, a blank. As for the reasons why he was there, standing on the deck of a Tirrenia Line ferry at five o'clock in the morning, they seemed utterly unreal and irrelevant.

When he looked again, it was over. The wall of darkness ahead had divided in two: a high mountain range below, dappled with a suggestion of contours, and the sky above, hollow with the coming dawn. Harbour lights emerged from behind the spit of land which had concealed them earlier, now differentiated from the open sea and the small bay beyond. Reading them like constellations, Zen mapped out quays and jetties, cranes and roads in the half-light. Things were beginning to put on shape and form, waking up to get dressed and make themselves presentable. The moment had passed. Soon it would be just another day.

Down below in the bar, the process was already well advanced. A predominantly male crowd, more or less dishevelled and bad-tempered, clustered around a sleepy cashier to but a printed receipt which they then took to the bar and traded in for a plastic thimble filled with strong black coffee. On the bench seats all around, young people were awakening from a rough night, rubbing their eyes, scratching their backs, exchanging little jokes and caresses. Zen had just succeeded in ordering his coffee when a robotic voice from the tannoy directed all drivers disembarking to make their way to the car deck. He downed the coffee hurriedly, scalding his mouth and throat, before heading down into the bowels of the ship.

The vehicles bound for this small port of call on the way to Cagliari, the ship's destination, were almost exclusively commercial and military. Neither category took the slightest notice of the signs asking drivers not to switch on their engines until the bow doors had been opened. Zen made his way through clouds of diesel fumes to his car, sandwiched between a large lorry and a coach filled with military conscripts looking considerably less lively than they had the night before when they had made the harbour at Civitavecchia ring with the forced gaiety of desperate men. He unlocked the door and climbed in. Fausto Arcuti had done him well, there was no question about that. Returning to the Rally Bar the previous afternoon, Zen had collected an envelope containing a set of keys and a piece of paper reading, Outside Via Florio, 63. He turned the paper over and wrote: Many thanks for prompt delivery. The Parrucci affair has nothing, repeat nothing, to do with you. Regards.

He handed the note to the barman and walked round the corner to Via Florio.

There was no need to check the house number. The car, a white Mercedes sedan with cream leather upholstery, stood out a mile among the battered compacts of the Testaccio residents. It had been fitted with Zurich numberplates, fairly recently to judge by the bright scratches on the rusty nuts. No registration or insurance documents were displayed on the windscreen, but this would have been a bit much to expect at such short notice. Zen took out his wallet and inspected the Swiss identity card in the name of Reto Gurtner which he had retained following an undercover job six years earlier. It was a fake, but extremely high quality, a product of the secret service's operation at Prato where, it was rumoured, a large number of the top forgers in the country offered their skills to SISMI in lieu of a prison sentence. The primitive lighting and Zen's constrained pose made the photograph look like a police mug shot, not surprisingly, since it had been taken on the same equipment. Herr Gurtner of Zurich looked capable of just about anything, thought Zen, even framing an innocent man to order.

As he sat there, the Mercedes' luxurious coachwork muffling him from the farting lorries and buses all around, Zen reflected that whatever happened in Sardinia, he had at least been able to clear up his outstanding problems in Rome before leaving. The *Volante* patrol summoned by his 113 call from the flat had arrested a man attempting to escape in the red Alfa Romeo. He turned out to be one Giuliano Acciari, a local hoodlum with a lengthy criminal record for housebreaking and minor thuggery. Zen thought he recognised him as the man who had picked his pocket in the bus queue, although he did not mention this to the police. Acciari was unarmed, and a search failed to turn up the shotgun which he was assumed to have dumped on hearing the sirens. But the police were holding Acciari for the theft of the Alfa Romeo and had assured Zen that they would spare no effort to extract any information Acciari might have as to the whereabouts of Vasco Spadola.

A series of shudders and a change in the pitch of the turbines announced that the ship had docked, but another ten minutes passed before a crack of daylight finally penetrated the murky reaches of the car deck.

The coaches and lorries to either side of Zen rumbled into motion and then, too soon, it was his turn.

Zen had learnt to drive back in the late fifties, but he had never really developed a taste for it. As the roads filled up, speeds increased, and drivers' tempers short-ened, he had seen no reason to change his views, al-though he was careful to keep them to himself, well aware that they would be considered dissident, if not heretical. But in the present case there had been no alternative: he couldn't drag anyone else along to act as his chauffeur, and it would not be credible for Herr Reto Gurtner, the wealthy burgher of Zurich, to travel through the wilds of Sardinia by public transport.

Zen's style behind the wheel was that of an elderly peasant farmer phut-phutting along at 20 kph in a worn-out Fiat truck with bald tyres and no acceleration, blithely oblivious to the hooting, light-flashing hysteria building up in his wake. The drive from Rome to the port at Civitavecchia the day before had been a two-and-a-half-hour ordeal, but getting off the ferry presented even greater problems of clutch control and touch steer-ing than the innumerable traffic lights of the Via Aurelia, at each of which the Mercedes had seemed to take fright like a horse at a fence. Having stalled three times and then nearly rammed the side of the ship by overrev-ving, Zen finally managed to negotiate the metal ramp leading to Sardinian soil, or rather the stone jetty to which the ferry was moored. Rather to his surprise, there were no formalities, no passports, no customs. But bureaucratically, of course, he was still in Italy.

The port amounted to no more than a couple of wharves where the ferries to and from the mainland touched once a week and Russian freighters periodically unloaded cargoes of timber pulp for the local papermill. At the end of the quay a narrow, badly surfaced road curved away between outcrops of jagged pink rock. Zen drove through a straggling collection of makeshift houses that never quite became a village and along the spit of land projecting out to the harbour from the main coastline. The sun was still hidden behind the mountains, but the sky overhead was clear, a delicate pale wintry blue. Seagulls swept back and forth foraging for food, their cries pealing out in the crisp air. It was Zen's first visit to the island. All police officials have to do a stint in one of the three problem areas of the country, but Zen had chosen the Alto Adige rather than Sicily or Sardinia because from there he could easily get back to Venice to see his mother. As he drove through the small town where the road inland crossed the main coastal highway, his instinct was to stop the car, drop into a cafe, and start picking up the clues, sniffing the air, getting his bearings. But he couldn't, for in Sardinia he was not Aurelio Zen but Reto Gurtner, and although he had as yet only a vague idea of Gurtner's character, he was sure that pausing to soak up the atmosphere formed no part of it. Or rather, he was sure that that was what the locals would assume, and it was their view of things that mattered. A rich Swiss stopping his Mercedes outside some rural dive for an early morning cappucino would instantly become a suspect Swiss, and that of all things was the one Zen could least afford.

For he must not let the clear sky, pure air and early morning sense of elation go to his head, he knew. In those mountains blocking off the sun, turning their back on the sea, lived men who had survived thousands of years of foreign domination by using their wits and their intimate knowledge of the land. Thousands of policemen, occasionally supplemented by the army, had been drafted there in a succession of attempts to break the complex, archaic, unwritten rules of the *Codice Barbaricine* and impose the laws passed in Rome. They had failed. Even Mussolini's strong-arm tactics, successful against the largely urban Mafia, had been ineffective with these shepherds who could simply vanish into the mountains. The mass arrests of their relatives in raids on whole villages merely served to strengthen the hands of the outlaws, making them into folk heroes. Any collaboration with the authorities was considered treachery of the most vile kind and punished accordingly. To Sardinians, mainland Italians were either policemen, soldiers, teachers, tax gatherers, bureaucrats, or more recently, tourists. They stayed for a while, took what they wanted, and then left, as ignorant as when they had arrived of the local inhabitants, the harsh brand of Latin they spoke, and the complex and often violent code for resolving conflicts among shepherds whose flocks roamed freely across the open mountains. This was why Zen had decided to go about this unofficial undercover operation in the guise of a foreigner. All outsiders were suspect in Sardinia, but a foreigner was much less likely to attract suspicion than a lone Italian, who would automatically be assumed to be a government spy of some type. Besides, Herr Reto Gurtner had a good reason for visiting this out-of-the-way corner of the island at this unseasonable time of the year. He was looking for a property.

The Mercedes hummed purposefully along the road that wound and twisted its way up from the coast through a parched, scorched landscape. To either side, jagged crags of limestone rose like molars out of acres of sterile red soil. Giant cactuses with enormous prickly ears grew there along with small groves of eucalyptus and olive and the odd patch of stunted vines that seemed to be wild. There was a gratifying absence of traffic about, and Zen was just getting into his stride when he was brought to a halt at a level crossing consisting of a chain with a metal plate dangling from it. He had been vaguely aware of a set of narrow-gauge railway tracks running alongside the road, but they looked so poorly maintained that he had assumed the line was disused.

On the other side of the chain, an elderly woman was chatting to a schoolboy wearing a satchel with the inscription Iron Maiden in fluorescent orange and green. They both turned to stare at the Mercedes. Zen gave them a bland, blank look he imagined to be typically Swiss. They continued to stare. Zen took the opportunity of consulting the map. That too was surely a typically Swiss thing to do.

A train consisting of an ancient diesel locomotive

and two decrepit coaches staggered to a stop at the crossing. The Iron Maiden fan climbed in to join a mob of other schoolchildren, the locomotive belched a cloud of fumes, and a moment later the road was clear again. Zen put the car in gear, stalled, let off the handbrake, started to roll backward, engaged the clutch, restarted the motor, stalled, engaged the handbrake, disengaged the clutch, restarted the motor, released the handbrake, engaged the clutch, and drove away. None of this, he felt, was typically Swiss. The look the crossing-keeper gave him suggested that she felt the same.

Fortified by the information from the map and the occasional faded and rusted road sign, Zen continued inland for a dozen kilometres before turning left up a steep road twisting up the mountainside in a series of switchback loops. At each corner he caught a glimpse of the village above. The nearer he got, the less attractive it looked. From a distance, it resembled some natural disaster, a landslip perhaps. Close up, it looked like a gigantic rubbish tip. There was nothing distinctively Sardinian about it. It could have been any one of thousands of communities in the South kept alive by injections of cash from migrant workers, the houses piled together higgledy-piggledy, many of them unfinished, awaiting the next cheque from abroad. The dominant colours were white and ochre, the basic shape the rectangle. Strewn across the steep slope, the place had a freakish, temporary air, as though by the next day it might all have been dismantled and moved elsewhere. And yet it might well have been there when Rome itself was but a village.

The final curves of the road had already been colonised by the zone of new buildings. Some were mere skeletons of reinforced concrete, others had a shell of outer walling but remained uninhabited. A few were being built story by story, the lower floor already in use while the first floor formed a temporary flat roof from which the rusted reinforcement wires for the next stage protruded like the stalks of some superhardy local plant that had learned to flourish in cement. The road gradually narrowed and became the main street of the village proper. Zen painfully squeezed the Mercedes past parked vans and lorries, cravenly giving way to any oncoming traffic, until he reached a small piazza that was really no more than a broadening of the main street. The line of buildings was broken here by a terrace planted with stocky trees overlooking a stunning panorama that stretched all the way down to the distant coastline and the sea beyond. Somewhere down there, Zen knew, indistinguishable to the naked eye, lay the Villa Burolo.

He parked on the other side of the piazza, in front of a squat, fairly new building with a sign reading, Bar— Restaurant—Hotel. It was still early and the few people about were all intent on business of one kind or another, but Zen was conscious of their eyes on him as he got out of the car and removed his suitcase from the boot. Stranger in town, they were thinking. Foreign car. Tourist? At this time of year? Zen was acutely aware of their puzzlement, their suspicion. He wanted to cultivate it briefly, letting the questions form and the implications be raised before he supplied an answer which, he hoped, would then come as a satisfying relief.

He pushed through the plate-glass doors into a bar which might have looked glamorously stylish when it had been built, some time in the mid-sixties, but which had aged gracelessly. The stippled plaster was laden with dust, the tinted metal facades were dented and scratched, the pine trim had been bleached by sunlight and stained by liquids and was warping off the wall in places. All these details were mercilessly reflected from every angle by a series of mirrors designed to increase the apparent size of the room, but which in fact reduced it to a nightmarish maze of illusory perspectives and visual cul-de-sacs.

"With or without?" the proprietor demanded when Zen asked if he had a room available.

Zen had given some thought to the question of how Reto Gurtner should speak, eventually deciding against funny accents or deliberate mistakes. It would be typically Swiss, he decided, to speak pedantically correct Italian, but slowly and heavily, as though all the words were equal citizens and it would be invidious and undemocratic to emphasise some at the expense of others.

"I beg your pardon?"

"A shower."

"Yes, please. With a shower."

The proprietor plucked a key from a row of hooks and slapped it down on the counter. He was plump, with a bushy black beard and receding hair. His manner was deliberately ungracious, as though the shameful calling of taking in guests for money had been forced on him by stern necessity and he loathed it as a form of prostitution. He took Zen's faked papers without a second glance and started copying the relevant details onto a police registration form.

"Would it be possible to have a *cappucino?*" Zen enquired politely.

"At the bar."

Zen duly took the four paces needed to reach this installation. The proprietor completed the form, held it up to the light as though to admire the watermark, folded it in two with exaggerated precision, and placed it with the papers in a small safe let into the wall. He then walked over to the bar, where he set about washing up some glasses.

An elderly man came into the bar. He was wearing a brown corduroy suit with leather patches at the seat and behind the knees and a flat cap. His face was as hard and smooth and irregular as a piece of granite exposed to centuries of harsh weather.

"Oh, Tommaso!" the proprietor called, setting a glass of wine on the counter. The man knocked the wine back in one gulp and started rolling a cigarette. Meanwhile he and the proprietor conversed animatedly in a language that might have been Arabic as far as Zen was concerned.

"May I have my *cappucino,* please?" he asked plaintively.

The proprietor glanced at him as though he had never seen him before and was both puzzled and annoyed to find him there.

"Cappucino?" he demanded in a tone which suggested that this drink was some exotic foreign speciality.

Zen's instinct was to match rudeness with rudeness, but Reto Gurtner, he felt sure, would remain palely polite under any provocation.

"If you please. Perhaps you would also be good enough to direct me to the offices of Dottor Confalone," he added.

The elderly man looked up from licking the gummed edge of his cigarette paper. He spat out a shred of tobacco which had found its way on to his tongue.

"Opposite the post office," he said.

"Is it far?"

There was a brief roar as the proprietor frothed the milk with steam.

"Five minutes," he said quickly, as though to forestall the old man from making any further unwise disclosures.

Zen stirred sugar into his coffee. He himself never took sugar, but he felt that Reto Gurtner would have a sweet tooth. Similarly, the cigarettes he produced were not his usual Nazionali but cosmopolitan Marlboros.

"I have an appointment, you see," he explained laboriously to no one in particular. "In half an hour. I don't know how it is here in Italy, but in Switzerland it is very important to be punctual. Especially when it's business."

Neither the proprietor nor the old man showed the slightest interest in this observation, but from the studious way they avoided glancing at each other Zen knew that the point had been taken. The disturbing mystery of Herr Gurtner's descent on the village had been reduced to a specific, localised puzzle.

It was just after nine o'clock when Aurelio Zen, spruce and clean-shaven, emerged from the hotel. The main street of the village was a deep canyon of shadow, but the alleys and steps running off to either side were slashed with sunshine, revealing panels of brilliant white walling inset with dark rectangular openings. Behind and above them rose a rugged chaos of rock and tough green shrubs, the ancient mountain backbone of the island, last vestige of the submerged Tyrrhenian continent.

Zen walked purposefully along, smiling in a pleasant, meaningless way at everyone he passed like a benevolent but rather simple-minded giant. The Sards were the shortest of all Mediterranean races, while Zen was above average height for an Italian, thanks to his father's quirky theories about food. A self-educated Socialist, he had been an enthusiast for many useless things, of which Mussolini's vapid patriotism had, briefly, been the last. Among these had been a primitive vegetarianism, in particular the notion that beans and milk were the foundation of a healthy diet. From the moment Aurelio was weaned, he had eaten a large dish of these two ingredients mashed together every lunchtime. His father's belief in the virtues of this wonder food had been based on a hodgepodge of half-baked ideas culled from his wide but eclectic reading, but by the purest chance he had happened to hit on two cheap and easily obtainable sources of complementary protein, with the result that Zen had grown up unaffected by the shortages of meat and fish which stunted the development of other children in wartime Venice.

The reactions to Herr Gurtner's bland Swiss smile varied interestingly. The young men hanging about in the piazza, as though work were not so much unavailable as beneath their dignity, surveyed the tall stranger like an exotic animal on display in a travelling circus: odd and slightly absurd, but also potentially dangerous. To their elders, clustered on the stone benches between the trees, he was just another piece in the hopeless puzzle which life had become, over which they shook their heads loosely and muttered incoherent comments.

The men, old and young, massed in groups, using the public spaces as an extension of their living rooms, but the women Zen saw were always alone and on the move. They had rights of passage only and scurried along as though liable to be challenged at any moment, clutching their wicker shopping baskets like official permits. The married ones ignored Zen totally, the nubile shot him glances as keen and challenging as a thrown knife. Only the old women, having nothing more to fear or hope from the enemy, gave him cool but not unfriendly looks of appraisal. Dressed all in black, they looked like pyramids of different-sized tyres narrowing from massive hips through bulbous waists to the tiny scarf-wrapped heads.

The exception which proved this rule of female purpose and activity was a half-witted woman who approached Zen just as he reached his destination, asking for money. Even by Sardinian standards, she was exceptionally small, almost dwarflike. She was wearing a dark brown pullover and a long full skirt of some heavy, navy blue material. Her head and feet were bare and dirty, and she limped so aggressively that Zen assumed that she was faking or at least exaggerating her disability for professional reasons. He offered her five hundred lire before realising that Herr Reto Gurtner, coming from a nation which prided itself on providing for all its citizens, would disapprove of begging on principle. Fortunately the woman was clearly too crazy to pick up on any such subtleties. Zen forced the money into her hand while she stared fixedly at him like someone who has mistaken a stranger for an old acquaintance. He turned away into the doorway flanked by a large plastic sign: Dott. Angelo Confalone—Solicitor—Notary Public—Estate Agent—Chartered Accountant—Insurance Broker—Tax and Investment Specialist. Also, teeth pulled and horoscopes cast, thought Zen as he climbed the steps to the second floor.

Angelo Confalone was a plush young man who received Herr Gurtner with an expansive warmth, in marked contrast to the cold stares and hostile glances which had been his lot thus far. It was a pleasure, he intimated, to have dealings with someone so distinguished and sophisticated, so different from the usual run of his clients. He wasn't Sardinian himself, it soon emerged, from Genoa in fact, but his sister had married someone from the area who had pointed out that there was an opening in the village, it was a long story and one he would not bore Herr Gurtner with, but the long and short of it was that one had to start somewhere.

Zen nodded his agreement. "We have a saying in my country: No matter how high the mountain, you have to start climbing at the bottom."

The lawyer laughed with vivacious insincerity and complimented Herr Gurtner on his Italian.

"And now to business, if you please," Zen told him. "You have, I believe, something for me to look at."

"Indeed."

Indeed! When Reto Gurtner had phoned him the day before with regard to finding a suitable holiday property for a client in Switzerland, Angelo Confalone could hardly believe his luck. Ever since Oscar Burolo's son had instructed him to put his father's ill-fated Sardinian retreat on the market, Confalone had been asking himself who on earth in his right mind would ever want to buy the Villa Burolo after the lurid publicity given to the horrors that had occurred there. Mindful of this, Enzo Burolo had offered to double the usual commission in order to get the place off their hands quickly, but Confalone still couldn't see any way that he would be able to take advantage of this desirable sweetener. Unless some rich foreigner happens along, he had concluded, I'm just wasting my time.

And lo and behold, just a few weeks later, Reto Gurtner had telephoned. He had inspected several properties in the north of the island, he said, but his client had specifically asked him to look on the east coast, where he had vacationed several years earlier and of whose spectacular and rugged beauty he retained fond memories. If Dottor Confalone by any chance knew of any suitable properties on the market . . .

A man wearing even one of the many hats mentioned on Angelo Confalone's business plate should perhaps have been shrewd enough to frown momentarily at this happy coincidence, but the young lawyer was too busy calculating his percentage from the sale of the property, which was now of course in a very different price bracket from the subsistence-level farm whose original purchase by Oscar Burolo he had also negotiated.

Confalone regarded his visitor complacently.

"As you are no doubt aware, Herr Gurtner, properties of a standard high enough to satisfy your client's requirements are few and far in this area. As for one coming on the market, you would normally have to wait years. It so happens, however, that I am in a position to offer you a villa which has only just become available, and which I can truly and honestly describe without risk of hyperbole as the finest example of its type to be found anywhere in the island, the Costa Smeralda included."

He went on in this vein for some time, expatiating on the imaginative way in which the original farmhouse had been modernised and extended without sacrificing the unique authenticity of its humble origins.

"The original owner was a man of vision and daring who brought his unlimited resources and great expertise in the construction business to bear on the . . ."

"He was realising a dream?" Zen suggested.

Confalone nodded vigorously. "Exactly. Precisely. I couldn't have put it better myself. He was realising a dream."

"And why is he now selling it, his dream?"

The lawyer's vivacity vanished.

"For family reasons," he murmured. "There was . . . a death. In the family."

He awaited Herr Gurtner's response with some trepidation. For the kind of commission the Burolos were offering, Confalone was quite prepared to try and conceal the truth. But commission wasn't everything. He had his career to consider, and that meant that he couldn't afford to lie.

But Reto Gurtner appeared satisfied.

"I should like to see this most interesting property at once," he declared, rising to his feet.

Confalone's relief was apparent in his voice.

"Certainly, certainly! I shall be privileged to accompany you personally and—"

"Thank you, that will not be necessary. There is a caretaker at the house? If you will be good enough to ring and let them know that I am coming, I prefer to look around on my own. We Swiss, you know, are very methodical. I do not wish to try your patience!"

After some polite insistence, Angelo Confalone gave way gracefully. Double commission and no time wasted doing the honours! He could hardly believe his luck.

Zen emerged from the lawyer's offices to a chorus of horns. The street had been blocked by a lorry delivering cartons of dairy produce to a nearby grocery. He slipped through the narrow space between the lorry and the wall and made his way along the cracked concrete slabs with which the street was paved, well pleased with the way things were going. Back in Rome, the idea of forestalling his official mission with a bit of private enterprise had appeared at best a forlorn attempt to leave no stone unturned, at worst a foolhardy scheme which might well end in disaster and humiliation. But from his present perspective, Rome itself seemed a city as distant and as foreign as Marseilles or Madrid. It was here, and only here, that Zen could hope to find the solution to his problems.

Not that he expected to crack the Burolo case, of course! There was nothing to crack, anyway. The evidence against Renato Favelloni was overwhelming. The only question was whether the architect had done the job personally or hired it out to a professional. The key to the whole affair had been the video tapes and computer diskettes stored in the underground vault at Oscar's villa. Here Oscar had kept in electronic form all the information recording in meticulous detail the history of his construction company's irresistible rise. After the murders, this material had been impounded by the authorities, but when the investigating magistrate's staff came to examine them, they found that the computer data had been irretrievably corrupted, probably by exposure to a powerful magnetic field.

Insistent rumours began to circulate to the effect that the disks had been in perfect condition when they were seized by the Carabinieri, and these rumours were strengthened about a month later when a leading news magazine published what purported to be a transcription of part of Oscar's records. The material concerned a contract agreed in 1979 for the construction of a new prison near Latina, a creation of the Fascist era on the Lazio coast, popularly known as Latrina. Burolo Construction had undercut the estimated minimum tender for the project by almost sixty percent. Their bid was duly accepted, despite the fact that the plan which accompanied it was vague in some places and full of inaccuracies in others.

No sooner had work begun than the site proved to be marshy and totally unsuitable for the type of construction envisaged. Burolo Construction promptly applied to the Ministry of Public Works for the first of a series of revised budgets which eventually pushed the cost of the prison from the 4 thousand million lire specified in the original contract to over 36 thousand million. This much was public knowledge. What the news magazine's article showed was how it had been done.

The central figure was a politician referred to in Burolo's electronic notes as *l'onorevole*. Although the article did not name him, it left little doubt in the reader's mind that the person referred to was a leading figure in one of the smaller parties making up the governing coalition, who had been Minister of Public Works at the time the prison contract was agreed. According to his notes, Oscar had paid Renato Favelloni 350 million lire to ensure that Burolo Construction would get the contract. A comment which some claimed to find typical of Oscar's sardonic style noted that this handout exceeded the normal rate, which apparently varied between six and eight percent of the contract fee. The records also listed the dates and places on which Oscar had contacted Favelloni and one on which he had met *l'onorevole* himself.

No sooner has this article appeared than the journalists responsible were summoned to the law courts in Nuoro and directed to disclose where they had obtained the information. On refusing, they were promptly jailed for culpable reticence. But that wasn't the end of the affair, for the following issue of the magazine contained an interview with Oscar's son. Enzo Burolo not only substantiated the claims made in the original article, but advanced new and even more damaging allegations. In particular, he claimed that six months prior to the killings his father had paid 70 million lire to obtain the contract for a new generating station for ENEL, the electricity board. Despite this exorbitant backhander, Burolo Construction did not get the contract.

According to Enzo, Oscar Burolo was so infuriated that he vowed to stop paying kickbacks altogether. From that point on, his company's fortunes went into a nosedive. In a desperate attempt to break the system, Oscar had leagued together with other construction firms to form a ring that tendered for contracts at realistic prices, but in each case the bidding was declared invalid on some technicality and the contract subsequently awarded to a company outside the ring.

Burolo Construction soon found itself on the verge of bankruptcy, but when Oscar applied to the banks for a line of credit he discovered that he was no longer a favoured client. His letters were mislaid, his calls not returned, the people he had plied with gifts and favours were permanently unavailable. Furious and desperate, Oscar had played his last card, contacting Renato Favelloni to demand the protection of *l'onorevole* himself. If this was not forthcoming, he warned Favelloni, he would reveal the full extent of their collaboration, including detailed accounts of the payoffs over the Latina prison job and a video tape showing Favelloni himself in an unguarded moment discussing his relationship with various men of power, *l'onorevole* included. Discussions and negotiations had continued throughout the summer, but according to Enzo this had been a mere delaying tactic which his father's enemies used to gain time in which to prepare their definitive response, which duly came on that fateful day in August, just hours after Renato Favelloni had left the Villa Burolo.

From that moment on, the case against Favelloni developed an irresistible momentum. True, there were still those who raised doubts. For example, if the destruction of Burolo's records had been as vital to the success of the conspiracy as the murder of Oscar himself, how was it that the magazine had been able to obtain an uncorrupted copy of one of the most incriminating of the disks? Even more to the point, why did the killer use a weapon as noisy as a shotgun if he needed time to destroy the records and make good his escape? But these questions were soon answered. The magazine's information, it was suggested, came not from the original disk but from a copy which the wily Burolo had deposited elsewhere, to be made public in the event of his death. As for the noise factor, there was nothing to show that the disks and videos had not been erased before the killings. Indeed, the metallic crash reproduced on the video recording seemed to strengthen this hypothesis. As for the weapon, this had presumably been chosen with a view to making the crime appear a savage act of casual violence. In short, such details appeared niggling attempts to undermine the case against Renato Favelloni and his masters at Palazzo Sisti, a case which now appeared overwhelming.

Luckily for Zen, the case itself was not his only concern. There was no way he could realistically hope to get Favelloni off the hook. His aim was simply to avoid making powerful and dangerous enemies at Palazzo Sisti, and the best way to do this seemed to be to take a leaf out of Vincenzo Fabri's book. In other words, he had to make it look as if he had done his crooked best to frame Padedda, but that his best just hadn't been good enough. This wasn't as easy as it sounded. The situation had to be handled very carefully indeed if he was to avoid sending an innocent man to prison and yet convince Palazzo Sisti that he was not a disloyal employee to be ruthlessly disposed of, but like Fabri, a well-meaning sympathiser who was unfortunately not up to the demands of the job. In Rome his prospects of achieving this had appeared extremely dubious, but he was now beginning to feel that he could bring it off. The tide had turned with the arrest of Giuliano Acciari and—yes, why not admit it?—with that lunch with Tania and the embrace with which it had concluded. A fatalist at heart, Zen had learnt from bitter experience that when things weren't going his way, there was no point in trying to force them to do so. Now that they were, it would be equally foolish not to take advantage of the situation.

He strolled along the street, glancing into shop windows and along the dark alleys that opened off to either side, scanning the features and gestures of the people he met. He felt that he was beginning to get the feel of the place, to sense the possibilities it offered.

Then he saw—or seemed to see—something that brought all his confident reasoning crashing down around him. In an alleyway to the left of the main street, a cul-de-sac filled with plastic rubbish sacks, a few empty oil drums, and some building debris, stood a figure holding what looked like a gun.

A moment later it was gone, and a moment after that Zen found himself questioning whether it had ever existed. Don't be absurd, he told himself as he stepped into the alley, determined to dispel this mirage created by his own overheated imagination. The man who had broken into his house in Rome was safely under arrest, and even if Spadola had taken up his twenty-year-old vendetta in person, how could he have tracked his quarry down so quickly? Zen had had every reason to take the greatest care when collecting the Mercedes and driving it to Civitavecchia. He wasn't thinking of Spadola so much as Vincenzo Fabri and the people at Palazzo Sisti. But he hadn't been followed, he was sure of that.

The alley narrowed to a crevice between the buildings on either side, barely wide enough for one person to pass. As his eyes adjusted to the gloom, Zen saw that it continued for some distance, dipped steeply, and then turned sharply left, presumably leading to a street below. There was no sign that anyone had been there recently.

When he heard the footsteps behind him, closing off his escape, he whirled around. For a moment everything seemed to be repeating itself in mirror image: once again he was faced with a figure holding a gun. But this time the weapon was a stubby submachine gun, the man was wearing battle dress, and there was no doubt about the reality of the experience. At the end of the alley, in the street, stood a blue jeep marked Carabinieri.

"Papers!" the man barked.

Zen reached automatically for his wallet. Then his hand dropped again.

"They took them at the hotel," he explained, accentuating his Northern intonation slightly.

The Carabiniere looked him up and down. "This isn't the way to the hotel."

"I know. I was just curious. I'm from Switzerland, you see. Our towns are more rationally built, but they lack these interesting and picturesque aspects."

The Carabiniere appeared to relax slightly. "Tourist?" he asked.

Zen ran through his well rehearsed spiel, taking care to mention Angelo Confalone several times. The Carabiniere's expression gradually shifted from suspicion to a slightly patronising complacency. Finally he ushered Zen back to the street.

"All the same," he said as they reached the jeep, "it's maybe better not to go exploring too much. There was a case last spring, a couple of German tourists in a camper found shot through the head. They must have stumbled on something they weren't supposed to see. It can happen to anyone, round here. All you need is to be in the wrong place at the wrong time."

The jeep roared away.

I thought their deaths would change everything, but nothing changed. Night after night I returned, as though next time the sentence might be revoked, the dream broken. In vain. Even here, where the darkness is entire, I knew I was only on parole. Nothing would ever change that. I was banished, exiled for life into this world of light which divides and pierces, driving its aching distances into us.

Perhaps I had not done enough, I thought. Perhaps a further offering was required, another death. But whose? I lost myself in futile speculations. There is a power that punishes us, that much seemed clear. Its influence extends everywhere, pervasive and mysterious, but can it also be influenced? Since we are punished, we must have offended. Can that offence be redeemed? And so on endlessly, round and round, dizzying myself in the search for some flaw in the walls that shut me in, that shut me out.

*   *   *

A good butcher doesn't stain the meat, my father used to say, though everything else was stained, clothes and skin and face, as he wrestled the animal to the ground and stuck the long knife into its throat, panting, drenched in blood from head to toe, the pig still twitching. Yet when he strung it up and peeled away the skin, the meat was unblemished. That's all I need be, I thought. A good butcher, calm, patient, and indifferent. All I lacked was the chosen victim.

Then the policeman came.

SATURDAY: 2010 — 2225

BY EIGHT O'CLOCK THAT evening, Herr Reto Gurtner was in a philosophical mood. Aurelio Zen, on the other hand, was drunk and lonely.

The night was heavy and close, with occasional rumbles of thunder. The bar was crowded with men of all ages, talking, smoking, drinking, playing cards. Apart from the occasional oblique glance, they ignored the stranger sitting at a table near the back of the room. But his presence disturbed them, no question about that. They would much rather that he had not been there. In an earlier, rougher era they would have seen him off the premises and out of the village. That was no longer possible, and so, reflected the philosophical Gurtner, they were willing him into nonexistence, freezing him out, closing the circle against him.

Despite evident differences in age, education, and income, all the men were dressed in very similar clothes: sturdy, drab, and functional. In Rome it was the clothes you noticed first these days, not the mass-produced figures whose purpose seemed to be to display them to advantage. But here in this dingy backward Sardinian bar it was still the people that mattered. We've thrown out the baby with the bath water, reflected the philosophical Gurtner. Eradicating poverty and prejudice, we've eradicated something else too, something as rare as any of the threatened species the ecologists make so much fuss about, and just as impossible to replace once it has become extinct.

Bullshit, Aurelio Zen exclaimed angrily, pouring himself another glass of *vernaccia* from the carafe he had ordered. The storm-laden atmosphere, the distasteful nature of his business, his sense of total isolation, the fact that he was missing Tania badly, all these had combined to put him in a sour and irrational mood. This priggish, patronising Zuricher was the last straw. Who did he think he was, coming over here and going on as though poverty were something romantic and valuable? Only a nation as crassly and smugly materialistic as the Swiss could afford to indulge in that sort of sentimentality.

He gulped the tawny wine that clung to the sides of the glass like spirits. It was tasting better all the time. Once again he thought of phoning Tania, and once again he rejected the idea. The more he lovingly recalled, detail by detail, what had happened that lunchtime, the more unlikely it appeared. He must surely have imagined the light in her eyes, the lift in her voice. The facts were not in dispute, it was a question of how you interpreted them. It was the same with the Burolo case. It was the same with *everything!*

Zen peered intently at the tabletop, which swam in and out of focus in a fascinating way. For a moment he seemed to have caught a glimpse of a great truth, a unified field theory of human existence, a simple basic formula that explained everything.

This wine is very strong, Reto Gurtner explained in his slightly pedantic accent. You have drunk a lot of it on an empty stomach. It has gone to your head. The thing to do now is to get something to eat.

Well, it was easy to say that! Hadn't he been waiting for all this time for some sign of life in the restaurant

area? It was now nearly a quarter past eight, and the
lights were still dimmed and the curtain drawn. What
time did they eat here, for God's sake?

Once again the thunder growled distantly, re-
minding Zen of the jet fighter which had startled him at
the villa earlier that day. There had been no hint of a
storm then. On the contrary, the sky was free of any
suspicion of cloud, a perfect dome of pale bleached blue
from which the winter sun shone brilliantly yet without
ferocity, a tyrant mellowed by age. The route to the villa
lay along the same road by which he had arrived, but in
this direction it looked quite different. Instead of a forbidding wall of mountains closing off the view, the land
swept down and away, rippling over hillocks and outcrops, reaching down to the sea, a shimmering inconclusive extension of the panorama like the row of dots
after an incomplete sentence. In all that vast landscape
there was no sign of man's presence, except for a distant plume of smoke from the paper mill near the harbour where he had disembarked that morning. The only
eyesore was a large patch of greenery off to the left on
the flanks of the mountain range. Its almost fluorescent
shade reminded Zen of the unsuccessful colour postcards of his youth. Presumably it was a forest, but how
did any forest rooted in that grudging soil come to glow
in that hysterical way?

The road looped down to the main road leading up
over the mountains toward Nuoro, the provincial capital
where Renato Favelloni now languished in judicial cus-
tody. According to the map, the unsurfaced track opposite petered out after a short distance at an isolated
station on the metre-gauge railway. Zen turned right,
then after a few kilometres, he forked left onto a road in
bad need of repair which ran across the lower slopes of
the valley and crossed the railway line before climbing
the other side to join the main coastal highway.

Some distance before the junction, a high, wire-
mesh fence came down from the ridge to Zen's left to
run alongside the road. At regular intervals, large signs
warned: Private Property, Keep Out, Electrified Fencing,

Beware of the Lions. The landscape was bare and wind-swept, a desolate chaos of rock, scrub, and stunted trees. After some distance, a surfaced driveway opened off the road to the left, leading to a gate of solid steel set in the wire-mesh fence.

Even before the Mercedes had come to a complete halt, the gate started to swing open. Zen pressed his foot down on the accelerator and the car, still in third gear, promptly stalled. Managing to restart it at the third attempt, he drove through the barrier, only to find his way blocked by a second gate identical to the first, which had meanwhile closed behind him, trapping the car between the wire-mesh fencing and a parallel inner perimeter of razor-barbed wire. Remote control cameras mounted on the inner gateposts scanned the Mercedes with impersonal curiosity. Thirty seconds later, the inner gate swung silently open, admitting Zen to the late Oscar Burolo's private domain.

The narrow strip of tarmac wound lazily up the hillside. After about fifty metres, Zen spotted the line of stumpy metal posts planted at irregular intervals, depending on the contours of the land. The posts marked the villa's third and most sophisticated defence of all: a phase-seeking microwave fence, invisible, intangible, impossible to cross undetected. Within the triply defended perimeter, the whole property was protected by heat-seeking infrared detectors, a move-alarm TV system, and microwave radar. All the experts agreed that security at the Villa Burolo was, if anything, excessive. It just hadn't been sufficient.

Oscar's private road continued to climb steadily upward, smashing its way through ancient stretches of dry-stone walling that were almost indistinguishable from outbreaks of the rock that was never far from the surface. Loose boulders of all sizes lying scattered about like some kind of crop, but in fact nothing grew there except a low scrub of juniper, privet, laurel, heather, rosemary, and gorse, a prickly stubble as tough and enduring as the rocks themselves.

Finally the land levelled out briefly, then fell away

more steeply to a hollow where the house appeared, sheltered from the bitter northerly winds. From this angle, the Villa Burolo seemed a completely modern creation. The south and east sides of the original farmhouse were concealed by new wings containing the guest suites, kitchen, scullery, laundry room, garage, and service accommodation. To the right, in a quarrylike area scooped out of the hillside, was the helicopter landing pad and a steel mast housing the radio beacon for night landings and aerials for Oscar's extensive communications equipment.

Zen parked the Mercedes and walked over to the main entrance, surmounted by a pointed arch of vaguely Moorish appearance. There was no bell or knocker in sight, but when the door opened at his approach and the caretaker appeared, Zen suddenly realised that it had been absurd to expect one. No one dropped in unexpectedly at the Villa Burolo, not when their every movement from the entrance gate to the front door was being monitored by four independent electronic surveillance systems.

As soon as he set eyes on Alfonso Bini, Zen knew why the caretaker had been ruled out as a suspect virtually from the start. Bini was one of those men so neutered by a lifetime of service that it was difficult to imagine him being able to tie his own shoelaces unless instructed to do so. He greeted the distinguished foreign visitor with pallid correctness. Yes, Dottor Confalone had explained the situation. Yes, he would be glad to show Signor Gurtner around.

No doubt on Confalone's instructions, the tour started with the new wing in order to dispel any idea that the property was in any way primitive or rustic. Zen patiently endured an interminable exhibition of modern conveniences ranging from en suite Jacuzzis and a fully equipped gymnasium to a kitchen that would have done credit to a three-star hotel. In the laundry room, a frightened-looking woman was folding towels. Zen guessed that this was the caretaker's wife, although Bini ignored her as though she were just another of the appliances stacked in neat, forbidding ranks along the wall. The only aspect of all this which was of any interest to Zen was a small room packed with video monitors and banks of switches.

"Security?" he queried.

Bini nodded and pointed to a row of red switches near the door, labelled with the names of the various alarm systems. The only ones switched on were the field sensors on the inner perimeter fence and the micro-wave radar.

"So someone has to be here all the time?" Zen asked.

Bini made a negative tutting sound.

"Only if you want to check the screens. If any of the systems picks up anything irregular, an alarm goes off."

He threw a switch marked Test. A chorus of electronic shrieks rose from every part of the building.

"Very impressive," murmured Zen. "My client certainly need have no worries about anyone breaking in."

The caretaker said nothing. His face was set so hard it looked as though it might crack.

Once the villa's luxury credentials had been established, Zen was taken into the older part of the house to appreciate its aesthetic qualities. A short passageway cut through the thick outer walls of the original farm brought them into a large lounge furnished with leather armchairs, inlaid hardwood tables, Afghan carpets, and bookcases full of antique bindings. The head of a disgruntled-looking wild boar emerged from the stonework above an enormous open fireplace as though the animal had charged through the wall and got stuck.

Zen walked over to a carved rosewood gun rack near the door and inspected the shotguns on display, including an early Beretta and a fine Purdy.

"Do they go with the property?" he asked.

The caretaker shrugged.

"There seems to be one missing," Zen pursued, indicating the empty slot.

Bini turned pointedly away toward the sliding doors opening on to the terrace.

"What's this?" Zen called after him, pointing to a wooden hatch in the flooring.

"The cellar," replied the caretaker tonelessly.

"And next door?"

Bini pretended not to hear. Ignoring him, Zen walked through the doorway into the dining room of the villa. In the lounge, the stones of the original walls had been left uncovered as a design feature, but here they had been plastered and painted white. Zen looked around the room that was horribly familiar to him from the video. It was a shock, somehow, to find the walls not splashed and flecked and streaked with blood, but pristine and spotless. A shuffling in the doorway behind him announced the caretaker's presence.

"Fresh paint?" Zen queried, sniffing the air.

Just for a moment, something stirred in the old man's passive gaze. Angelo Confalone would have briefed him carefully, of course. "Say nothing about what happened! Don't mention Burolo's name! Just keep your mouth shut and with any luck you might keep your job."

Bini had done his best to obey these instructions so far, but now the strain was beginning to show.

"Nice and clean," Zen commented approvingly.

The caretaker's mouth cracked open in a ghastly grin. "My wife, she cleans everything, every day . . ."

Zen nodded. He had read the investigators' reports on the couple. Giuseppina Bini was one of those elderly women who, having grown up when doctors were expensive and often ineffective, strove obsessively to keep the powers of sickness and death at bay by banishing their agents, dirt and dust, from every corner of the house. This had made it virtually certain that the dried spots of blood found on the dining room floor and on the steps leading to the cellar must have been deposited by the lightly wounded killer. In which case, thought Zen, he must have destroyed the disks and tapes *after* the murders, despite the horrendous risks involved in staying at the scene once the alarm had been raised and the police were on their way. It didn't make any sense, he told himself for the fiftieth time. If the object was to destroy both Burolo and his records, surely the killer would either have used a silenced weapon or eliminated Bini and his wife as well, thus giving himself ample time to erase Burolo's records before making good his escape. And if the disks and tapes had been erased after they were seized by the Carabinieri—the long arm of Palazzo Sisti would no doubt have been capable of this —then why did the killer make his way down to the cellar and ransack the shelves at all?

It made no sense, no sense at all, although Zen had a tantalising feeling that the solution was actually right under his nose, simple and obvious. But that was no concern of his. His reason for visiting the villa had nothing to do with viewing the scene of the crime. Nevertheless, for the sake of appearances he asked Bini to show him the cellar before they went outside. The caretaker duly levered up a brass ring and lifted the hatch to reveal a set of worn stone steps leading down.

"It's not locked?" Zen asked.

Bini clicked a switch on the wall and a neon light flickered into life below. "There are no locks here," he said. "If you keep your jewels in a safe, you don't need to lock the jewel case."

The cellar was large, stretching the entire width of the original farm. Zen sniffed the air.

"Nice and fresh down here."

The caretaker indicated a narrow fissure at floor level.

"The air comes in there. They used to cure cheeses and hams here in the old days. Even in the summer it stays cool."

Zen nodded. This constant temperature was no doubt why Oscar had used the place as a storage vault. But now the twin neon bars illuminated an empty expanse of whitewashed walls and bare stone floor. There was nothing to show that this had once been the nerve centre of an operation which had apparently succeeded in fulfilling the alchemists' dreams of turning dross into gold.

Once they got above ground again, the caretaker led Zen out on to the terrace.

"The swimming pool," he announced.

Wild follies and outrageous whims die with the outsized ego that created them, and their corpses make depressing viewing. Even drained and boarded over, a swimming pool is still a swimming pool, but Oscar's designer beach was an all-or-nothing affair. Once the plug had been pulled and the machinery turned off, it stood revealed for what it was: a tacky, pretentious monstrosity. The transplanted sand was dirty and threadbare, the rocks showed their cement joints, and the mystery of those azure depths laid bare as a coat of blue paint applied to the vast concrete pit, where the body of some small animal lay drowned in a shrinking puddle of water.

"We can get everything going again," Bini assured his visitor. "It's all set up."

But he sounded unconvinced. Even if some crazy foreigner did buy the place, nothing would ever be the same again. Villa Burolo was not a house, it was a performance. Now that the star was dead, it would always be a flop.

"Well, it certainly seems to be a very pleasant and impressive property," Zen remarked with a suitably Swiss lack of enthusiasm. "I'll just have a look around the grounds on my own."

Bini turned back into the house, clearly relieved that his ordeal was over.

When he had gone, Zen strolled slowly along the terrace, rounding the corner of the original farmhouse. Despite the encircling wire, there was no sense of being in a guarded enclosure, for the boundaries of the property had been cleverly situated so as to be invisible from the villa. The view was extensive, ranging from the sea across the wide valley he had crossed in the Mercedes, to the mountain slopes where the village was just visible as an intrusive smudge.

When he reached the dining-room window, Zen looked round to ensure that he was unobserved, then crouched down to examine the slight discolouration of the flagstones marking the spot where Rita Burolo had bled to death. Another thing that made no sense, he thought. None of the investigators had commented on the remarkable fact that the murderer had made no attempt to find out whether Signora Burolo was dead or not. As it happened, she had gone into an irreversible coma by the time she was found, but how was the killer to know that? A few minutes either way, a stronger constitution or a lesser loss of blood, and the Burolo case would have been solved before it began.

Nor was this the only instance in which the killer had displayed a most unprofessional carelessness. For although Oscar Burolo had concealed video equipment about the villa to tape the compromising material he stored in the vault, he camouflaged these clandestine operations behind a very public obsession with recording poolside frolics and informal dinner parties. Thus no attempt had been made to disguise the large video camera mounted on its tripod in the corner of the dining room. No glimpse of the murderer had been recorded on the tape, but how could he have been absolutely sure of that? And if there was even the slightest possibility that some damning clue had been captured by the camera, why had the assassin made no attempt to remove or destroy the tape?

Once again, Zen felt his reason swamped by the sense of something grossly abnormal about the Burolo case. What did this almost supernatural indifference indicate if not the killer's knowledge that he was *invulnerable?* There was no need for him to take precautions. The efforts of the police and judiciary were as vain as Oscar Burolo's expensive security measures. The murderer could not be caught any more than he could be stopped.

He walked back along the terrace to the west face of the villa. Beyond the sad ruins of the pool, the land sloped steeply upward toward the lurid forest he had noticed earlier. The trees were conifers of some kind, packed together in a tight, orderly mass that looked like a reforestation project. Beyond them lay the main mountain range, a mass of shattered granite briefly interrupted by a smooth grey wall, presumably a dam. Zen continued along the terrace to the wall which concealed the service block and helicopter pad, a half-hearted imitation of the traditional pasture enclosures, higher and with the stones cemented together. On the other side was a neat kitchen garden with a system of channels to carry water to the growing vegetables from the hosepipe connected to an outside tap. Zen took a path leading uphill toward a group of low concrete huts about fifty metres away from the house and partially concealed by a row of cherry trees.

As he passed the line of trees, a low growl made the air vibrate with a melancholy resonance that brought Zen out in gooseflesh. There were three huts, one small one and two larger structures which backed on to an enclosure of heavy-duty mesh fencing. Both of these had metal doors mounted on runners. One of them was slightly open, and it was from here that the noise had come.

The inside of the hut was in complete darkness. A hot, acrid odour filled the air. Something rustled restlessly in the further reaches of the dark. As Zen's eyes gradually adjusted, he made out a figure bending over a heap of some sort on the ground. The resonant vibration thrilled the air again, like a giant breathing stertorously in a drunken slumber. The bending figure suddenly whirled round, as though caught in some guilty act.

"Who are you?"

Zen advanced a step or two into the hut.

"Stay there!"

The man walked toward him with swift, light strides. He was short and stocky, with wiry black hair and the face of a pugnacious gnome.

"What are you doing?"

"Looking over the house."

"This is not the house."

Zen switched on his fatuous Swiss smile. "Looking over the property, I should have said."

The man was staring at him with an air of deep suspicion. "Who are you?" he repeated.

Zen held out his hand, which was ignored. "Reto Gurtner."

"You're Italian?"

"Swiss."

The low growl sounded out again. Inside the hut, its weight of emotion seemed even greater, an expression of grief and loss that was almost unbearable.

"What was that noise?" Zen asked with polite curiosity.

The man continued to eye him with open hostility, as though trying to stare him down.

"A lion," he said at last.

"Ah, a lion." ·

Zen's tone remained conversational, as though lions were an amenity without which no home was complete.

"Where in Switzerland?" the man demanded.

He was wearing jeans and a blue T-shirt. A large hunting knife in a leather sheath was attached to his belt. His bare arms were hairy and muscular. A long white scar ran in a straight line from just below his right elbow to his wrist.

"From Zurich," Zen replied.

"You want to buy the house?"

"Not personally. I am here on behalf of a client."

Before the man could speak again, something inconceivably huge and fast passed overhead, blocking out the light for an instant like a rapid eclipse of the sun. An instant later there was an earth-shattering noise, as if a tall stone column had collapsed on top of the hut. Even after the moment had passed, the rumbles and echoes continued to reverberate in the walls and ground for several seconds.

The lion-keeper was on his knees at the far end of

the hut, bent over the heap on the ground. Zen started toward him, his shoes rustling on the straw underfoot.

"Stay there!" the man shouted.

Zen stopped. He looked around the hot, fetid gloom of the hut. Two pitchforks, some large plastic buckets, a shovel, and lengths of rope and chain were strewn about the floor in disorder. A coiled whip and a pump-action shotgun hung from nails hammered into the roof supports.

"What was that?" Zen called.

The man got to his feet.

"The air force. They come here to practise flying low over the mountains. When Signor Burolo was . . ."

He broke off.

"Yes?" Zen prompted.

"They didn't bother us then."

I bet they didn't, thought Zen. A few phone calls and a hefty contribution to the officers' mess fund would have seen to that.

The low melancholy growl was repeated once more, a feeble echo of the jet's brief uproar like a child softly imitating a word it does not understand.

"It does not sound happy, the lion," Zen observed.

"It is dying."

"Of what?"

"Of old age."

"The planes disturb it?"

"Strangers, too."

The man's tone was uncompromising. Zen pointed to the scar on his forearm.

"But it is still dangerous, I see."

The man brushed past him toward the door.

"A very neat job, though," Zen commented, following him out. "More like a knife or a bullet than claws."

"You know a lot about lions?" the keeper demanded sarcastically as they emerged into the brilliant sunlight and pure air.

"Only what I read in the papers."

The man walked over to the smaller hut and

brought out a plastic bucket filled with a bloody mixture of hearts, lungs, and intestines.

"I notice that you keep a shotgun in there," Zen pursued, "so I assume there is reason for fear."

The man regarded him with blank eyes. "There is always reason for fear when you are dealing with creatures to whom killing comes naturally."

Seeing him standing there in open defiance, the bucket of guts in his hand, ready to feed the great beasts that he alone could manage, it was easy to see Furio Padedda's attraction for a certain type of woman. It was to these concrete huts that Rita Burolo had come to disport herself with the lion-keeper, unaware that their antics were being recorded by the infrared video equipment her husband had rigged up under the roof.

How had Oscar felt, viewing those tapes which—according to gloating sources in the investigating magistrate's office—made hard-core porno videos look tame by comparison? Had his motive for making them been simple voyeurism or was he intending to blackmail his wife? Was she independently wealthy? Had he hoped in this way to stave off bankruptcy until his threats forced *l'onorevole* to intervene in his favour? Supposing he had mentioned the existence of the tapes to her and she had passed on the information to her lover. To a proud and fiery Sardinian, the fact that his amorous exploits had been recorded for posterity might well have seemed a sufficient justification for murder. Or rather, Zen corrected himself as he left the Villa Burolo, it could easily be made to appear that it had. Which was all that concerned him, after all.

Zen stared blearily at his watch, eventually deciphering the time as twenty to nine. The bar had emptied appreciably as the men drifted home to eat the meals their wives and mothers had shopped for that morning. Zen pushed his chair back, rose unsteadily, and walked over to the counter where the burly proprietor was rinsing glasses.

"When can I get something to eat?"

Reto Gurtner would have phrased the question more politely, but he had stayed behind at the table.

"Tomorrow," the proprietor replied without looking up from his work.

"How do you mean, tomorrow?"

"Out of season the restaurant's only open for Sunday lunch."

"You didn't tell me that!"

"You didn't ask."

Zen turned away with a muttered obscenity.

"There's a pizzeria down the street," the proprietor added grudgingly.

Zen pushed through the glass doors of the hotel. The piazza was deserted and silent. As he passed the Mercedes, Zen patted it like a faithful, friendly pet, a reassuring presence in this alien place. A roll of thunder sounded out, closer yet still quiet, a massively restrained gesture.

In the corner of the piazza stood the village's only public phone box, a high-tech glass booth perched there as if it had just landed from outer space. Zen eyed it wistfully, but the risk was just too great. Tania would have had time to think things over by now. Supposing she was offhand or indifferent, a cold compensation for her excessive warmth the day before? He would have to deal with that eventually, of course, but not now, not here with all the other problems he had.

The village was as still and dead as a ghost town. Zen shambled along, looking for the pizzeria. All of a sudden he stopped in his tracks, then whirled around wildly, scanning the empty street behind him. No one. What had it been? A noise? Or just drunken fancy? "They must have stumbled on something they weren't supposed to see," the Carabiniere had said of the murdered couple in the camper. "It can happen to anyone, round here. All you need is to be in the wrong place at the wrong time."

As the alcoholic mists in Zen's mind cleared for a moment, he had an image of a child scurrying along an alleyway running parallel to the main street, appearing at intervals in the dark passages with steps leading up. A child playing hide and seek in the darkness. But had he imagined it or had he really caught sight of something out of the corner of his eye on the extreme periphery of vision, something seen but not registered until now?

He shook his head sharply, as though to empty it of all this nonsense. Then he set off again, a little more hurriedly now.

The pizzeria was just around the corner where the street curved downhill among the new blocks on the outskirts of the village. The exterior was grimly basic— reinforced concrete framework, bare brickwork infill, adhesive plastic letters spelling Pizza Tavola Calda on the window—but inside, the place was bright, brash, and cheerful, decorated with traditional masks, dolls, straw baskets, and woven and embroidered hangings. To Zen's astonishment, the young man in charge even welcomed him warmly. Things were definitely looking up.

After a generous antipasto of local air-cured ham and salami, a large pizza, and most of a flask of red wine, they looked even better. Zen lit a cigarette and looked around at the group of teenagers huddled conspiratorially in the corner, the tabletop laden with empty soft drink bottles. If only he had had someone to talk to, it would have been perfect. As it was, his only source of entertainment was the label of the bottled mineral water he had ordered. This consisted of an assurance by a professor at Cagliari University that the contents were free of microbacteriological impurities, together with an encomium on the water's virtues which seemed to imply that in sufficient quantities it would cure everything but old age. Zen studied the chemical analysis, which listed among other things the *abbassamento crioscopico, concentrazione osmotica* and *conducibilitá elettrica specifica a 18 C.* Each litre contained 0.00009 grams of barium. Was this a good thing or a bad thing?

The door of the pizzeria opened to admit the half-witted midget he had seen outside Confalone's office that morning. She was dripping wet, and Zen realised suddenly that the hushing sound he had been hearing for some time now, like static on a radio programme, was caused by a downpour of rain. The next instant a deafening peal of thunder rang out right overhead. One of the teenagers shrieked in mock terror, the others giggled nervously. The beggar woman limped theatrically over to Zen's table and demanded money.

"I gave you something this morning," Reto Gurtner replied in a tone of distaste.

The owner shouted angrily in Sardinian and the woman turned away with a face as blank as the wooden carnival masks hanging on the wall and went to sit on a chair near the door, looking out at the torrential rain. She must know a thing or two, thought Zen, wandering about from place to place, privileged by madness.

When the owner came to clear Zen's table, he apologised for the fact that he'd been bothered.

"I try to keep her out of here, but what can you do? She's got nowhere to go."

"Homeless?"

The man shrugged. "She's got a brother, but she won't live with him. Claims he's an imposter. She sleeps rough, in caves and shepherd's huts, even on the street. She's harmless, but quite mad. Not that it's surprising, after what happened to her."

He made no effort to lower his voice, although the woman was sitting quite nearby, perched on her chair like a large doll. Zen glanced at her, but she was still staring rigidly at the door.

"It's all right," the owner explained. "She doesn't understand Italian, only dialect."

"What happened to her?"

The young man shook his head and sighed.

"I wasn't around then, but people say she just disappeared one day, years ago. She was about fifteen at the time. The family said she'd gone to stay with relatives who'd emigrated to Tuscany. Then a few years ago her parents died in . . . in an accident. The son was away doing his military service at the time. When the police went to the house, they found Elia shut up in the cellar like an animal, almost blind, covered in filth and half crazy.''

Reto Gurtner looked suitably horrified by this example of Mediterranean barbarism. ''But why?''

The young man sighed. ''Now, you understand, this village is just like anywhere else. Televisions, pop music, motorbikes.'' He waved at the teenagers in the corner. ''The young people stay out till all hours, even the girls. They do what they like. Twenty years ago it was different. People say that Elia was seeing a man from a nearby farm. Perhaps she stayed out too late one summer night, and—''

He broke off as the door banged open and three men walked in. The beggar woman sprang to her feet, staring at them like a wild animal about to pounce or flee. One of the men spat a few words of dialect at her, and she flinched as though he had struck her, then ran out. The rain had stopped as suddenly as it had begun.

The three newcomers were wearing the local heavyweight gear, durable, anonymous and mass-produced, but there was nothing faceless or conventional about their behaviour. They took over the pizzeria as though it were the venue for a party being given in their honour. The leader, who had obviously had quite a lot to drink already, threw his weight around in a way that seemed almost offensively familiar, going behind the counter and sampling the various plates of toppings, talking continuously in a loud voice. Zen could understand nothing of what was being said. Although the owner kept smiling and responded in the required jocular fashion, it seemed an effort, and Zen thought he would have been happier if the men had gone away.

Having done the rounds, chaffed the owner and his wife, and grabbed a plate of olives and salami and a litre of wine, the trio seated themselves at the table next to Zen's. Once their initial high spirits had subsided, their mood rapidly turned sombre, as though all three had immense grievances which could never be redressed. The leader in particular not only looked fiercely malcontent, but was scowling at Zen as though he was the origin of all his troubles. His bristly jet-black beard, curly hair, and enormous hook nose gave him a Middle Eastern appearance, like a throwback to the island's Phoenician past. He reminded Zen of someone he had seen earlier, although he couldn't think whom. From time to time, between gulped half-glassfuls of wine, the man muttered to his companions, bitter interjections in dialect which received no reply.

Zen began to feel alarmed. The man was clearly drunk, his mood explosive and unpredictable, and he was staring at him more and more directly, as though beating up this stranger might be just what was needed to make his evening. To defuse the situation before it got out of hand, Zen leaned over to the three men.

"Excuse me," he said in his best Reto Gurtner manner. "Could you tell me if there's a garage round here?"

"A garage?" the leader replied after a momentary hesitation. "For what?"

Zen explained that his car was making a strange knocking noise and he was worried that it might break down.

"What kind of car?"

"A Mercedes."

After a brief discussion in dialect with his companions, the man replied that Vasco did repairs locally, but he wouldn't have the parts for a Mercedes. Otherwise there was a mechanic in Lanusei, but he was closed tomorrow, it being Sunday.

"You're on holiday?" he asked.

As Zen recited his usual explanation of who he was and what he was doing, the man's expression gradually changed from hostility to sympathetic interest. After a few minutes, he invited Zen to join them at their table. Zen hesitated, but only for a fraction of a moment. This was an invitation which he felt it would be decidedly unwise to refuse.

Three quarters of an hour and another flask of wine later, he was being treated almost like an old friend. The hook-nosed man, who introduced himself as Turiddu, was clearly delighted to have a fresh audience for his long and rather rambling monologues. His companions said hardly a word. Turiddu talked and Zen listened, occasionally throwing in a polite question with an air of wide-eyed and disinterested fascination with all things Sardinian. Turiddu's grievances, it turned out, were global rather than personal. Everything was wrong, everything was bad and getting worse. The country, by which he appeared to mean that particular part of the Oliastra, was in a total mess. It was a disaster. The government in Rome poured in money, but it was all going to waste, leaking away through the sievelike conduits of the development agencies, provincial agricultural inspectorates, the irrigation consortia, and land reclamation bodies.

"In the old days the landowner, he arranged everything, decided everything. You couldn't fart without his permission, but at least there was only one of him. Now we've got these new bosses instead, these pen pushers in the regional government, hundreds and hundreds of them! And what do they do? Just like the landowner, they look after themselves!"

Turiddu broke off briefly to gulp some more wine and accept one of Zen's cigarettes.

"And when they do finally get around to doing something, it's even worse! The old owners, they understood the land. It belonged to them, so they made damn sure it was looked after, even though we had to break our bums doing the work. But these bureaucrats, what do they know? All they do is sit in some office down in Cagliari and look at maps all day!"

Turiddu's companions sat listening to this harangue with indulgent and slightly embarrassed smiles, as what he was saying was true enough but it was pointless and rather demeaning to mention it, particularly to a stranger.

"There's a lake up there in the mountains," Turiddu continued, striking a match casually on his thumbnail. "A river used to flow down toward the valley, where it disappeared underground into the caves. The rock down here is too soft, the water runs through it. So what did those bastards in Cagliari do? They looked at their maps, saw this river that seemed to go nowhere, and they said, 'Let's dam the lake, so instead of all that water going to waste we can pipe it down to Oristano to grow crops.' "

Turiddu broke off to shout something at the pizzeria owner in Sardinian. The young man came over with an unlabelled bottle and four new glasses.

"Be careful!" the barman warned Zen with humorous exaggeration, tapping the bottle. "Dynamite!"

"Dynamite, my arse," Turiddu grumbled when he had gone. "I've got stuff at home, the *real* stuff, makes this taste like water."

He filled the four tumblers to the brim, spilling some on the tablecloth, and downed his at one gulp.

"Anyway, what those clever fuckers in Cagliari didn't realise was that all that water from the lake didn't just disappear. It was there, underground, if you knew where to look for it. All the farms round here were built over caves where the river ran underground. With that and a bit of fodder, you could keep cattle alive through the winter, then let them loose up in the mountains when spring came. But once that fucking dam was built, all the water—*our* water—went down the other side to those soft idle bastards on the west coast. As if they didn't have an easy enough life already! Oh, they paid us compensation, of course. A few lousy million lire to build a new house here in the village. And what are we supposed to do here? There's no work. The mountains take what little rain there is, the winter pasture isn't worth a shit. What's the matter? You're not drinking."

Zen obediently gulped down the liquid in his glass as the Sardinian had done and almost gagged. It was raw grappa, steely, unfiltered, virtually pure alcohol.

"Good," he gasped. "Strong."

Turiddu shrugged. "I've got some at home makes this taste like water."

The door of the pizzeria swung open. Zen looked round and recognised Furio Padedda. The lion-keeper had just walked in with another man. Zen turned back to his new companions, glad of their company, their protection.

"Tell me, why is that bit of forest on the other side of the valley so green? It almost looks as though some-one is watering it."

Turiddu gave an explosive laugh that turned into a coughing fit.

"They are! We are, with our water!"

He refilled all the glasses with grappa.

"The dam they built, it was done on the cheap. Bunch of crooks from Naples. It leaks, not much but all the time. On the surface the soil is dry, but those trees have roots that go down twenty metres or more. Down there it's like a marsh. The trees grow like geese stuffed for market."

Zen glanced round at Furio Padedda and his com-panion, who were sitting near the door drinking beer. Despite his drunkenness, Turiddu had not missed Zen's interest in the newcomers.

"You know them?" he demanded with a contemp-tuous jerk of his thumb at the other table.

"One of them. We met today at the villa where he works."

Turiddu regarded him with a stupefied expression.

"That place? You're not thinking of buying it?"

Zen looked suitably discreet.

"My client will make the final decision. But it seems an attractive house."

The three men glanced at each other, their looks dense with exchanged information, like deaf people communicating in sign language.

"Why, is there something wrong with it?"

Zen's expression remained as smooth as processed cheese. Turiddu struggled visibly with his thoughts for a moment.

"It used to belong to my family," he announced finally. "Before they took our water away."

He stared drunkenly at Zen, daring him to disbe-lieve his story. Zen nodded thoughtfully. It might be true, but he doubted it. Turiddu was a bit of a fantasist, he guessed, a man with longings and ambitions that were too big for his small-town habitat but not quite big enough to give him the courage to leave.

The Sardinian laughed again.

"You saw the electric fences and the gates and all that? He spent a fortune on that place to make it safe, the poor fool. And it's all useless!"

Zen frowned.

"Do you mean to say that the security system is defective in some way?"

But Turiddu did not pursue the matter. He was looking around with a vague expression, a cigarette which he had forgotten to light dangling from his lips.

"Just take my advice, my friend," he said. "Have nothing to do with that place. Terrible things have happened there, things you can't wash away with water, even if there was any. There are plenty of nice villas up north on the coast, houses for rich foreigners. Down here is not the place for them. There are too many naughty boys. Like that one over there, for instance."

He nodded toward Furio Padedda, who was just finishing his beer.

"Is he a friend of yours?" asked Zen.

Turiddu slapped the table so hard that the bottle nearly fell over.

"Him? He's no one's friend, not round here! He's a foreigner. He's got friends all right, up in the mountains."

He lowered his voice to a sly whisper.

"They don't grow crops up there, you know. They don't grow anything, the lazy bastards. They just take whatever they want. Sheep, cattle. Sometimes people too. Then they get very rich very quick!"

One of his companions said something brief and forceful in Sardinian. Turiddu frowned but was silent.

A shadow fell across the table. Zen looked up to find Furio Padedda standing over him.

"Good evening, Herr Gurtner," he said, stressing the foreign title.

"What the fuck you want, Padedda?" growled Turiddu.

"I just wanted to greet our friend from Switzerland here. Been having a drink, have you? Several drinks, in fact."

"None of your fucking business," Turiddu told him.

"I was thinking of Herr Gurtner," Padedda continued in an even tone. "He should be careful. Our Sardinian grappa might be a little strong for him."

He waved his companion over.

"Let me introduce my friend Patrizio. Patrizio, Herr Reto Gurtner of Zurich."

Patrizio held out his hand and said something incomprehensible. Zen smiled politely.

"I'm sorry, I don't understand dialect."

Padedda's eyes narrowed. "Not even your own?"

A silence like thick fog fell over the pizzeria. You could feel it, taste it, smell it, see it.

"Enzo spent eight years in Switzerland working on the Saint Bernard tunnel," Padedda explained. "He speaks Swiss German fluently. Oddly enough, it seems that Herr Reto Gurtner does not."

I knew him at once. They think they're so clever, the others, but their cleverness is lost on me. It's a poison that doesn't take, a disease I'm immune to. Their conjuring tricks are meant for them, the children of the light to whom everything is what it seems, the way it looks. The policeman just provided himself with false papers and a big car and—presto!—he was magically transformed in his own eyes and theirs into a foreign businessman come to buy property. They believe in property, they believe in documents and papers, names and dates. How could they not believe in him? Living out a lie themselves, how could they recognise his lies?

But I knew who he was the moment I set eyes on him. I knew why he had come and why he wanted to see the house. I knew what lay behind his sly questions and insinuating remarks, his prying and peeping.

*   *   *

I was very bold, I confronted him openly. He shied away, seeming not to know me. The darkness showed its hand for an instant, like a brief eclipse of the sun, and I read death in his eyes. I'd seen it before with the animals father killed. I knew what it meant.

Perhaps he too sensed that something was going on. Perhaps he even suspected that his life was in danger. But how could he have had the slightest idea who it was that represented that danger?

SUNDAY: 0700 — 1120

PERHAPS IF THE KIDNAP attempt had not occurred when he
had been driving back from it, Oscar Burolo might have
shown his appreciation to the local church by donating
a set of real bells. It was the kind of showy gesture he
was fond of, stage-managed to look like an impulsive act
of generosity, although in fact he would have costed the
whole thing down to the last lira and got a massive discount from the foundry in return for some building
work using materials recycled from another contract.
Nevertheless, the village church would have got its
bells. As it was, it had to make do with a gramophone
record of a carillon played through loudspeakers, and it
was this that woke Aurelio Zen shortly before dawn the
following morning. The gramophone record was very
old, with a loud scratch which Zen's befuddled brain
translated as high-velocity shots being fired at him by a
marksman perched in the bell tower. Luckily, by the
time they reached his room the bullets had slowed
down considerably, and in the end they just hovered in
the air about his face, darting this way and that like
dragonflies, a harmless nuisance.

As the recorded bells finally fell silent, Zen opened his eyes on a jumble of colours and blurred shapes. He waited patiently for things to start making sense, but when minutes went by and his surroundings still refused to snap into focus, he began to worry that he had done some permanent injury to his brain. He hauled himself upright in bed, slumping back against the wooden headboard.

Things improved somewhat. True, he still had a splitting headache and felt like he might throw up at any moment, but to his relief the objects in the room began —a little reluctantly, it seemed—to assume the shapes and relationships he vaguely remembered from the previous day. There was the large plywood wardrobe with the door that wouldn't close properly and the wire clothes hangers hanging like bats from a branch. There was the small table with its cumbersome ceramic lamp, and the three cheap ugly wooden chairs squatting like refugees awaiting bad news. From a ceiling the colour of spoiled milk, a long rusty chain supported a dim light whose irregular thick glass bowl must have looked very futuristic in about 1963.

There was the washbasin, the rack for glasses below the mirror and the dud bulb above, the metal rubbish bin with its plastic liner, the barred window lying open into the room. He must have forgotten to close it when he went to bed. That was why the air seemed stiff with cold and why the sound of the bells had wakened him. He didn't feel cold in bed, though, probably because he was still fully dressed except for his shoes and jacket. He laboriously transferred his gaze to the floor, a chilly expanse of speckled black and white aggregate polished to a hard shine. There they were, the two shoes on their sides and the discarded jacket on its back above them like the outline drawing of a murder victim.

He lay back, exhausted by this effort, trying to piece together the events of the previous evening. Quite apart from resulting in the worst hangover he had ever experienced, he knew that what had happened hadn't been good news. But what *had* happened?

He remembered arriving back at the hotel. The bar was empty except for the old man called Tommaso and a younger man playing the pinball machine in the corner. The proprietor called Zen over and handed him his identity card and a bill.

"The hotel's closing for repairs."

"You didn't tell me when I checked in."

"I'm telling you now."

The pinball player had turned to watch them, and Zen had recognised him. He had even known his name —Patrizio—although he had no recollection of how or where they had met. What had he been doing all evening?

Abandoning this intractable problem, Zen swung his feet down on to the icy floor and stood up. This was a mistake. Previously he had had to deal with the electrical storm in his head, a stomach badly corroded by the toxic waste swilling around inside it, limbs that twitched, joints that ached and a mouth that seemed to have been replaced by a plaster replica. The only good news, in fact, had been that the room wasn't spinning round and round like a fairground ride. That was why it had been a mistake standing up.

Washing, shaving, dressing, and packing were so many stations of the cross for Aurelio Zen that morning. But it wasn't until he lit a cigarette in the mistaken belief that it might make him feel better and found tucked inside the packet of Marlboros a book of matches whose cover read Pizzeria Il Nuraghe that the merciful fog obscuring the events of the previous evening suddenly lifted.

He collapsed on one of the rickety wooden chairs, its feet scraping atrociously on the polished floor slabs. Zen didn't notice. He wasn't in his hotel room any longer. He was sitting at the table in the pizzeria, drunker than he had ever been in his life: horribly, monstrously, terminally drunk. Five men, three seated and two standing, were staring at him with expressions of pure, malignant hostility. The situation was totally out of control. Nothing he could say or do would have any effect whatsoever.

For a moment he thought that they might be going to assault him, but in the end Furio Padedda and his friend Patrizio had just turned away and walked out. Then the man called Turiddu threw some banknotes on the table and he and his companions left, too, without a word.

Outside, the air was thick with scents brought out by the rain: creosote, wild thyme, wood smoke, urine, motor oil. To judge by the stillness of the street, it might have been the middle of the night. Then a motorcycle engine opened up the night like a crude tin-opener, all jagged, torn edges. The bike emerged from the shadows of an alley and moved slowly and menacingly toward Zen. By the volatile moonlight, he recognised the rider as Furio Padedda. The lion-keeper bestrode the machine like a horse, urging it on with tightenings of his knees. From a strap around his shoulders hung a double-barrelled shotgun.

Then a figure appeared in the street some distance ahead of Zen. One ahead and one behind, the classic ambush. The correct procedure was to go on the offensive, take out one or the other before they could complete the squeeze. But if Zen had been following correct procedures he would never have been there in the first place without any backup. Even in his prime, twenty years ago, he couldn't have handled either man, never mind both of them. As Zen approached the blocker, he saw that it was Turiddu. With drunken fatalism, he kept walking. Ten metres. Five. Two. One. He braced himself for the arm across the throat, the foot to the groin.

Then he was past and nothing had happened. He sensed rather than saw Turiddu fall in behind him, his footsteps blending with the raucous murmur of Padedda's motorcycle. Zen forced himself not to hurry or look round. He walked on past rows of darkened windows, closed shutters, and locked doors, followed by the two men, until at last he reached the piazza and the hotel.

Now, mulling it over in his room, his thoughts crawling through the wreckage of his brain like the stunned survivors of an earthquake, Zen realised that he owed his escape to the enmity between the two Sardinians. Both had no doubt intended to punish the imposter, but neither was prepared to allow the other that honour, and cooperation was out of the question. Back at the hotel, the proprietor, alerted by Padedda's associate Patrizio, had delivered his ultimatum. There was no other accommodation in the village, and in any case, there was no point in Zen remaining now that Reto Gurtner had been exposed as a fraud. Whatever he said or did, everyone would assume that he was a policeman, a government spy. The farce was over. He would drive to Cagliari that morning and book a ticket on the night ferry to the mainland. When he returned to the village, it would be in his official capacity. At least that way he could compel respect.

His inability to do so at present was amply demonstrated by the length of time it took him to get breakfast in the bar downstairs. At least half a dozen of the locals had drifted in and out again, replete with *cappucinos* and pastries, before Zen was finally served a lukewarm cup of coffee that tasted as though it had been made from secondhand grounds and watered milk.

"Good-bye for now," he told the proprietor as he stalked out.

The remark elicited a sharp glance that expressed anxious defiance as well as hostility. It gladdened Zen for a moment, until he reflected that his implied threat was the first step on the path that had led to the Gestapo tactics of the past.

The weather had changed. The sky was overcast, the air still and humid. Zen's hangover felt like an octopus clinging to every cell of his being. Every movement involved an exhausting struggle against its tenacious resistance. He found himself looking forward luxuriously to sinking into the Mercedes's leather upholstery and driving away from this damned village, listening to the radio broadcasts from Rome, that lovely, civilised city where Tania was even now rising from her bed, sipping her morning coffee, thinking of him perhaps. He could allow himself to dream. Given all he'd been through, he'd surely earned the right to a little harmless self-indulgence.

Halfway across the piazza, beside the village war memorial, Zen had to stop, put his suitcase down, and catch his breath. The dead of the 1915-18 war covered two sides of the rectangular slab, the same surname often repeated six or eight times like a litany. The Sardinians had formed the core of the Italian Army's mountain divisions; half the young men of the village must have died at Isonzo and on the Piave. The later conflicts had taken a lesser toll. Thirty had died in 1940-45, four in Spain and five in Abyssinia.

As Zen picked up the leaden suitcase again, he noticed a tall thin man in a beige overcoat staring at him. His deception would be common knowledge by now, he realised, and his every action a cause for suspicion. He dumped the suitcase in the boot of the Mercedes, got inside, and turned the ignition on. Nothing happened. It was a measure of his befuddlement that it took him several minutes to realise that nothing was going to happen, no matter how many times he twisted the key. At first he thought he might have drained the battery by leaving the lights on, but when he tried the windscreen wiper, it worked normally. He had invented problems with the Mercedes as a way of breaking the ice with Turiddu and his friends the night before, and the wretched car was apparently now taking its revenge by playing up just when he needed it most. Then he noticed the envelope tucked under the wiper blade like a parking ticket.

Zen got out of the car and plucked it free. The envelope was blank. Inside was a single sheet of paper. *Furio Padedda is a liar*, he read. *He was not in the bar the night the foreigners were killed, but the Melega clan of Orgosolo know where he was.*

The message had been printed by a hand seemingly used to wielding larger and heavier implements than a pen. The letters were uneven and dissimilar, laboriously crafted, starting big and bold but crowded together at the right-hand margin as though panicked by the prospect of falling off the edge of the page.

Despite his predicament, Zen couldn't help smiling. So the humiliating disaster of the previous night had worked to his advantage, after all. Turiddu had seen an opportunity to even the score with his rival, no doubt easing his conscience with the reflection that Zen had not yet been officially identified as a policeman. If the information was true, it might be just what Zen needed to fabricate a case against Padedda and so keep Palazzo Sisti off his back. Unfortunately Turiddu's hatred for the foreigner from the mountains, whatever its cause, did not make him a very reliable informant. Nevertheless, there was something about the note which made Zen feel that it wasn't pure fiction, although in his present condition he couldn't work out what it was.

He stuffed the letter into his pocket, wondering what to do next. For no reason at all, he decided to ring Tania.

The phone was of the new variety that accepted coins as well as tokens. Zen fed in his entire supply of change and dialled the distant number. Never had modern technology seemed more miraculous to him than it did then, stranded in a hostile, poverty-stricken, Sardinian village listening to a telephone ringing in Tania's flat, a universe away in Rome.

"Yes?"

It was a man's voice, abrupt and bad-tempered.

"Signora Biacis, please."

"Who's speaking?"

"I'm calling from the Ministry of the Interior."

"For Christ's sake! Don't you know this is Sunday?"

"Certainly I know!" he replied impatiently. The coins were dropping through the machine with alarming frequency. "Do you think I like having to work today either?"

"What do you want with my wife?"

"I'm afraid that's confidential. Just let me speak to her, please."

"Eh no, certainly not! And don't bother ringing any more, signor, because she isn't in! She won't be in! Not ever, not for you! Understand? Don't think I don't know what's going on behind my back! You think I'm a fool, don't you? A simpleton! Well, you're wrong about that! I'll teach you to play games with a Bevilacqua! Understand? I know what you've been doing, and I'll make you pay for it! Adulterer! Fornicator!"

At this point Zen's money ran out, sparing him the rest of Mauro Bevilacqua's tirade. He walked despondently back to the Mercedes. By now the octopus had slackened its grip somewhat, but it still took Zen five minutes to work out how to open the bonnet. Once he had done so, however, he realised at once why the car would not start. This was no credit to his mechanical knowledge, which was nonexistent. But even he could see that the spray of wires sticking out of the centre of the motor, each cut cleanly through, meant that some essential component had been deliberately removed.

He closed the bonnet and looked around the piazza. The phone box was now occupied by the man in the beige overcoat. With a deep sigh, Zen reluctantly returned to the hotel. Why on earth should anyone want to prevent him from leaving? Did Padedda need time to cover his tracks? Or was this sabotage Turiddu's way of reconciling his anonymous letter with the burdensome demands of *omertá?*

The proprietor greeted Zen's reappearance with a perfectly blank face, as though he had never seen him before.

"My car's broken down," Zen told him. "Is there a taxi service, a car hire, anything like that?"

"There's a bus."

"What time does it leave?"

"Six o'clock."

"In the evening?"

"In the morning."

Zen gritted his teeth. Then he remembered the railway down in the valley. It was a long walk, but by now he was prepared to consider anything to get out of this cursed place.

"And the train doesn't run on Sunday," the proprietor added, as though reading his thoughts.

A phone started ringing in the next room. The proprietor went to answer it. Zen sat down at one of the tables and lit a cigarette. He felt close to despair. Just as he had received information that might well make his mission a success, every door had suddenly slammed shut in his face. At this rate, he would have to phone the Carabinieri at Lanusei and ask them nicely to come and pick him up. It was the last thing he wanted to do. To avoid compromising his undercover operation, he had left behind all his official identification. Involving the rival force would involve lengthy explanations and verifications and his highly questionable business there would inevitably be revealed, probably stymieing his chances of bringing the affair to a satisfactory conclusion. But there appeared to be no alternative, unless he wanted to spend the night in the street or in a cave like the beggar woman.

He looked up as the thin man in the beige overcoat walked in. Instead of going up to the bar, however, he headed for the table where Zen was sitting.

"Good morning, dottore."

Zen stared at him.

"You don't recognise me?" the man asked.

He seemed disappointed. Zen inspected him more carefully. He was about forty years old, with the soft, pallid look of one who works indoors. At first sight he had seemed tall, but Zen now realised that this was due to the man's extreme thinness. As far as he knew, he had never seen him before in his life.

"Why should I?" he retorted crossly.

The man drew up a chair and sat down.

"Why indeed? It's like at school, isn't it? The pupils all remember their teacher, even years later, but you can't expect the teacher to recall all the thousands of kids who have passed through their hands at one time or other. But I still recognise you, dottore. I knew you right away. You haven't aged very much. Or perhaps you were already old, even then."

He took out a packet of the domestic *toscani* cigars and broke one in half, replacing one end in the packet and putting the other between his lips.

"Have you got a light?"

Zen automatically handed over his lighter. He felt as though all this was happening to someone else, someone who perhaps understood what was going on. Certainly he didn't.

The man lit the cigar with great care, rotating it constantly, never letting the flame touch the tobacco. When it was glowing satisfactorily, he slipped the lighter into his pocket.

"But that's mine!" Zen protested, sounding like a child whose toy has been taken away.

"You won't be needing it any more. I'll keep it as a souvenir."

He stood up and took his coat off, draping it over a chair, then walked over to the bar and rapped on the chrome surface with his knuckles.

"Eh, service!"

The proprietor emerged from the back room, scowling furiously.

"Give me a glass of beer. Something decent, not any of your local crap."

Shorn of his coat, the man's extreme thinness was even more apparent. It gave him a disturbing two-dimensional appearance, as though when he turned sideways he might disappear altogether.

The proprietor banged a bottle and a glass down on the counter.

"Three thousand lire."

The thin man threw a banknote down negligently.

"There's five. Have a drink on me. Maybe it'll cheer you up."

He carried the bottle and glass back to the table and proceeded to pour the beer as carefully as he had lit the cigar, tilting the glass and the bottle toward each other so that only a slight head formed.

"Miserable fuckers, these Sardinians," he commented to Zen. "Forgive me if I don't shake hands. Someone once told me that it's bad luck, and I certainly don't need any more of that. Strange, though, you not remembering my face. Maybe the name means something. Vasco Spadola."

Time passed, a lot perhaps, or a little. The thin man sat and smoked and sipped his beer until Zen finally found his voice.

"How did you know where I was?"

It was a stupid question. But perhaps all questions were stupid at this point.

Spadola picked up his overcoat, patted the pockets, and pulled out the previous day's edition of *La Nazione*, which he tossed on the table.

"I read about it in the paper."

Zen turned the newspaper round. Halfway down the page was a photograph of himself he barely recognised. It must have been taken years ago, dug out of the newspaper's morgue. He looked callow and cocksure, ridiculously self-important. Beneath the photograph was an article headed, "New Evidence in Burolo Affair?" Zen skimmed the text.

ACCORDING TO SOURCES CLOSE TO THE FAMILY OF RENATO FAVELLONI, ACCUSED OF PLOTTING THE MURDERS AT THE VILLA BUROLO, DRAMATIC NEW EVIDENCE HAS RECENTLY COME TO LIGHT IN THIS CASE RESULTING IN THE REOPENING OF A LINE OF INVESTIGATION PREVIOUSLY REGARDED AS CLOSED. A SENIOR OFFICIAL OF THE MINISTRY'S ELITE CRIMINALPOL SQUAD, VICE-QUESTORE AURELIO ZEN, IS BEING SENT TO SARDINIA TO ASSESS AND COORDINATE DEVELOPMENTS AT THE SCENE. FURTHER ANNOUNCEMENTS ARE EXPECTED SHORTLY.

Zen put the paper down. Of course. He should have guessed that Palazzo Sisti would take care to publicise his imminent trip to the area in order to ensure that the "dramatic new evidence" he fabricated got proper attention from the judiciary.

"Shame I missed you in Rome," Spadola told him. "Giuliano spent over a week setting the whole thing up, watching your apartment, picking the locks, leaving those little messages to soften you up. By that Friday we were all set to go. I didn't know you'd sussed out the car, though. Giuliano was always a bit careless about things like that. Same with that tape he took instead of your wallet. It comes of being an eldest son, I reckon, Mamma's favourite. You think you can get away with anything."

He paused to draw on his cigar.

"When the cops rolled up, I had to beat it out the back way. I was lucky to get away, carrying the gun and all. I had to dump it in a rubbish skip and come back for it later. All that effort gone to waste, and what was worse, they'd got Giuliano. I knew he wouldn't have the balls to hold out once they got to work on him. I reckoned I'd have to lie low for months, waiting for you to get fed up being shepherded about by a minder or holed up in some safe house. I certainly didn't expect to be sitting chatting to you in a cafe two days later!"

He broke out in gleeful laughter.

"Even when I read the report in the paper, I never expected it to be this easy! I thought you would be staying in some barracks somewhere, guarded day and night, escorted around in bulletproof limousines. Still, I had to come. You never know your luck, I thought. But never in my wildest dreams did I imagine anything like this!"

The door of the bar swung open to admit Tommaso and another elderly man. They greeted the proprietor loudly and shot nervous glances at Zen and Spadola.

Zen ground out his cigarette. "All right, so you've found me. What now?"

Spadola released a breath of cigar smoke into the air above Zen's head.

"What now? Why, I'm going to kill you of course!"

He took a gulp of beer.

"That's why I didn't want to shake hands. One of the people I met in prison used to be a soldier for the Pariolo family in Naples. You worked there once, didn't you? Gianni Ferrazzi. Does the name ring a bell? It might have been after your time. Anyway, this lad had twenty or thirty hits to his credit, he couldn't remember exactly how many himself, and everything went fine until he shook hands with the victim before doing the job. He hadn't meant to, he knew it was bad luck, but they were presented, the man stuck out his paw, what was he supposed to do? It would have looked suspicious if he'd refused. He still went ahead and made the hit, even though he knew he'd go down for it. That's what I call real professionalism.

"To be honest, I thought that it would be a bit like that with you. Impersonal, I mean, anonymous, like a paid hit. That's the way it was with that judge Bertolini, unfortunately. I just hadn't thought the thing through that first time. The bastard never even knew why he died. I had enough to cope with, what with his driver pulling a gun and his wife screaming her head off from the house. I realised afterwards that I wanted a lot more than that, otherwise I might just as well hire it out and save myself the trouble. I mean the victim's got to understand, he's got to know who you are and why you're doing it, otherwise what kind of revenge is it?

"So I swore that you and Parrucci would be different. I certainly got my money's worth out of him, but you were more difficult. Once this terrorist scare started after I shot Bertolini, it seemed too risky to try and kidnap someone from the Ministry. They would have cracked down hard. I had no intention of getting caught. I've done twenty years for a murder I didn't commit, so they owe me this one free!"

He leant back in his chair with a blissful smile.

"Ah, but I never imagined anything like this! To sit here like this, two old friends chatting at a table, and tell you that I'm going to kill you, and you knowing it's true, that you're going to die! And all the time those two old bastards over there are discussing the price of sheep's milk or some fucking thing, and the barman's cleaning the coffee machine, and the television's blatting away next door, and the ice-cream freezer in the corner is humming. And you're going to die! I'm going to kill you while all this is going on! And it'll still go on once you're dead. Because you're not needed, Zen. None of us is. Have you ever thought about that? I have. I spent twenty years thinking about it. Twenty years, locked up for a murder I didn't even do!"

Spadola squeezed the last puff of acrid smoke from his cigar and threw the butt on the floor.

"You want to know who killed Tondelli? His cousin, that's who. It was over a woman, a barroom scuffle. Once he was dead, the Tondellis saw a way to use it against me and paid that cunt Parrucci to perjure himself. You bastards did the rest. But even supposing I had killed him, so what? People die all the time, one way or another. It doesn't make a fucking bit of difference to anything.

"*That's* what you can't admit, you others. That's what scares you shitless. And so you make little rules and regulations, like at school, and anyone who breaks them has to stand in the corner with a dunce's cap on. What a load of bullshit! The truth of it is that *you're* the first to break the rules, to cheat and lie and perjure yourselves to get a lousy raise, a better job or a fatter pension! *You're* the ones who ought to be punished! And believe it or not, my friend, that's what's going to happen, just this once. Take it in, Zen! You're going to die. Soon. Today. And I'm telling you this, warning you, and you know it's true, and yet there's absolutely nothing whatsoever that you can do about it! Not a single fucking thing!"

Spadola put his fingers to his lips and blew a kiss up into the air like a connoisseur appreciating a fine wine.

"This is the ultimate! I've never felt anything like it. It makes up for everything. Well, no, let's not exaggerate. Nothing could make up for what I've been through. But if it's any consolation, you've made me a very happy man today. You destroyed my life, it's true, but you have also given me this moment. My mother, may she rest in peace, used to say that I was destined to great sorrows and great joys. And she was right. She was so right."

He broke off, biting his lip; tears welled up in his eyes.

"I suppose it's no use telling you that I had nothing to do with the evidence against you being faked," Zen said dully.

Spadola rocked violently back and forth in his chair as though seized by an involuntary spasm.

"I don't believe it! This is too much! It's too good to be true!" He panted for breath. "Do you remember what you said that morning at the farm near Melzo? I told you I was innocent. I told you I hadn't done it. I knew I'd been betrayed, and that made it all the harder to bear. If I'd really knifed that fucking Southerner, you'd never have got a word out of me, but knowing it was all a fix, I thought I'd go crazy. And do you know what you said when I screamed my innocence in your face? You said, 'Yes, well you would say that, wouldn't you?' And you looked at me in that sly way you educated people have when you're feeling pleased with yourselves. *Of course* you had nothing to do with it, dottore! Just like this what's-his-name, the politician in this murder case you're investigating. *He* didn't have anything to do with it either, did he? People like you never do have anything to do with it!"

"I don't mean that I didn't plant the knife myself. I mean I didn't even know that it had been planted. It was done without my knowledge, behind my back."

"Then you're an incompetent bastard. It was your case, your responsibility! I've spent twenty years of my life, the only one I'll ever have, shut up in a stinking damp cell with barely room to turn around, locked up for hours in the freezing-cold darkness . . ."

He broke off, shuddering uncontrollably, his cheeks glistening wet.

"Go on, take a good look! I'm not ashamed of my tears! Why should I be? They're pearls of suffering, *my* suffering. I should make you lick them up, one by one, before I blow your evil head off!''

"Cut the crap, Spadola!" Zen exploded. "Even if you didn't do the Tondelli job, you were guilty as hell of at least four other murders. What about Ugo Trocchio and his brother? You had them killed and you know it. We knew it, everyone knew it. We couldn't prove it because people were too scared to talk. And so it went on, until some of my colleagues decided that it was time you were taken out of circulation. Since they couldn't do it straight, they did it crooked. As I say, I didn't know. If I had known, I would have tried to stop it. But the fact remains that you earned that twenty-year sentence several times over."

"That's not the point!" Spadola shouted, so loudly that the men at the bar turned to stare at him.

"Christ almighty, if everyone who broke the law in this country was sent to prison, who'd be left to guard them? We'd need a whole new set of politicians, for a start! But it doesn't work that way, does it? It's a game! And I was good! I was fucking brilliant! You couldn't pin a damn thing on me. I had you beat inside out. So you moved the goalposts!"

"That's part of the game too."

Spadola drained off his beer and stood up.

"Maybe. But the game stops here, Zen. What happens now is real."

His voice was perfectly calm again. He stood staring down at Zen.

"I know what you're thinking. You think I'm crazy, telling you what I'm going to do, warning you, giving you a chance to escape. There's no way I can get away with it, that's what you're thinking, isn't it? Not in broad daylight, not in the middle of this village. Well, we'll see. Maybe you're right. I agree that that's a possibility. Maybe you're cleverer than me. Maybe you'll figure out a way to save your skin this time around. That doesn't worry me. I'll get you in the end, whatever happens. And meanwhile that slim hope is part of your punishment, Zen, just like I was tormented with talk of appeals and parole that never came to anything."

He put on his overcoat.

"You've probably noticed that your car's not working. I removed the distributor and cut the leads. Just to save you time, I'll tell you that the phone box is out of order now, too. As for the locals, I doubt if they'd tell you the time by the clock on the wall. I showed them the paper, you see, told them who you are. Oddly enough, they didn't seem terribly surprised. Between the two of us, I think they must have sussed you out already.

"So I'll see you later, dottore. I can't say when exactly. That's part of the punishment, too. It could be in a few minutes. I might suddenly get the urge. Or it might not be until late tonight. It all depends on my mood, how I'm feeling. I'll know when the moment has come. I'll sense it. Don't worry about the pain. It'll be quick and clean, I promise. Nothing fancy like with Parrucci. I really had it in for him in a big way. They used to call him the nightingale, didn't they? Because of how beautifully he sang, I suppose. He turned out to be more of a screamer in the end. I had to take a walk, I couldn't handle it myself. He was tougher than he looked, though. When I got back an hour or so later, he was still whimpering, what was left of him. I had to finish him off with a pistol. Sickening, really. Well, I'm off for a piss."

He walked across the restaurant area and disappeared through a door marked Toilets.

"Let me use your phone!" Zen told the proprietor. "That man is a criminal. He has threatened to kill me. I'm a Vice-Questore at the Ministry of the Interior. If you don't help, you'll be an accessory to murder."

The proprietor gazed at him stonily.

"But your name is Reto Gurtner. I've seen your papers. You're a Swiss businessman from Zurich."

"My name is Aurelio Zen! I'm a high-ranking official!"

"Prove it."

"Let me use the phone! Quickly, before he comes back!"

"There's no phone here."

"But I heard it ringing when I came in."

"That was the television."

Given a few more minutes, Zen might have been able to change the man's mind with a combination of threats and pleas. But the few seconds before Vasco Spadola reappeared were too precious to gamble on that slim possibility. Besides, it would take the Carabinieri at least fifteen minutes to reach the village, and that would be plenty of time for Spadola to carry out his threat. Zen turned and ran.

Outside in the piazza, people had begun to gather for the promenade before lunch. Zen stood uncertainly by the door. Who could he turn to? Angelo Confalone? But it was Sunday. The lawyer's office would be closed and Zen had no idea where he lived. For a moment he thought of appealing to the crowd, throwing himself on their mercy. But there was no time to indulge in public oratory, and besides, he had been branded a spy, a proven liar, an agent of the hated government in Rome. Anyone who helped him would risk placing his own position in the community in jeopardy. Spadola was right. He was on his own.

Then he saw the Mercedes and realised that there was just one faint hope. It hung by the slenderest of threads, but he had nothing to lose. Anything was better than staying in the village, hiding in corners waiting to be rooted out and killed.

As he shoved his way unceremoniously through the knots of bystanders, Zen noticed Turiddu standing in a group of other men. They were all staring at him, talking in low voices and pointing at a yellow Fiat Uno with Rome numberplates parked nearby. To one side, all alone, stood Elia, the mad beggar woman. Zen belatedly noted the resemblance between her and Turiddu, and realised that he must be the brother she had rejected. That explained his anger on finding her at the pizzeria

the night before. In a community like this, a mentally ill
relative would be a perpetual source of shame.

   He released the handbrake of the Mercedes and put
the gear lever into neutral. Then he got out and started
to push with all his might, struggling to overcome the
vehicle's inertia and the slight incline leading up to the
main street. His headache sprang back into active life
and his aching limbs protested. After a violent effort, the
car rolled onto the cracked concrete slabs of the street.
Zen turned the wheel so that it was facing downhill,
then got it moving, and jumped back inside. Soon the
car was moving quite fast on the steeply inclined main
street and round the curve leading out of the village. He
wasn't in the clear yet, not by a long way, but he was
exhilarated by his initial success. By the time he reached
the new houses on the outskirts, the car was moving as
fast as he would have wanted to go anyway. He even
had to use the horn several times to warn groups of
villagers of his silent approach.

When I saw him leaving I thought everything was lost. I'd followed him everywhere, gun in hand, flitting through the shadows like a swift at dusk. All for nothing. There was always someone there, foiling my plans, as though some god protected him! And now he was beyond my reach.

He thought he was safe, I thought I'd failed. What neither of us understood was that his death was already installed in him, lodged in his body like our sins in the Bleeding Heart above the fireplace. I used to think the heart was from one of the pigs father had slaughtered. I kept expecting to find the beast's guts on another wall and its cock and balls nailed to the door. Once the lamp went out in the middle of a thunderstorm and Mother made me get down on my knees and pray to be forgiven or God would strike us dead on the spot. So I knelt to the great pig in the sky whose farts terrified mother, praying it wouldn't shit all over us.

*   *   *

Which is just what it did, a little later on. Be careful what you pray for. You might give God ideas.

I wandered off, neither knowing nor caring where I went. All places were equal now. My feet brought me here like a horse that knows its own way home. He would be far away, I thought, speeding through the corridors of light in his big white car.

But there was only one exit from the maze in which we both were trapped. Even as I despaired, he was on his way there, bringing me the death I needed.

SUNDAY: 0940 — 1325

IT WAS ONLY AS he approached the series of hairpin bends by which the road descended from the village that Zen realised Vasco Spadola might well have sabotaged the Mercedes' brakes as well as its engine. By then the car was doing almost 50 kph and accelerating all the time.

The brakes engaged normally, and a moment later Zen saw that his fears had been groundless. Spadola's exacting sense of what was due to him made it unthinkable that he would choose such an indirect and mechanical means of executing his revenge. His desires were urgent and personal. They had to be satisfied personally, face to face, like a perverted sex act.

The car drifted downhill in a lush silence cushioned by the hum of the tyres and the hushing of the wind. The hairpin bends followed one another with barely a pause. Zen found himself reminded of sailing on the Venetian lagoons, continually putting the boat about from one tack to the other as he negotiated the narrow channels between the low, muddy islets. He felt strangely exhilarated by that moment when life and death had seemed balanced on the response of a brake

lever as on the toss of a coin. In Rome, when he had
first sensed that someone was on his trail, he had felt
nothing but cold, clammy terror, a paralysing suffoca-
tion. But here in this primitive landscape, what was happening seemed perfectly natural and right. This is what
men were made for, he thought. The rest we have to
work at, but this comes naturally. This is what we are
good at.

Even in this euphoric state, however, he realised
that some men were better at it than others, and that
Vasco Spadola was certainly too good for him. If he was
to survive, he had to start thinking. Fortunately his brain
seemed to be working with exceptional clarity, despite
his hangover. There was as yet no sign of pursuit on the
road above, but as soon as Spadola emerged from the
hotel he was bound to notice that the Mercedes was
gone and realise that it could only have moved under
the force of gravity. All he needed to do after that was
follow the road downhill, and sooner or later—and it
was likely to be sooner rather than later—he would
catch up.

Below, the road wound down to the junction
where Zen had stopped to consult the map on his way
to the Villa Burolo twenty-four hours earlier. On the
other side of the junction, he remembered, an unsurfaced track led to the station built to serve the village
in the days when people were prepared to walk four or
five kilometres to take advantage of the new railway.
This station was Zen's desperate goal. It didn't matter
that there were no trains on Sunday. The station was
bound to have a telephone, and the stationmaster, owing his allegiance—and more importantly his job—not
to the locals but to the State, was bound to let Zen
use it. All Criminalpol officials were provided with a
codeword, changed monthly, which acted as a turnkey
providing the user with powers to dispose of the facilities of the forces of order from one end of the country
to the other. One brief phone call, and helicopters and
jeeps full of armed police would descend on the area,
leaving Spadola the choice of returning to the prison

cell he had so recently vacated or of dying in a hail of machine-gun fire. All Zen had to do was make sure the police arrived before Spadola.

He had banked on being able to freewheel the Mercedes all the way, but as soon as he got close enough to see the track, he noticed a feature not shown on the map: a low rise of land intervening between the road and the railway. It was difficult to estimate exactly how steep it was from the brief glances he was able to spare as he approached the last of the treacherous hairpin bends. For a moment he was tempted to let the car gather speed on the final straight stretch, gambling that the accumulated momentum would be enough to carry it over the ridge. But the risk was too great. If he didn't make it, he would be forced to abandon the Mercedes at the bottom of the slope, in full view of the road, which would be tantamount to leaving a sign explaining his intentions. When Spadola arrived, he would simply drive along the track, easily overtaking Zen before he could reach the station on foot.

By now he was seconds away from the junction. The only alternative was to turn onto the main road, which ran gently downhill to the right. Trying to conserve speed, he took the turn so fast that the tyres lost their grip on a triangular patch of gravel in the centre of the junction and the Mercedes started to drift sideways toward the ditch on the other side. At the last moment the steering abruptly came back, almost wrenching the wheel from Zen's hands. He steered back to the right-hand side, thankful that there was so little traffic on these Sardinian roads. As the car started to gather speed again, he glanced at the road winding its way up to the village. Several hundred metres above, he spotted a small patch of bright yellow approaching the second hairpin. Then a fold of land rose between like a passing wave and he lost sight of it.

The road stretched invitingly away in a gentle downward slope. Zen felt his anxieties being lulled by the car's smooth, even motion, but he knew that this sense of security was an illusion. Once on the main road, Spadola's Fiat would outstrip the engineless Mercedes in a matter of minutes, while every kilometre Zen travelled away from the station was a kilometre he would have to retrace painfully on foot. The car was not the asset it seemed, but a liability. He had to get rid of it, but how? If he left it by the roadside, Spadola would know he was close by. He had to ditch it somewhere out of sight, buying time to get back to the station on foot while Spadola continued to scour the roads for the elusive white Mercedes. Unfortunately, the barren, scrub-covered hills offered scant possibilities for concealing a bicycle, never mind a car.

He reached the junction with the side road to the Villa Burolo, but did not take it, remembering that it bottomed out in a valley where he would be stranded. What he needed was a smaller, less conspicuous turnoff, something Spadola might overlook. But time was getting desperately short! He kept glancing compulsively in the rearview mirror, dreading the moment when he saw the yellow Fiat on his tail. Once that happened, his fate would be sealed.

Almost too late, he caught sight of a faint dirt track opening off the other side of the road. There was no time for mature reflection or second thoughts. With a flick of his wrists, he sent the Mercedes squealing across the asphalt onto the twin ruts of bare red earth. Within moments a low hummock had almost brought the car to a halt, but in the end its forward momentum prevailed, and after that, it was all Zen could do to keep it on the track, which curved back on itself, becoming progressively rougher and steeper. The steering wheel writhed and twisted in Zen's hands, but he managed to hold on. Eventually the track straightened out and ran down more gently into a hollow sunk between steep, rocky slopes where a small windowless stone hut stood in a grove of mangy trees.

Zen stopped the Mercedes at the very end of the track. He got out and stood listening intently. Out of sight of the main road, the land curved up all around, containing the silence like liquid in a pot, its surface faintly troubled by a distant sound that might have been a flying insect. Zen turned his head, tracking the car as it drove past along the road above, the engine noise fading away without any change in pitch or intensity. His shoulders slumped in relief. Spadola had not seen him turn off and had not noticed the tyre marks in the earth.

He walked over to the hut, a crude affair of stones piled one on top of the other, with a corrugated iron roof. He stooped down and peered in through the low, narrow, open doorway inside. A faint draught blew toward him from the darkness within, carrying a strong smell of sheep. It must once have been a shepherd's hut, used for storing cheese and curing hides, but was now clearly abandoned. Zen knelt down and wriggled inside, crouching on the floor of bare rock. The reek was overpowering. As his eyes adjusted to the obscurity, Zen discovered that he was standing at the edge of a large irregular fissure in the rock. When he held his hand over the opening, he discovered that this was the source of the draught that stirred the fetid air in the hut.

Then he remembered Turiddu saying that the whole area was riddled with caves which had once brought water down underground from the lake in the mountains. The idea of water was very attractive. His hangover had left him with the most atrocious thirst. But of course there was no more water in the caves since they had built the dam. That's why the hut had been abandoned like so many of the local farms, including the one Oscar Burolo had bought for a song. This was presumably one of the entrances to that system of caves. It was large enough to climb down into, but of course there was no saying what that impenetrable darkness concealed, a cosy hollow he could hide in or a sheer drop into a cavern the size of a church.

Nevertheless, he was strongly tempted to stay put. He felt safe in the hut, magically concealed and protected. In fact he knew that it would be suicidal to stay. Indeed, he had already wasted far too much precious time. Before long, the road Spadola was following would start to go uphill, and he would know that Zen could

240   VENDETTA

not have passed that way. The network of side roads
would complicate his search slightly, but in the end a
process of elimination was bound to lead him to this
gully and the stranded Mercedes. The first thing he
would do then would be to search the hut.

But this knowledge didn't make the alternative any
more palatable. The idea of setting out on foot across
country with only the vaguest idea of where he was
going was something Zen found quite horrifying. His
preferred view of nature was through the window of a
train whisking him from one city to another. Men's con-
trivances he understood, but in the open he was as
vulnerable as a fox in the streets, his survival skills nonexistent, his native cunning an irrelevance. Nothing less
than the knowledge that his life was at stake could have
impelled him to leave the hut and start to climb the
boulder-strewn slope opposite.

He laboured up the hillside, using his hands to
scramble up the steeper sections, grasping at rocks and
shrubs, his clothes and shoes already soiled with the
sterile red dirt, the leaden sky weighing down on him.
He felt terrible. His limbs ached, thirst plagued him, and
his headache had swollen to monstrous dimensions.
Halfway to the top he stopped to rest. As he stood there,
panting for breath, cruelly aware how unfit he was for
this kind of thing, his brain blithely presented him with
the information it had withheld earlier. The anonymous
note left under the windscreen wiper of the Mercedes
had claimed that Padedda's whereabouts for the night
of the murders was known to "the Melega clan of
Orgosolo." It was that name which had seemed to au-
thenticate the writer's allegations. Antonio Melega, he
belatedly remembered, was the young shepherd who
had been buried a few days after the abortive kidnapping of Oscar Burolo, having been run over by an unidentified vehicle.

The faint hum of a passing car stirred the heavy
silence. The main road was still out of sight, so there
was no particular reason to suppose that the vehicle had
been Spadola's yellow Fiat. But the incident served as a

reminder of Zen's exposed position on the hillside above the hollow where the Mercedes stood out as prominently as a trashed refrigerator in a ravine. Putting every other thought out of his head, Zen attacked the slope as though it were an enemy, kicking and punching, grunting and cursing, until at last he reached the summit and the ground levelled off, conceding defeat.

Before him the landscape stretched monotonously away toward undesirable horizons. Zen trudged on through a wilderness of armour-plated plants that might have been dead for all the signs of life they showed. To take his mind off the brutal realities of his situation, Zen struggled to work out how the information he had obtained might be brought to bear on the Burolo case. And the more he thought about it, the more convinced he became that he had stumbled on the key to the whole mystery.

The irony was that having been sent to Sardinia to rig the Burolo case by incriminating Furio Padedda, he now possessed evidence which strongly suggested that the Sardinian was in fact guilty. With the lions, which Oscar had bought to patrol the grounds of his villa after the kidnap attempt, had come a man calling himself Furio Pizzoni. His real name, Palazzo Sisti had discovered, was Padedda, and he was not from the Abruzzo mountains but from those around Nuoro. And Padedda's friends, according to Turiddu's drunken revelations the night before, in addition to the traditional sheep-rustling, were also engaged in its more lucrative modern variation, kidnapping. Turiddu's companions had shut him up at that point, but the implications were clear.

There had never been any question that the Melega family, with a dead brother to avenge, had an excellent motive for murdering Oscar Burolo and the ruthless dedication to carry it out. What no one had been able to explain was how a gang of Sardinian shepherds had been able to gain entrance to the villa despite its sophisticated electronic defences, but given an ally within Burolo's gates, this obstacle could easily have been overcome. According to their testimony, Alfonso Bini and his wife had been watching television in their quarters at the time of the murder. If Padedda, instead of drinking in the village, had concealed himself at the villa, there was nothing to stop him entering the room from which the alarms were controlled and throwing the cut-out switches. For that matter, he could have carried out the killings himself. The wound on his arm, which had looked suspiciously like a bullet mark to Zen, corresponded to the fact that the assassin had been lightly wounded by Vianello. Padedda would no doubt have used his own shotgun, familiar and reliable, to do the killings, removing one of Burolo's weapons to confuse the issue. Zen recalled the ventilation hole in the wall of the underground vault to which the trail of blood stains led. Had that been searched for the missing weapon? And had ejected cartridges from the shotgun which Padedda kept hanging in the lions' house been compared with those found at the scene of the crime? Such checks should have been routine, but Zen knew only too well how often routine broke down under the pressure of preconceived ideas about guilt and innocence.

A car engine suddenly roared up out of nowhere and Zen threw himself to the ground. He lay holding his breath, his face pressed to the dirt, cowering for cover in the sparse scrub as a yellow car flashed by a few metres in front of him. It seemed impossible that he had escaped notice, but the car kept going. A few moments later it had disappeared.

He stood up cautiously, rubbing the cuts on his face and hands caused by his crash landing in the prickly shrubbery. Now that he knew it was there, he could see the thin grey line of asphalt cutting through the landscape just ahead of him. There was no time to lose. Spadola had taken the direction leading down into the valley. He would soon see that the Mercedes was not there and couldn't have climbed the other side, and so he would cross this road off his list, turn back and try again. Zen's only consolation was that Spadola had not yet found the abandoned car and therefore did not know that Zen was on foot.

He ran across the raised strip of asphalt and on through the scrub on the other side, hurrying forward until the contours of the hill hid him from the road. He could see the railway now, running along a ledge cut into the slope below. Rather than lose height by climbing down to it, he continued across the top on a converging course which he hoped would bring him more or less directly to the station. Meanwhile the bits and pieces of the puzzle continued to put themselves together in his mind without the slightest effort on his part.

As with Favelloni, it was impossible to know whether Padedda had actually carried out the killings or merely provided access to the villa. On balance, Zen thought the latter more likely. The Melegas, like Vasco Spadola, would have wanted the satisfaction of taking vengeance in person. This also explained the bizarre fact that no attempt had been made to destroy the video tape. Unlike Renato Favelloni, such unsophisticated men might well have ignored the camera as just another bit of the incomprehensible gadgetry the house was full of. Afterwards, the Melegas would have had no difficulty in persuading a few of the villagers to come forward and claim that they had seen Padedda in the local bar that evening, while the age-old traditions of *omertà* would stop anyone else from contradicting their testimony. It all made sense, it all fitted together.

Zen hurried on, forcing himself to maintain a punishing pace. To his right, he could see the whole of the valley stretching across to the ridge on the other side where the Villa Burolo was visible as a white blur. Further up, toward the mountains, the unnatural green of the forest fed by the leaking dam stained the landscape like a spillage of some pollutant. A distant rumble gave him pause for a moment until he realised that it was not a car but two distant aircraft. After some time, he made out the speeding black specks of the jet fighters swooping across the mountain slopes on their low-altitude manoeuvres. Then they disappeared up a valley and silence fell again. He pushed on, torn between satisfaction at having finally cracked the Burolo case and frustration at the thought that unless he managed to get to a telephone before Spadola caught up with him, the villagers' silence would remain unbroken forever and Renato Favelloni would be sent to prison for a crime he had not committed. Of course, Favelloni no doubt royally deserved any number of prison terms for other crimes which would never be brought home to him, protected as he was by *l'onorevole.* But as Vasco Spadola had remarked, that was not the point.

The going was not easy. The baked red earth, baked hard by months of drought, supported nothing but low bushes, bristling like porcupines with wiry branches, abrasive leaves, and sharp thorns that snagged his clothing continually. Fortunately the plants never grew very close together, so it was possible to find a way through. But the constant turning and winding through the labyrinth of bush increased the distance he had to cover and made his progress much more tiring. And he *was* tired. His dissipations the night before had resulted in a shallow, drunken sleep that had only scratched the surface of his immense weariness.

At last he reached the crest of a small ridge which had formed his horizon for some time and caught sight of the station for the first time, about half a kilometre away to his right, a squat building with a steeply pitched roof. The railway itself was invisible at that distance, so the buildings looked as if they had been set down at random in the middle of nowhere. Below, the track he had originally been planning to take in the car wound through the scrub. Zen ran down the hill to join it. The track showed no signs of recent use. Low bushes were growing over the wheel ruts, and rocks had sprouted everywhere. But now that he was within sight of his goal, the walking was almost a pleasure.

The first sign of what was to come was that one end of the station roof had fallen in. Then he saw that the windows and doors were just gaping holes. By the time he reached the yard, it was evident that the station was a complete ruin. The ground floor rooms were gutted, strewn with beams and plaster from the fallen ceiling, the walls charred where someone had lit a fire in one corner. Outside, the gable wall still proclaimed the name of the village in faded letters, with the height in metres above sea level, but it was clearly many years since the station had been manned. The whole line was a pointless anachronism whose one train a day served no purpose except to provide a few thousand people with jobs and, above all, keep the lucrative subsidies flowing in from Rome.

Zen shook his head. He couldn't believe this was happening. It was like a bad dream. Automatically he reached for a cigarette, only to remember that Spadola had taken his lighter. He blasphemed viciously, then tried to force himself to think. It was tempting to think of spending the night at the station and catching the train the next morning, but that would be as short-sighted as staying in the shepherd's hut. It would be equally foolish to try and make off across country. The Barbagia was one of the wildest and least populated areas of the country. Without a map and a compass, the chances of getting lost and dying of exposure were very high.

That left just two possibilities: he could walk back along the track to the main road and then try and hitch a lift to the nearest town, or he could follow the railway line up into the mountains. The problem with taking the road was that Vasco Spadola would surely see him. Walking the railway would be a long and tiring business, and he would probably have to spend a night in the open. But if the worst came to the worst, he could flag down the train the next morning or even jump aboard at the speed it would be going. But the decisive advantage was that the railway was out of sight of the road, which Spadola would now be patrolling in increasing frustration.

The unlit cigarette clenched between his lips, Zen stepped across the disused passing loop where pulpy cacti ran riot and started to walk along the line of rusty rails which curved off to the left, following the contours of the hillside. He had imagined walking along the railway as being tedious but relaxing, but in fact it was every bit as demanding as negotiating the scrub. The ancient rails, rough-hewn, weathered and split, were placed too close together to step comfortably on each one and too far to take them two at a time, while the ballast in between was jagged, uneven, and rife with plants.

A thunderous rumble sounded in the distance once again. Zen stopped and looked up to spot the jets at their sport in the mountains. It was only moments later that he realised another sound had been concealed in the cavernous booming of the jets, a rhythmic purr that was quieter but much closer. For a moment it seemed to be coming from the railway line, and Zen's hopes briefly flared. Then he swung round and saw the yellow Fiat driving along the track to the station.

Instinctively he crouched down, looking for cover. But this time it was too late. Its engine revving furiously, the Fiat had left the track and was smashing its way through the scrub toward him. Zen leapt up and started to run as fast as he could in the opposite direction. Almost immediately he tripped over a rusty signal wire and went flying, landing on a small boulder and turning his ankle agonisingly. Behind him, the frantic roaring of the car engine reached a peak, then abruptly died. A car door slammed. Zen forced himself to his knees. Some fifty metres away the yellow Fiat lay trapped in a thicket of scrub. Beside the car, a shotgun in his hand, stood Vasco Spadola.

Zen tried to stand up, but his left ankle gave way and he stumbled. He tried again. This time the ankle held, although it hurt atrociously. He now knew that Spadola was going to kill him, but he couldn't just stand there and let it happen, even though it meant torturing himself in vain. He started to hobble away as fast as he could, gasping at every step. Repeatedly he tripped, lost his precarious balance, and ended up on his hands and knees in the rocky dust. He did not look back. There was no point. Spadola would catch up with him in a matter of minutes. He wondered how good a shot Spadola was and whether he would hear the blast that killed him.

When he finally stopped to look round, he found that Spadola was still some fifty metres away, dawdling along, the shotgun balanced loosely in the crook of his arm. With a groan, Zen turned back to his calvary. So that was how it was going to be. Spadola was in no hurry to finish him off. On the contrary, the longer he could draw out the agony, the more complete his revenge would be. Only the approach of night would force him to close in for the kill, lest his prey escape under cover of darkness. But that was many hours away yet. In the meantime, he was content to dog Zen's footsteps, not trying to overtake him but not letting him rest either, harrying him on relentlessly toward the inevitable bloody conclusion.

Zen plodded blindly on in a nightmare of pain, confusion, and despair. He neither knew nor cared which direction he was going in. All his hopes and calculations had come to nothing. Unless Palazzo Sisti managed to throw a political wrench in the works at the last moment, Renato Favelloni would be convicted of the Burolo murders while Furio Padedda and the Melega family watched with ironic smiles, never guessing that they owed their freedom to a vendetta very similar to the one which had cost Oscar and the others their lives. To cap it all, Spadola would probably get away with it, too. The villagers would say nothing, particularly since it would involve them as accessories to Zen's murder. When his corpse was eventually discovered, it would be assumed that he had fallen victim to the long-running guerilla war between the islanders and the State. His colleagues in Rome would shake their heads and agree that it had been crazy to improvise a one-man undercover operation in Sardinia without even telling anyone what he was doing. "He was *asking* for it!" Vincenzo Fabri would crow triumphantly, just as people had said about Oscar when he chose a villa so close to the kidnappers' heartland. No one would want to tug too hard on any of the loose ends that remained. As Zen well knew, the police were part of the forces of order in more senses than one. They liked things to make sense, they liked files that could be closed. If this order happened to correspond to the truth, well and good, but in the last resort they'd rather have a false solution that was neat and tidy than no solution at all. Certainly there was never any encouragement to throw things back into chaos by suggesting that the things might not be quite what they appeared.

Without the slightest warning, something impossibly fast for its monstrous size overshadowed the world and the sky fell apart with a hellish roar. At first Zen thought that Spadola had fired at him. Then, swivelling round, he saw the second jet sharking silently through the air toward him. Absurdly, he started to wave, to shout for help! Vasco Spadola broke into hoots of derisory laughter that were lost in the din as the fighter screamed past overhead, not deigning to notice the antics of the petty creatures which crawled about on the bed of this sea of air it used as a playground.

After that, Zen lost all track of time. Reality was reduced to a patch of baked red soil, always different, always the same. His task was to find a way through the dense, prickly plants that grew there. Sometimes they were widely spaced. Then he had only the constant jarring pain from his ankle to contend with, the choking thirst and the hammering headache. But usually the plants formed patterns restricting his moves like hostile pieces in a board game. Then he had to raise his eyes and try to find a way through the maze. If he got it wrong or the plants ahead of him closed up entirely, then he had to force his way through. Branches poked him, thorns ripped his clothes and scratched his skin. Several times he almost got stuck, only to wrench himself free with a final effort. But stopping or turning back was not permitted, although by now he could hardly remember why.

At some point in this timeless torment he found himself confronted by a new obstacle, unforeseen by the rules of the game which had absorbed him hitherto. It was a wire mesh fence, about four metres high, supported on concrete stakes and stretching away in either direction as far as the eye could see. Some distance behind it stood a similar fence of barbed wire.

Zen's first thought was that it was some sort of military installation. It wasn't until he saw a sign reading Beware of the Lions that he realised he had blundered into the perimeter fence of the Villa Burolo. He started to follow the fence as it marched up the hillside. But where it cut effortlessly through the undergrowth, dividing the wilderness in two with surrealistic precision, Zen had to scramble, wriggle, dodge, and feint. Denser thickets in his path constantly forced him to seek alternate routes, and as he became more exhausted, he began to lose his footing on the steep slope. His hands were soon scuffed and scratched, his clothing tattered, his legs bruised and bleeding.

It was some time before it occurred to him that he might try to attract attention by setting off the villa's alarm systems. If he could set the sirens off, the caretaker might turn on the closed-circuit television scanners, see the armed figure of Spadola and phone the police. The problem was that in order to minimise false alarms, the outer fence was not connected to the system, so Zen had to lob stones at the inner fence with its attached sensors. This consisted of single strands of razor wire, and was very hard to hit. Zen's aim gradually improved, but before any of the stones connected with the target something that sounded like a swarm of bees whined past his head. An instant later he heard the gunshot.

When he turned round, Spadola had already broken open the shotgun and was reloading the spent barrel. He gestured angrily at Zen, waving him away from the fence. This incident served to remind Zen of the realities of his situation. The noise the shot made passing overhead suggested that it had been travelling fast enough to do significant damage to his hands, face, and neck. At the very least, such injuries would cause serious loss of blood, in turn inducing a shocked condition in which further resistance would become impossible. Spadola could do that any time he wanted to. The fact that he had deliberately aimed high proved that. He was in total command of the situation and would carry out the killing when it suited him and not before. Meanwhile, Zen could only struggle like an animal being used for scientific research, its agony the subject of dispassionate study, its feeble attempts to escape as predictable as they are vain.

Eventually the fence, obeying the forgotten whims of a dead man, changed direction to run north across the mountainside. Zen had now to choose between following it into unknown territory or continuing up the face of the mountain toward the lurid green forest massed at the head of the valley now closed by the dam. And he had to choose quickly because Spadola was suddenly forcing the pace. But as soon as he saw that his quarry was continuing to struggle up into ever higher and wilder regions, he slackened off again. What had concerned him, presumably, was that Zen might try to circle round the Burolo property to the main road. If he asked himself why his victim had selected the harder and more hopeless option, he probably put it down to his growing confusion and disorientation.

Zen toiled up the successive ridges of the mountainside toward the forest. Close to, it was not the upper surface of the forest that struck the eye but its lower depths, a dull brown stagnancy killed off by the tall victors of the struggle for survival. Their outspread branches formed a roof which closed off all light to the ground, condemning their own lower branches together with the losers of the race, whose spindly skeletons rose from a mulch of pine needles and rotting branches. This was what Zen had been hoping for. Vasco Spadola thought that he could play cat and mouse with his victim for hours yet, spinning out the game until the approach of night. What he hadn't realised was that in that unnatural forest, beneath those trees gorged on water seeping from the flawed dam, it was *always* night.

Zen glanced back to find that Spadola had broken into a run. Teeth gritted against the stabbing pain in his ankle, Zen ran, too. He ran with the desperation of a man who knows that his life depends on it, and for the first crucial moments, despite his injury, he ran faster. After that, Spadola rapidly started to narrow the gap, but by then it was too late. Zen had reached the cover of the trees. Another shot rang out, and Zen felt stinging pains all over his arms, legs, and back. When he clapped a hand to his neck, as though slapping a mosquito, it came away stained with blood. Then he saw the lead pellets in his hand, little black lumps lodged just under the skin like burrowing ticks.

As Zen made his way deeper into the forest, he knew that there would be no further reprieves. The sadistic pleasure of killing his enemy by degrees had been replaced in Spadola's mind by an urgent desire to finish him off before it was too late. Because unless he could do so before darkness fell, he had lost. There was no way he could patrol the perimeter of the forest and stop Zen from slipping away into the night.

After so many hours in the open, entering the forest was like stepping into a cathedral: hushed, mysterious, dim and intimate in details, vast and complex in design. Zen barged on, forcing aside the brittle tendrils that waved outward from the trunks like seaweed under water. The darkness thinned to a dimness that limited visibility to about ten metres, except when a clearing caused by a rocky outcrop punched a hole in the dense fabric of the forest. In one of these, he suddenly caught sight of a great curtain of concrete towering above the trees. The thought of that hanging lake increased his impression of being underwater. Beyond the immediate circle of bare columnlike trunks, nothing was visible. Despite the moisture that forced its way out through the faults in the dam to keep the undersoil perpetually damp, nothing grew beneath the killing cover of the trees. The forest was a reservoir of silence and darkness. No breezes entered, nothing stirred.

The bare soil, soft with composted droppings,

squelched underfoot. It was the sound that could give him away, he realised. In the deathly hush beneath the trees, the least noise would betray his position, and it was impossible to move without making a lot of noise. But by the same token, Spadola could only hear Zen if he himself stopped moving, in which case he would fall ever further behind, the sounds would grow fainter and his bearings on their source less precise. So Zen's strategy was to plough on without once stopping or looking back and then, once he was deep inside the forest, stop and stay absolutely still. Then the tables would be turned. Deprived of any clue as to Zen's whereabouts, Spadola could only beat about at random, while the noise he made doing so would give Zen ample warning of his approach. If necessary, he could simply repeat the process until darkness fell. The advantage now lay with him.

The floor of the forest sloped gently to the east, following the contours of the invisible mountainside. Zen pushed on, his arms held up to protect his face from the dead twigs sticking out from the tree trunks. Once he stumbled on a root surfacing like a monstrous worm and fell against a broken branch that laid his forehead open. But he felt nothing until he stopped, satisfied that he had gone far enough. Surrendering to his exhaustion, Zen stretched out on the ground and closed his eyes.

The noises woke him, crashing sounds close at hand, their source invisible in the eerie gloom. He looked round wildly, forgetting for a merciful moment where he was. Then he saw the line of scuffed footmarks running back across the undulating surface and the dangling branches he had broken in his reckless flight, and he understood. So, far from vanishing into the trackless wastes of the forest, he had left a trail a child could have followed. But the creature following him was no child, and it was almost upon him.

He knew this was the end. Physically exhausted by his ordeal, weakened by hunger, thirst, and loss of blood, this final blow had crippled his morale as well.

Further resistance was futile. Nothing he had done since leaving the village had made the slightest difference to the outcome. He might just as well have ordered a last drink and sat in the bar waiting to die. Yet to his disgust, for it seemed a kind of weakness, a cowardice, he was unable to let things take their course even now. Instead he must stagger on through that sunken landscape, that lumber room of dead growth, without direction or purpose, out of control to the last.

In this frame of mind, he was incapable of surprise, even when he stumbled across the path weaving through the forest like a road across the bed of a flooded valley. The trodden surface showed signs of recent use, no doubt by animals, though there were no signs of any droppings. In one direction it ran downhill, presumably leading out of the lower flank of the forest. Zen turned the other way. Encroaching branches were already broken off, and his own footsteps were invisible in the general disturbance of the forest floor. If Spadola went the wrong way when he reached the path, Zen would have gained ample time to find a secure sanctuary. Hope teased his heart, banishing the deathly calm of his fatalistic resignation.

The path wound uphill in a lazily purposeful way that lulled Zen's attention, until he suddenly found himself standing on the brink of a deep chasm in the forest floor, scanning the trough of darkness in front of him. He could see nothing: no path, no ground, no trees. It was as if the world ended there.

After standing there indecisively for some moments, he realised the ravine offered the perfect hiding place he had been seeking, if he could manage to scramble down the precipitous slope below him. Nevertheless, he had to overcome a strong reluctance to descend into that black hole. It was not the dark he should be afraid of but Spadola. He lowered himself onto a rocky outcrop and started to clamber down.

At first the descent was easier than he had imagined, with numerous ledges and projections. But the further down he went, the fainter grew the glimmers of

light from the surface far above, until at length he could
hardly make out his next foothold. The idea of losing his
footing and plunging off into nothingness made his
palms sweat and his limbs shake in a way that greatly
increased the chances of this happening. The only measure of how deep the chasm was came from the falling
rocks he dislodged. Gradually the clattering became
briefer and less resonant, until he sensed rather than
saw that he had reached the bottom.

As his pupils dilated fully, he could just make out
the hunched shapes of boulders all around and suddenly
realised that he was standing in the channel cut by the
river which had flowed down from the lake above before the dam was built. The huge rocks littering its bed
would have been washed down in the former torrent's
spectacular seasonal surges.

When he heard the scurry of falling stones behind
him, Zen's first thought was that the dam had given way
and the black tide, unpenned, was surging toward him,
sweeping away everything in its path. Then he realised
the sound had come from above.

Frantically he began to pick his way down the
riverbed, crawling round and over the shattered lumps
of granite, desperately trying to put as much distance as
possible between himself and the killer on his trail. As
soon as the noises of Spadola's descent ceased, Zen
would go to ground in some obscure nook or cranny. It
would take an army weeks to search that chaotic maze.

But to his dismay, the channel ended almost immediately, widening out into a circular gully closed off by a
wall of dull white rock rounded like the end of a bath.
The foliage above was thinned out by this space where
nothing grew, allowing a trace more light to filter down
to the depths. Zen gazed at the freakish rock formation
surrounding him. He did not understand what could
have caused it, but one thing was clear. The wall of
smooth white rock was at least ten metres high and
absolutely sheer. Zen couldn't possibly climb it, and
with Spadola hard on his heels he couldn't turn back.

He had fallen into a perfect natural trap, a killing ground from which there was no exit.

The sound of tumbling rocks announced the approach of the hunter. With a weary slackness of heart, as though performing a duty for the sake of appearances, Zen knelt and squeezed himself into a narrow crevice underneath a tilting boulder. As soon as Spadola reached the end of the gully, he would realise that Zen could not have climbed out and must therefore be hiding nearby. He would flush him out almost at once. This time it really was the end. There was nothing to do but wait. He lay absolutely still, as though he were part of the rock pressing in on him.

"Well, fuck me!"

Zen felt so lonely and scared that the words, the first he had heard since leaving the village, brought tears to his eyes. He was suddenly desperate to live, terrified of death, of extinction, of the unknown. How precious were the most banal moments of everyday life, precisely because they were banal!

A mighty roar scoured the enclosed confines of the gully. As the shot echoed away, Spadola's peals of manic laughter could be heard.

"Come on out, Zen! The game's over. Time to pay up."

The voice was close by, although Zen could see nothing but a jumble of rocks.

"Are you going to come out and die like a man, or do you want to play hide-and-seek? It's up to you, but if you piss me about I might just decide to kill you a little more slowly. Maybe a little shot in the balls, for openers. I'm not a vindictive man, but there are limits to my patience."

Like rats leaving a doomed ship, all Zen's faculties seemed to have fled the body wedged in its rocky tomb. He was incapable of movement, speech, or thought, as good as dead already.

Spadola laughed. "Ah, so there you are! Decided to spare me the trouble, have you? Very wise."

Zen still couldn't see Spadola, but somehow he had

been spotted. The anomaly didn't bother him. It was perfectly consistent with everything else that had happened. Footsteps approached. Zen tried to think of something significant in his last moments and failed. After all the ballyhoo, it looked as though death was going to prove a disappointment.

Something stirred the air close to his face. Less than a metre away, close enough to touch, a boot hit the ground and a trousered leg swished past.

"There's no point in trying to hide," Spadola shouted, his voice echoing slightly. "I can still see you. Let's just get it over with, shall we? It's been fun, but . . ."

There was a loud gunshot, followed by a scream of rage and fury. Then two more shots rang out simultaneously, one deafeningly close to Zen, the other a repetition of the first. Pellets bounced and rattled against the rocks, ricocheting about like hailstones.

It seemed impossible that the silence could ever recover from such a savage violation, but before long the echoes died away as though nothing had happened. Zen had no idea what *had* happened, so he waited, sampling the silence before emerging from his hiding place. He found Spadola almost immediately. His body was flung backward across the rocks, a limp, discarded carapace. Something had scooped a raw crater out of his belly, around which circles of lesser destruction spread out like ripples on a pond. The shotgun lay close by, wedged between two rocks.

Zen searched dispassionately through the dead man's pockets until he found his lighter, then sat down on a rock and lit a cigarette. From this perch he could see the end of the gully. Beneath the wall of white rock the ground opened up to form a cavernous sluice funnelling downward, the edges clean and rounded. As he sat there, the cigarette smoldering peacefully between his fingers, Zen recalled what Turiddu had said about the soft rocks and the hard rocks and realised that the white surface closing off the gully was the limestone that overlaid the granite at this point, rubbed to a smooth curve by the whirling water before it disappeared underground into the pool of darkness beneath, which was now the main entrance to the cave system underlying the whole area.

After that, things started to fall into place almost faster than he could keep up with them. Before the cigarette had burned out, the whole picture was clear in his mind: Spadola's death, the murders at the Villa Burolo, the villagers' hostility, everything. He'd had all the clues in his hand for some time, but he hadn't been able to put them together until now.

As he got up to start making his way back to civilisation, he caught a glimpse of something glinting in the darkness below. Like the immortal he had once seemed to be, playing God with the video of the Burolo killings, Zen made his way down as though immune to danger. Just inside the mouth of the cave he found the other shotgun, a double-barrel pump action Remington. The rock nearby was heavily stained with sticky, drying blood. It was merely a confirmation of what Zen already knew when, by the flickering flame of his cigarette lighter, he read the inscription engraved on the barrel of the gun: *To Oscar, Christmas 1979, from his loving wife Rita.*

How wrong I was! And how right! Yes, a death was needed, and he brought it. But how did I fail to see that the person whose death would set me free was me?

The darkness is closing in, touching me, taking me like a lover. There was blood then, too. He seemed to expect it, but I was shocked. No one had told me anything. I thought I was going to die. I didn't, though, not that time. But now my long labour is finally accomplished, and the death I have been carrying all these years is about to be delivered. A little more pain and everything will be over. There's nothing more to do, nothing to be done.

And then? I've tried to be a good girl, but trying is not enough. Everything depends on his mercy or his inattention. It's surprising what you can get away with sometimes, then at others he'll beat you viciously for nothing at all. So in the end justice is done. Who can say? Will my sufferings count for anything, my good deeds? Will I be judged worthy of forgiveness this time? Will I be judged worthy of love?

Rome

FRIDAY: 1120 — 2045

"He threatened to kill me?"

"Oh, yes! Me too, for that matter. But it's only talk. He has to call his mother if he finds a spider in the bath. Now if *she*'d said it we might have something to worry about."

The cafe on Via Veneto accurately reflected the faded glories of the street itself. The mellow tones of marble, leather, and wood predominated. Dim lighting discreetly revealed the understated splendours of an establishment so prestigious it had no need to put on a show. Its famous name appeared everywhere, on the cups and saucers, the spoons, the sugar bowl and ashtray, the peach-coloured napkins and tablecloth and the staff's azure jackets. The waiters conducted themselves like family retainers, studiously polite yet avoiding any hint of familiarity. A sumptuous calm reigned.

The cafe was too far from the Viminal to be one of the regular haunts of Ministry personnel, who in any case would have balked at paying four thousand lire for a cup of coffee they could get elsewhere for eight hundred with a hefty dose of Roman pandemonium thrown in for free. This was one reason why Zen had invited Tania there for their first meeting since his return from Sardinia. The other was a desire he still didn't completely understand, to do things differently, to break free of old habits, to change his life, himself.

"How did he find out?"

She smiled, anticipating his reaction.

"He hired a private detective."

"To follow you?"

"No, to follow *you!*"

So that was who Leather Jacket had been working for, thought Zen, not Spadola or Fabri, but Mauro Bevilacqua! Ironically, he might have considered that possibility earlier if it hadn't seemed wishful thinking to imagine that Tania's husband could have any reason to feel jealous of *him*.

"He didn't want to admit even to the detective that his wife might be unfaithful," Tania explained. "He was afraid people would laugh at him and call him a cuckold."

"Which he wasn't, of course. Isn't, I mean."

"Well, it depends on how you look at it. According to the strictest criteria, a husband is a cuckold if his wife has even *thought* of being unfaithful."

They exchanged a glance.

"In that case we're all cuckolds," Zen replied lightly.

"That's why Mauro would claim that his vigilance was completely justified."

This time they both laughed.

Zen lit a Nazionale and studied the young woman sitting opposite him, her legs crossed, her right foot rising and falling gently in time to her pulse. Clad in the currently fashionable outfit of black midi-length overcoat, short black skirt and black patterned tights, with bright scarlet lipstick and short wet-look hair, she looked very different from the last time that he had seen her. Not that he minded. The Tania he loved—he felt able to use the word now, at least to himself—was invulnerable to change, and as for this new image she had

chosen to show the world, he found it exciting, sophisticated, and sexy. A week ago he would have hated it, but
the life which had almost miraculously been returned to
him in Sardinia was no longer quite the same as it had
been before he had passed through that ordeal.

"It must be a nightmare for you," he said sympa-
thetically. "It was bad enough having to live there before, but now that his suspicions have been proven, or
apparently proven . . ."

"I don't live there any more."

For a moment they both remained silent, the news
lying on the table between them like an unopened letter
which might contain anything.

Tania lifted the pack of Nazionali and shook a cigarette loose.

"May I?"

"I didn't know you smoked."

"I do now."

He held the lighter for her. She lit up and blew out
smoke self-consciously, like a schoolgirl.

"He hit me, you see."

Zen signalled his shock with a sharp intake of
breath.

"So I hit him back. With the frying pan. It had hot
fat in it. Not much, but enough to give him a nasty burn.
When his mother found out, I thought she'd go for me
with the carving knife, but in the end she backed off
and started babbling to herself in this creepy way, hysterical but very controlled, saying I was a Northern
witch who had put her son under a spell but she knew
how to destroy my power. It scared me to death. I knew
then that I had to leave."

"Where did you go?"

He dropped the question casually like the experienced interrogator he was, as though it were a minor
detail of no significance.

"To a friend's."

"A friend's."

She took a notebook and pen from her handbag,
wrote down an address and handed it to him. He read,

*Tania Biacis, c/o Alessandra Bruni, Via dei Gelsi 47.
Tel. 788447.*

"It's in Centocelle. I'm staying there temporarily until I find something for myself. You know how difficult it is."

He nodded. "And Mauro?"

"Mauro? Mauro's still living with his mamma."

Everything about her had a new edge to it, and Zen couldn't be sure that this wasn't an ironical reference to his own situation.

Ignoring this, he said, "That restaurant in Piazza Navona, it's open tonight."

She waited for him to spell it out.

"Would you think of . . . I mean, I don't suppose you're free or anything, but . . ."

"I'd love to."

"Really?"

She laughed, this time without malice. "Don't look so surprised!"

"But I *am* surprised."

Her laughter abruptly subsided. "So am I, to tell you the truth. I can't quite see how we got here. Still, here we are."

"Here we are," he agreed, and signalled the waiter.

On the broad pavement outside, Zen pulled Tania against him and kissed her briefly on both cheeks in a way that might have been purely friendly, if they had been friends. She coloured a little, but said nothing. Then, having agreed to meet at the restaurant that evening, Tania hailed a taxi to take her to Palazzo di Montecitorio, the Parliament building, where she had to run an errand for Moscati, while Zen returned to the Ministry on foot.

The winter sunlight, hazy with air pollution, created a soothing warmth that eased the lingering aches in Zen's body. A surgeon in Nuoro had spent three hours picking shotgun pellets out of his limbs and lower back, but apart from those minor injuries and a slightly swollen ankle, his ordeal had left no permanent scars. He strolled along without haste, drinking in the sights and sounds. How precious it all seemed, how rich and various, unique and detailed! He spent five minutes watching an old man at work collecting cardboard boxes left outside a shoe shop, deftly collapsing and flattening each one. An unmarked grey delivery van with reflecting windows on the rear doors drove past with a roar and pulled in to the side of the street, squashing one of the cardboard boxes. The old man waved his fist impotently, then retrieved the box, straightened it out and brushed it clean before adding it to the tall pile already tied to the antique pram he used as a cart.

Zen walked on past the open doorway of a butcher's shop, from which came a series of loud regular bangs and a smell of blood. The delivery van roared by and double-parked at the corner of the street, engine running. Outside a pet shop, a row of plastic bags filled with water were hanging from a rack. In each bag, a solitary goldfish twitched to and fro, trapped in its fragile bubble-world. A mechanical street cleaner rolled past, leaving a swathe of glistening asphalt in its wake, looping around the obstruction caused by the grey van. No one got in or out of the van. Nothing was loaded or unloaded. A tough-looking young man, clean-shaven with short, cropped hair, sat behind the wheel, staring straight ahead. He paid no attention to Zen.

Up in the Criminalpol suite on the third floor of the Ministry, the other officials were in the midst of a heated discussion centered on Vincenzo Fabri.

"The British have got the right idea," Fabri was proclaiming loudly. "Catch them on the job and gun them down. Forget the legal bullshit."

"But that's different!" Bernardo Travaglini protested. "The IRA are terrorists."

"There's no difference! Sicily, Naples, Sardinia, they're our Northern Ireland! Except we're dumb enough to respect everyone's rights and do things by the book."

"That's not the point, Vincenzo," De Angelis interrupted. "Thatcher's got an absolute majority, she can do what she wants. But here in Italy we've got a democracy. You've got to take account of people's opinions."

"Screw people's opinions!" Fabri exploded. "This is war! The only thing that matters is who is going to win, the state or a bunch of gangsters. And the answer is they are, unless we stop pissing about and match them for ruthlessness."

He caught sight of Zen sliding past and broke off suddenly.

"Now there's somebody who's got the right idea," he exclaimed. "While the rest of us are sweating it out down in Naples trying to protect a bunch of criminals who would be better off dead, Aurelio here pops over to Sardinia and turns up quote 'new evidence in the Burolo case' unquote, which just happens to put a certain politician's chum in the clear. That's the way to do things! Never mind the rights and wrongs of the situation. Results are all that matters."

Resignedly Zen turned to face his tormentor. This was a showdown he could not dodge.

"What do you mean by that?"

Fabri faked a smile of complicity.

"Oh, come on! No hard feelings! In your shoes I'd have done the same. But it just goes to prove what I've been saying. Do things by the book like us poor suckers and what do you get? A lot of headaches, long hours, and a boot up the bum if things go wrong. Whereas if you look after number one, cultivate the right contacts, and forget about procedures, you get covered in glory, name in the paper, and friends in high places!"

"To be fair, you should take some of the credit," Zen replied.

"Me? What are you talking about?"

"Well, you recommended me, didn't you?"

Fabri's eyes narrowed dangerously. "Recommended you to who?"

"To Palazzo Sisti."

A moment's silence was broken by a rather forced laugh from Vincenzo Fabri.

"Do me a favour, will you? I don't go to bed with

politicians, and if I did, I certainly wouldn't choose that bunch of losers!''

"It's all right, Vincenzo," Zen reassured him. "They told me. I asked who had put them on to me and they said it was their contact at the Ministry.''

Fabri laughed dismissively. "And what's that got to do with me?''

"Well, they said this person, this contact, had already tried to fiddle the Burolo case for them, except he'd made a complete balls-up of it. As far as I know, you're the only person here who's done any work on that case.''

"You're lying!''

It was Zen's turn to switch on a smile of complicity.

"Look, it's all right, Vincenzo! We're among friends here. No hard feelings, as you said yourself. I for one certainly don't hold it against you. But then I'm hardly in a position to, of course.''

Fabri stared at him furiously. "I tell you once and for all that I have nothing whatever to do with Palazzo Sisti! Is that clear?''

Zen appeared taken aback by this ringing denial. "Are you sure?''

"Of course I'm fucking sure!''

Zen shook his head slowly. "Well, that's very odd. Very odd indeed. All I can say is that's what I was told. But if you say it's not true . . .''

"Of course it's not true! How dare you even suggest such a thing?''

"Admittedly, I can't prove anything," Zen muttered.

"Of course you can't!''

"Can *you*?''

The reply was quick and pointed. Fabri recoiled from it as from a drawn knife.

"What? Can I what?''

"Can you prove that the allegations made by *l'onorevole*'s private secretary are untrue?''

"I don't *need* to prove it!'' Fabri shouted.

No one had moved, yet Zen sensed that the arrangement of the group had changed subtly. Before, he had been confronted by a coherent mass of officials, united in their opposition to the outsider. Now, a looser gathering of individuals stood between him and Fabri, shuffling their feet and looking uncertainly from one man to the other.

"Don't you?" Zen replied calmly. "Oh well, in that case, of course, there's nothing more to be said."

He turned away.

"Exactly!" Fabri called after him. "There's nothing more to be said!"

When Zen reached the line of screens that closed off his desk, he glanced back. The group of officials had broken up into smaller clusters, chatting together in low voices. Vincenzo Fabri was talking at full speed in an undertone, gesticulating dramatically, demanding the undivided attention he felt was his by right. But some of his listeners were gazing down at the floor in a way which suggested that they were not totally convinced by Fabri's protestations. They accepted that Zen was an unscrupulous grafter on the make. The difference was that they now suspected that Fabri was one, too, and the reason for his bitterness was not moral indignation but the fact that his rival was more successful.

Giorgio De Angelis, keeping a foot in both camps as usual, patted Fabri on the shoulder in a slightly patronising way before walking over to join Zen.

"Congratulations. It was about time something like that happened to Vincenzo."

A wan smile brightened Zen's face.

"So tell me all about it!" De Angelis continued. "How on earth did you manage to do it?"

Zen's smile died. Of all his colleagues, De Angelis was the one with whom he had the closest relationship, yet the Calabrian clearly took it for granted that Zen had fixed the Burolo case. Well, if no one was going to believe him anyway, he might as well take the credit for his supposed villainy!

He turned his smile on again. "The funny thing is, I hadn't been going to use the woman at all originally.

The person I had in mind was Furio Padedda. He seemed the perfect candidate from everyone's point of view.''

"But Padedda was involved, too, wasn't he?" said De Angelis.

Zen shook his head. No one seemed to be able to get the story straight, no doubt because the only thing that really concerned them was the headline news which the media, carefully orchestrated by Palazzo Sisti, had been trumpeting all week: that the case against Renato Favelloni had collapsed.

"Padedda and the Melega family were planning to kidnap Burolo, successfully this time, and extort a huge sum of money from the family. They might well have killed him, too, after they got paid, but that was all in the future. On the night of the murders, Padedda was attending a meeting of the gang up in the mountains. But I certainly could have used him, if all else had failed. He even had a convenient wound on his arm. His blood group is different from that of the stains at the villa, but we could have got around that somehow.''

One by one, the other officials had approached to hear Zen's story. It was a situation new to him, and one he found rather embarrassing. Unlike Fabri, he had never enjoyed being the centre of attention. But things had changed. If Fabri could no longer count on star billing, neither could Zen avoid the fame—or rather notoriety—which had been thrust upon him.

"But I didn't need Paddeda. As soon as I'd visited the scene, I knew how I was going to work it. As you probably know, Burolo's villa was originally a farmhouse. The farms in that area were all built over caves giving access to an underground stream where they got their water. When I inspected the cellar of the Villa Burolo, I noticed that the air was very fresh. The caretaker explained that it was naturally ventilated and pointed out an opening at floor level. Since we were underground, I realised right away that the air could only have come from the cave system.''

The assembled officials nodded admiringly.

"No one else had thought of this as a way around the famous problem of access, for the simple reason that the vent was too small to admit a normal adult. But that was precisely what attracted me to the idea. There were already indications suggesting that the killer might have been exceptionally small. The upward angle of fire, for one thing, and the fact that on the video Burolo and even Vianello's wife, who was tiny herself, look *down* at the person confronting them. Then there was the ghost that child claimed to have seen one night, a woman who looked like a little old witch. As soon as this woman Elia hobbled up to me in the village, asking for money, I put two and two together and made five."

This elicited a ripple of appreciative laughter.

"But mightn't she have done it?" asked Carlo Romizi earnestly. "I mean, I saw this thing on the television which seemed to be suggesting that . . ."

Zen gestured impatiently. "Of course she might! She wouldn't have been much use to me otherwise, would she?"

"No, I mean *really*."

Zen turned to the others. "Quick, someone! Get on the phone to Palazzo Sisti. They'll have your mug all over the morning papers, Carlo. 'Italian Believes Favelloni Innocent! After months of research, Palazzo Sisti announced last night that they had located someone who believes in the innocence of Renato Favelloni. "It's true he's an Umbrian," admitted a spokesman for *l'onorevole*, "but we feel this may be the beginning of a significant swing in public opinion." ' "

Zen stood back, letting the waves of laughter wash over him. I could grow to like this, he thought, the good-humoured, easy-going chaffing, the mutual admiration of male society. As a fatherless child with no one to teach him the unwritten rules, he had always found it difficult to play the game with the necessary confidence and naturalness. But perhaps it wasn't too late even now.

"What I still don't understand is how you managed to tie it up so neatly at the end," Travaglini commented.

"There was nothing to it really," Zen replied modestly. "There were various ways I could have worked it, but when Spadola showed up in the village, it seemed a good idea to kill two jailbirds with one stone, so to speak. I couldn't predict exactly what would happen if I brought him and Elia together, but there seemed a good chance that one or both might not survive. Which suited me down to the ground, of course. The last thing I wanted was the magistrates getting a chance to interrogate her."

"Have they found her body yet?" someone asked.

Zen shook his head.

"The cave system is very extensive and has never been mapped. As you can imagine, the locals don't have much time for speleology. They used the cave mouths for storage and shelter, but no one had bothered to explore any further. The Carabinieri flew in a special team trained in pot-holing . . ."

"Complete with designer wet suits by Armani," De Angelis put in.

Everyone laughed. The glamorous image of their paramilitary rivals was always a sore point with the police.

"By Wednesday, two of the Carabinieri had managed to get lost themselves," Zen resumed, "and the others were busy looking for them. All they found of the woman was a few bloodstains matching those at the villa and a collection of odds and ends she'd apparently stolen, things of no value."

Travaglini offered Zen a cigarette, which he felt constrained to accept even though it wasn't a brand he favoured. Such are the burdens of popularity, he reflected.

"What are you doing about a motive?"

"No problem. One of the villagers, a man called Turiddu, claimed that his family had once owned the farmhouse which Burolo bought. At the time I thought he was bragging, but it turned out to be true. The Carabinieri also confirmed that Elia was Turiddu's sister, and that she'd been found locked up in a cellar. The story is

that when she was fifteen she fell in love with someone
her father disapproved of. The man suggested that he
get her pregnant to force her father to consent to their
marriage. Simpleminded Elia agreed. Once he'd had her
a few times, the young man changed his mind about
marriage, of course. Although she wasn't pregnant, Elia
told her father what had happened, hoping he would
force the man to keep his word. Unfortunately her lover
got wind of this and ran off to a branch of the family in
Turin.

   "Since he was out of reach, Elia's father took revenge on his daughter instead, locking her up in the
cellar and telling everyone that she had gone away to
stay with relatives on the mainland. She spent the next
thirteen years there, in total darkness and solitude,
sleeping on the bare floor in her own filth. Twice a day
her mother brought her some food, but she never spoke
to her or touched her again. Turiddu told us that he was
forbidden to mention her existence, even within the
family. This naturally made him even more curious
about this strange sister of his who had committed this
terrible nameless sin. He started sneaking down to the
cellar when his parents were out to gawp at her. And
then one day, to his astonishment, he found she wasn't
there.

   "There was nowhere she could be hiding, and it
was inconceivable that she had escaped through the
bolted door leading up to the house. Eventually he realised that she must have managed to get through the hole
leading to the underground stream. He put out his lantern and kept watch, and sure enough, a few hours later
he heard her coming back. He struck a match and
caught her wriggling in through the hole, which she
had gradually worn away by continual rubbing until it
was just wide enough for her to get through. His father's
ban on acknowledging Elia's existence made it impossible for Turiddu to betray her secret even if he had
wanted to. Anyway, it didn't seem important. As far as
he was concerned, the caves where the stream flowed
were just an extension of the cellar. Elia's prison might

be a little larger than her father supposed, but it was still a prison.

"All this came out when we interrogated Turiddu on Monday and Tuesday. At first he played the tough guy, but once I made it clear that his sister was dead, that she was going to take the rap for Favelloni, and that unless he cooperated he would get five to ten for aiding and abetting, he changed his mind. Underneath the bluster, he was a coward with a guilty conscience. There was a running feud between his family and a clan in the mountains. The usual story, rustling and encroachment. Turiddu's father 'accidentally' shot one of the mountain men while out hunting, and they got their own back by bombing his van. Both parents were killed. It was Turiddu's responsibility to carry on the vendetta, but he shirked it. That sense of shame fed his hatred for anyone connected with the mountains, like Padedda. Still, he gave us what we wanted. Once he got started, he poured out details so fast that the sergeant taking notes could hardly keep up. 'Eh, excuse me, would you mind confessing a little more slowly?' he kept saying."

Once again, laughter spread through the officials grouped around, hanging on Zen's words.

"So the motive is revenge," said De Angelis. "As far as this woman was concerned, whoever lived upstairs in that house was the person who was responsible for punishing her."

Zen shrugged. "Something like that. It doesn't matter anyway. She was crazy, capable of anything. And we don't need a confession. The gun she dropped after shooting Spadola was the one used in the Burolo killings, and her fingerprints match the unidentified ones on the gun rack at the villa."

"But how do you explain the fact that Burolo's records had been tampered with?" Travaglini objected.

"Easy. They weren't. In our version, the chaos in the cellar was due to the fact that the new shelving Burolo had put up blocked the vent Elia used to get in and out of her old home. On the night of the murders she worked the fittings loose, then pushed the whole unit over, sending the tapes and floppy disks flying, which is what caused the crash audible on the video recording. By the way, lads, how do you think this is going to make our friends of the flickering flame look? The Carabinieri seized all that material right after the killings. If our murderer didn't erase the compromising data on those disks, who did?"

De Angelis shook his head in admiration. "You're a genius, Aurelio! How the hell did you ever manage to balls it up so badly in the Moro business?"

For a moment Zen thought his facade of cool cynicism would crack. This was too near the bone, too painful. But in the end he managed to carry it off.

"We all make mistakes, Giorgio. The best we can hope for is not to go on making the same one over and over again."

"I still don't see how you arranged for the shotgun used in the Burolo murders to turn up in the cave where this Elia was," Romizi insisted. "Or how you fixed the fingerprints."

Zen smiled condescendingly. "Now, now. You can't expect me to tell you all my little secrets!"

"So Renato Favelloni walks free," Travaglini concluded heavily.

"Not to mention *l'onorevole*," added Romizi.

For a moment it seemed as though the atmosphere might turn sour. Then De Angelis struck a theatrical pose.

" 'I have examined my conscience,' " he declaimed, quoting a celebrated statement by the politician in question, " 'and I find that it is perfectly clean.' "

"Not surprisingly," Zen chipped in, "given that he never uses it."

The discussion broke up amid hoots of cynical laughter.

Before meeting Tania Biacis for dinner that evening, Zen had a number of chores to perform. The first of these was to return the white Mercedes. Early on Monday morning a Carabinieri jeep had towed the car back to Lanusei, where it had been repaired. On his return to

Rome Zen left a note for Fausto Arcuti at the Rally Bar, and earlier that morning Arcuti had phoned and told Zen to leave the car opposite the main gates of the former abattoir.

"What about locking the doors?" Zen had asked.

"Lock them, dottore, lock them! The Testaccio is a den of thieves."

"And the keys?"

"Leave them in the car."

"But how are you going to open it, then?"

"How do you think we opened it in the first place?" Fausto demanded. Now that the informer was no longer in fear of his life, his naturally irreverent manner had reasserted itself.

After lunch with De Angelis and Travaglini, Zen set off in the Mercedes, reflecting on his conflicting feelings about being readmitted to the male freemasonry which ran not only the Criminalpol department but also the Ministry, the Mafia, the Church, and the government. It all seemed very attractive at first, the mutual back-scratching and ego-boosting, the shared values and unchallenged assumptions. Yet even before the end of lunch a reaction set in, and Zen found that the cosy back-chat and the smug sense of innate superiority was beginning to pall. It was all a bit cloying, a bit too reminiscent of the self-congratulatory nationalism of the Fascist epoch. Whatever happened between him and Tania, he knew it would never be easy. But that, perhaps, was what made it worthwhile.

As he queued up to enter the maelstrom of traffic around the Colosseum, Zen noticed an unmarked grey delivery van three or four vehicles behind him. He adjusted the rearview mirror until he could see the driver. It didn't look like the man he had seen that morning, but of course they might be working shifts.

He continued south past the flank of the Palatine, then turned right along the Circus Maximus and crossed the river into Trastevere. The grey van followed faithfully. He was being tailed, no question about that. This in itself was bad enough. What made it infinitely worse was that Zen felt absolutely sure he knew who was responsible.

Despite his bluster, Vasco Spadola must have known that he couldn't be certain of success in his twenty-year-old vendetta. Things can always go wrong; that's why people take out insurance. There seemed very little doubt that the grey van represented Spadola's insurance. The men he had seen were not slavering psychotics like Spadola himself, getting a hard-on at the idea of killing. Neither were they third-rate cowboys like Leather Jacket. They were professionals, doing what they had been paid to do, carrying out a contract to be put into effect in the event of Spadola's death. The only other explanation was that Mauro Bevilacqua was pursuing revenge secondhand, but that seemed wildly unlikely. Tania clearly hadn't taken his threats seriously. In any case, professional killers didn't advertise in the Yellow Pages, and a bank clerk wouldn't have known how to contact them.

Zen turned off the Lungotevere and steered at random through the back streets around the factory where his favourite Nazionali cigarettes were made. The incident had plunged him into apathetic despair. These men wouldn't give up, whatever happened. They had their reputation to consider. There was no point in having the team in the van arrested. They would simply be replaced by another crew. His only hope, a very slim one, was to find out who Spadola had placed the contract with and try to renegotiate the deal. But that was for the future. His immediate task was to lose the tail. Unfortunately this called for virtuoso driving skills Zen didn't possess.

In the end, his very incompetence proved to be his salvation. As he turned out of the backstreets by Porta Portese, he was so deep in thought about his problems that he failed to notice that the traffic light had just changed to red. The white Mercedes just managed to squeeze between the lines of the traffic closing in from either side, but the grey van remained trapped. Zen crossed the river again, veered round into Via Marmorata and then, once he was out of sight of the van, turned right into the Testaccio. He abandoned the car with the keys locked inside, as Arcuti had instructed him, then worked his way back on foot to Via Marmorata, taking refuge in the doorway of the ornate fire station at the corner until he saw a Number 30 tram approaching the stop.

He got off the tram near Portomaggiore and walked round to Gilberto Nieddu's flat, where his mother had been staying for the past week. Zen had promised to collect her that afternoon, but now he was going to have to ask for more time. Gilberto had insisted that everything had gone well, but he was bound to say that. Zen knew that looking after his mother must have been a terrible imposition and one that would now have to be prolonged. Until he had resolved the problem of the grey van, his mother could not return home. He did not look forward to breaking this news to the Nieddus.

Gilberto was at work, so it was Rosa Nieddu who greeted Zen at the door of their pleasant, modern flat in Via Carlo Emanuele. To Zen's amazement, his mother was playing a board game with the two youngest Nieddu daughters. It was so long since he had seen his mother do anything except slump in a comatose state in front of the television that this perfectly ordinary scene of domestic life seemed as bizarre and alarming as if the tram he had just been on had suddenly veered off the rails and started careering freely about the streets, menacing the passers-by.

"Hello, Aurelio!" she called gaily, beaming a distracted smile in his direction. "Everything all right?"

Without waiting for his response, she turned back to the children.

"No, not there! Otherwise I'll gobble you up like this, bang bang bang bang bang!"

The girls tittered nervously.

"But Auntie, you can't go there, it's the wrong way," the elder pointed out.

"Oh! So it is! Silly old me. Silly old Auntie."

Zen felt a pang of jealous hurt, all the stronger for

being completely absurd. She's not your auntie, he felt like shouting, she's my mamma! Mine! Mine!

Taking Rosa Nieddu aside, he hesitantly broached the subject of his mother staying one more night.

"That's wonderful!" she replied, interrupting his deliberately vague explanations. "Did you hear that, kids? Auntie Zen's not leaving today after all!"

A look of sheer delight instantly appeared on the children's faces. They rushed about, doing a war dance around the old lady, screaming at the top of their voices while she looked on happily, a benign totem pole.

"What a treasure your mother is!" Rosa Nieddu enthused.

"Why, er, yes. Yes, of course."

"She's been absolutely tireless with those two. I love them dearly, of course, but sometimes I think they're going to drive me round the bend. But your mother has the patience of a saint. And she knows all these wonderful games and tricks and stories! I haven't had to do a thing. It's been a real holiday for me. I've finally been able to catch up with my own life a bit. Gilberto helps as much as he can, of course, but he's so busy at work these days. Anyway, we've arranged that your mother's going to come round every week, once she goes home I mean. That's all right, I hope."

Zen stared at her.

"You *want* her to come?"

Rosa Nieddu's serene features contracted in puzzlement.

"Of course I do! And just as important, *she* wants to. She said she was . . . well, anyway, she wants to come."

Zen eyed her.

"What did she say?"

"I don't expect she meant it."

"Meant what?"

"Well . . ."

"Yes?"

"It was just a manner of speaking, you know, but she said she'd had enough of being locked up at home."

"Locked up?" Zen shouted angrily. "What the hell do you mean? She's the one who refuses to set foot outside the flat!"

"Well, she's been out a lot while she's been with us."

"She never wanted to move here in the first place. She hates Rome!"

"No, she doesn't! We all went to the Borghese gardens on Sunday. She couldn't believe all the joggers and cyclists and the fathers pushing babies. Afterwards, we went to the zoo and then had lunch out. We had a really good time. She said she hadn't enjoyed herself so much for years."

Zen stood open-mouthed. This is not my mother, he wanted to protest, it's an imposter! My mother is a crabby old woman who spends her time shut up at home in front of the television. I don't want this wonderful, patient, inventive old lady with a zest for life! I want my mamma! *I want my mamma!*

"I'm glad to hear it, I'm sure," he said drily. "So it'll be no trouble if she stays another night, then?"

"It'll be a pleasure."

Zen rode the lift downstairs feeling irritated, relieved, and obscurely guilty. It wasn't his fault, of course. How could it be? He hadn't locked his mother up in the flat. She'd locked herself up. It was true that he had accepted that because it was convenient, because it had left him free to do what he wanted, particularly when he had been seeing Ellen. He'd always avoided confronting his mother with that relationship, preferring to shut her out of that area of his life. That was apparently one of the things that had made Ellen leave him in the end. Perhaps it *was* partly his fault, in a way. He hadn't created the situation, but he'd connived at it, used it, acquiesced. He hadn't been cruel, but he'd been lazy. He'd been thoughtless and selfish.

He stopped in the first cafe he came to and phoned the caretaker at home. Then he walked back to Portomaggiore and took the Number 19 tram all the way round the city to its terminus a short walk from where he lived. As he had expected, there was no sign of the grey van, but the chances were that the house was under surveillance. Zen walked casually down the street and into the shop next door to his house, an outmoded emporium selling everything from corkscrews and hot-water bottles to dried beans and herbal remedies. It had the air of a museum rather than a shop, and the elderly woman who ran it had the haughty, disinterested manner of a curator.

"You're from the Electricity?" she demanded as Zen threaded his way through the shelves and cupboards to the counter.

"That's right."

She jerked her thumb at a door at the rear of the shop. The array of mops and brooms which normally concealed it had been cleared to one side.

"Don't you dare touch anything!" she admonished. "I know where everything is! If anything's missing, there'll be trouble, I promise you."

Zen opened the door. Inside was a dark passageway almost completely filled with boxes of various sizes. At the end was a second door, opening into the courtyard of his own house. In the hall he found Giuseppe and thanked him for getting the shopkeeper to unlock the doors.

"So what's the problem, dottore?" the caretaker asked anxiously.

"Just a jealous husband."

Giuseppe cackled and waggled a finger on either side of his forehead.

"He has good reason, I'll bet!"

Zen shrugged modestly. Giuseppe redoubled his cackles.

"Like we say in Lucania, there may be snow on the roof but there's still fire in the furnace! Eh, dottore!"

Once he had showered and shaved, Zen put on a suit of evening dress exhumed from the oak chest in which it had lain entombed since the last time he had had occasion to attend a formal gathering. He wandered dispiritedly through to the living room, struggling with a recalcitrant stud. In the absence of his mother and Maria Grazia, the lares and penates of the place, the flat felt hollow and unreal, like a stage set which despite its scrupulous accuracy does not quite convince.

Catching sight of himself in the mirror above the sideboard, Zen was surprised to find that he did not look flustered and absurd, as he felt, but elegant and distinguished. What a shame that Tania would not see him in his finery! But it was clearly out of the question to keep their appointment as long as hired assassins were pursuing Spadola's vendetta from beyond the grave. He had already put her life at risk once too often.

He picked up the smooth pasteboard card propped against the mirror and scanned the lines of engraved italic copperplate requesting the pleasure of his company at a reception at Palazzo Sisti that evening at seven o'clock. Even *l'onorevole* and his cronies didn't have the gall to celebrate openly the collapse of the case against Renato Favelloni, so the reception was nominally in honour of one of the party's rising stars who had recently been appointed to a crucial portfolio in the government's newly reshuffled cabinet. Zen had been very much in two minds about attending, particularly after Vincenzo Fabri's attack on him that morning, but the appearance of the grey van had removed his lingering doubts.

There was no point in trying to buy off the people Spadola had hired. Even if he'd had the money to do so, the underworld has a strict code of consumer protection in such matters. Spadola would have made a substantial payment up front, with the balance in the hands of a trusted third party. The deposit was unreturnable now that Spadola was dead, so any failure to carry out the hit would amount to breach of contract. These rules of conduct were extremely rigid. Zen's only recourse was to try and persuade the organisation involved that it was in its own interests to make an exception in this case. He himself didn't have the necessary clout to do

this, but *l'onorevole* should, or would know who did.
And *l'onorevole* owed him.

He reached for the phone and dialled the number
Tania had given him that morning to cancel their date,
but there was no reply. By now it was ten to seven, and
there was no sign of the taxi he had ordered, so he rang
to complain before trying Tania's friend again. To his
dismay, the dispatcher not only disclaimed all knowledge of his previous call but even hinted that Zen had
invented it in order to jump the forty-five minute waiting period that now existed. After a brief acrimonious
exchange, Zen slammed down the receiver and headed
for the door. The evening was fine and it was not too far
to walk. Even if he didn't manage to pick up a taxi on
the way, he would arrive no more than fashionably late.

He raced down the stairs two at a time and out to
the street, trying to work out how best to phrase his
petition without making it look as though he took
Palazzo Sisti's underworld connections for granted. So
preoccupied was he that he didn't notice the unmarked
grey delivery van that was now double-parked further
down the street nor the dark figure that slipped out of a
doorway nearby and began to follow him.

His route was the same as he and Tania had taken a
week earlier: past the law courts, across the river, and
south through Piazza Navona. He strode rapidly along,
oblivious to the stares he was attracting from passers-by
curious about this image of sartorial rectitude hoofing it
through their vulgar streets like Cinderella going home
from the ball. When he reached the small piazza facing
the grimy baroque church of Sant' Andrea della Valle, he
was halted for some time by the traffic on Corso Vittorio
Emmanuele. A woman getting out of a car parked by the
fountain shouted something and pointed. Zen turned to
find a slight, swarthy man brandishing a pistol at him.

"You have disgraced my marriage bed and . . ."

He paused, breathless with the effort of running to
keep up with Zen.

". . . and brought dishonour on my house! For
this you shall pay, as my name is Mauro Bevilacqua!"

So this is the way it's going to end, thought Zen. He almost laughed to think he had survived the worst a Vasco Spadola could do, only to fall victim to the ravings of a jealous bank clerk.

"You thought you had it all worked out, you two, didn't you?" Bevilacqua sneered. "You thought you could have fun and games at my expense and get away scot-free. Well, let me tell you . . ."

Tyres squealed as the grey van slewed to a halt by the neat Fascist office block at the other side of the piazza. Men in grey overalls bearing the word Police in fluorescent yellow leapt out clutching submachine guns.

"Don't move!" boomed a harshly amplified voice. "Drop your weapon!"

Mauro Bevilacqua looked about him in utter bewilderment. He turned to face the van, the pistol still in his hand. A volley of shots rang out. There was a sound of breaking glass and a woman's scream.

"For Christ's sake, drop the fucking thing before they kill us all!" Zen hissed.

The pistol clattered to the cobblestones.

"It's only a replica," Bevilacqua muttered.

The woman who had shouted to Zen stood looking with a shocked expression at her car, whose windscreen was now crazed and punctured by bullet holes. Two of the men in grey overalls threw Bevilacqua against the side of the car, arms on the roof, and searched him roughly. Another walked up to Zen and saluted.

"Ispettore Ligato, NOCS unit 42! I trust you're unharmed, dottore?"

Zen nodded.

"Sorry about losing contact this afternoon," Ligato went on. "You were a bit too quick for us at the lights. Still, no harm done. We were here when it counted."

He walked over to Bevilacqua, who was now lying face down on the cobblestones, his arms tightly handcuffed behind his back. Ligato gave him an exploratory kick in the ribs.

"As for you, you bastard, you can count yourself lucky you're still alive!"

Zen laid a restraining hand on the official's shoulder.

"Don't be too hard on him," he said. "His wife's just left him."

Palazzo Sisti was lit up and humming like the power-station it was. A queue of limousines tailed back from the courtyard, waiting to discharge their illustrious passengers. The miniscule porter, beside himself with the importance of the occasion, was haranguing a chauffeur who was trying to park in a space reserved for some Party dignitary.

At the top of the staircase lounged a familiar apelike figure, unconvincingly got up in a footman's apparel.

"Good evening, Lino."

The bodyguard scowled at Zen.

"That way," he said, jerking his thumb.

"This way?" Zen enquired brightly.

Lino's scowl intensified. "Don't push me too far!" he warned.

"Sorry, too late. Someone already threatened to kill me this evening. In fact there's a waiting list, I'm afraid. I could pencil you in for some time next month."

"You're crazy," muttered Lino.

Zen walked past a mutilated classical torso which revived memories of a particularly nasty murder case he had once been involved in. A pair of rosewood doors opened into a series of salons whose modest dimensions and exquisite decoration reflected the tone of the palace as a whole. The rooms were packed with people. Those nearest the door scanned Zen's features briefly, then turned away. But though they did not recognise him, he saw many faces familiar from the television and newspapers. As he hovered on the fringes of the gathering, unable to find an opening, Zen found himself reminded oddly of the village bar in Sardinia. If the contrasts were obvious, so were the similarities. He couldn't get a drink here either. For one thing, the white-jacketed waiters always passing by were just out of his reach, ignoring his signals. But more important, here too he was an intruder, a gate-crasher at a private club. These people were constant presences in each other's lives, meeting regularly at functions such as this, not to mention other more significant reunions. Nothing any of them did or said could be indifferent to the others. They were a family, a tribe to which Zen did not belong. They had felt obliged to invite the man who did their dirty work for them, but in fact his presence was an unwelcome embarrassment to himself and everyone else.

To Zen's dismay, the first familiar face he saw was that of Vincenzo Fabri, resplendent in an aerodynamically styled outfit that made Zen's look as though it had been rented from a fancy-dress agency. Fabri approached with a smile that boded no good.

"I didn't know you'd be here, Zen."

"Life's full of surprises."

"Isn't it just?"

Fabri beckoned him closer with a crooked finger. "Guess what?"

Zen gazed at him bleakly.

"I've made Questore!" Fabri crowed in a triumphant whisper.

He extended the forefinger of his right hand and poked Zen in the chest.

"To be fair, I suppose you should take some of the credit, as you said this morning. But it's results that count in the end, isn't it? Bari or Ferrara seem the most likely prospects at the moment, unless I decide to take a few months' leave and wait for something better to come up. They say Pacini won't last much longer in Venice. Now there's a thought, eh? Well, I must circulate. See you at the Ministry. I'll be in to clear my desk."

Zen knew he had to leave quickly before he said or did something unforgivable. As he pushed through the crowd, not caring who he offended, he felt a grip on his arm.

"Wherever are you going in such a hurry, dottore? I

was just about to, ah . . . that's to say, I was on the point of, ah, introducing you to a certain person who has taken a very close, very *personal* interest in the events of the past few days.''

The young secretary steered Zen toward a distinguished-looking figure in his midsixties who was holding court in the centre of the room where the throng was thickest. Zen recognised him immediately. Unlike the other celebrities whose fleshly reality often jarred uncomfortably with their etherealised media image, this man's appearance coincided perfectly with the photographs Zen had seen of him. Elderly without frailty, experienced but not resigned, he gave the impression of having reached just the prime of life.

"We were talking about you earlier," the young man resumed, effortlessly inserting himself and Zen into the inner circle of initiates. "Indeed, I trust you will not think me indiscreet if I mention that *l'onorevole* was pleased to remark how deeply indebted we are to you for your, ah, effective and timely intervention.''

The distinguished figure, deep in conversation with two younger men whose enthusiastic servility was embarrassing to behold, paid not the slightest attention.

"It would be no exaggeration to say that the Party has been spared a most trying experience as the result of your, ah, initiative," the young man went on. "It's true that we were initially somewhat surprised by the choice of . . . that's to say, by the fact that this woman, ah, proved to be the guilty party. However, on mature consideration we unreservedly approve of this solution, more especially since it allows us to retain the Padedda option as a fall-back position should any further problems arise. We are really most grateful, most grateful indeed. Isn't that so, *l'onorevole?*''

For a second, the elder man's eyes swept over Zen's face like the revolving beam of a lighthouse.

"If there's ever anything you need . . ." he murmured.

Zen made the appropriate noises, then gracefully

withdrew. As he headed toward the door, toward his evening with Tania, the words were still ringing in his ears: *If there's ever anything you need* . . . Better than money in the bank, he thought. Better than money in the bank!

ABOUT THE AUTHOR

MICHAEL DIBDIN attended schools in Scotland and in Northern Ireland, where he grew up, and universities in England and Western Canada. He spent four years in Italy, teaching English at the University of Perugia, and now lives in Oxford, England. Dibdin's first two novels, *Ratking* and *The Tryst*, were both winners of the Golden Dagger Award for Best Crime Novel. His most recent Aurelio Zen novel is *Cabal*.